BRAIN DEAD BLUES

MATT HAYWARD

POLTERGEIST PRESS

POLTERGEIST PRESS

www.sundancecrow.com

This is a work of collected fiction. All characters depicted in this book are ficticious, and any resemblance to actual events or persons, living or dead, is purely coincidental.

ISBN: 978-1-9993419-3-0

First Edition

Originally published in paperback by Sinister Grin Press

www.poltergeistpress.com

PRAISE FOR MATT HAYWARD

"Not content to conquer the rock music world via Lace Weeper and his own phenomenal solo work, Matt Hayward has now turned his attention to dark fiction, and how much richer we all are as a result. Brain Dead Blues *is everything you'd expect from a rock star turned horror writer, documenting not only facets of the music world but also the darkness that can result from obsessions both creative and violent. I have long been a fan of both the music and the man behind it. Now I'm a fan of his writing too."*

—**Kealan Patrick Burke**, author of *The Turtle Boy* and *Kin*

"In Brain Dead Blues, *Matt Hayward shows that he is one of horror's most distinctive new voices. This collection is full of evocative storytelling, vivid characterizations, and fresh takes on old tropes. Do yourself a favor and read it."*

—**Bryan Smith**, author of *Depraved* and *68 Kill*

"...the future of the horror genre is changing hands, and there is a whole new brew of writers assuming the task. Matt Hayward leading that pack."

—**Edward Lee**, author of *The Bighead* and *White Trash Gothic*

"Hayward bleeds onto the page..."

—**Brian Keene**, author of *The Rising* and *Ghoul*

"Hayward has forged his way to the head of the latest generation of horror writers, developing a distinctive voice and writing style that I am incredibly eager to see developed in further work."

—Sci-Fi and Fantasy Reviewer

"The writing is crisp and clear. The characters are all relatable and the monsters, oh man, the monsters. Hayward understands what fear is. And that a lot of times the monsters we see and fight are just skewed reflections of ourselves. But then sometimes, they are monsters."

—Ginger Nuts of Horror

Acknowledgements

Thanks to Anna Hayward, Melissa & Fionnuala Hayward, Patrick Lacey, Kealan Patrick Burke, Bryan Smith, Robert Ford, Brian Keene, Edward Lee, Mary SanGiovanni, Kelli Owen, Jeff Angell, Csaba Mester, Rachel Autumn Deering, Jessica Deering, Tim Meyer, Seán O'Connor, and Josh Jabcuga

CONTENTS

GOD IS IN THE RADIO

THE NOTE TREMBLED in Elliot's hand as he read for a second time.

Couldn't hear that song again...So, I'm going to kill myself. I looked for it everywhere, but I couldn't find it. Are you hiding it from me, Bill? Because, us fans, us who understand *it, will do* anything *to get another listen...*Anything. *Why hasn't it been released? Why would you do this to me, Billy, why? My skin prickled when you played it last night. My hair stood on end. I'm not embarrassed to say that I think I orgasmed. Twice.*

I could see that song, see it in my mind...Sounds turned to colours, took shape and danced, danced...like ballroom ballerinas. That noise raced through my veins and filled me with something that I imagine a syringe, plump with heroin, would be for a junkie. That song is mine. It's all for me. Pure and absolute magic, nothing less...Do you get the same experience from it?

Either way, I can't hear it now, Billy, and that's driving me insane.

Other people heard it too. I know, I know...And I'm so jealous that I'm shaking. I can hardly see straight. I can't stand knowing that...You made your song a slut, Billy. A filthy fucking whore. It's been inside so many people now that you should be checking for diseases. You've tainted its purity...

Oh, but I need to hear it. Not tomorrow, not next week. Now. I need it, I need it, I need it.

Elliot lowered the note and took a deep, shaking breath. He squeezed at the bridge of his nose before continuing.

But I can't have it all the time, can I? And there's no way I can have it all to myself...Not when you've already whored it out to every Tom, Dick and Harry with ears. Even the people that don't get it...I'm crying here. How could you give such a beautiful thing away? I can't understand...

So...I'm out. I mean it. I have a bottle of whiskey (your favourite, by the way), and about forty caps of Kadian that I robbed from work. 30 mg, the good stuff. I worked in a hospital, Billy, did you even know that about me?

The note was unsigned. Dropping it back to the table, Elliot stepped away as the cabin spun around him.

"Why are you in here?"

He turned at the sound of the voice, coming face to face with Bill Jennings. He tried to swallow but found himself unable.

"The door was open," Elliot said. "I let myself in."

Bill Jennings crossed the room with a sigh, his boot heels clicking off the hardwood. A bruise darkened his left cheek but Elliot said nothing. Instead, he watched as Bill settled into the wicker chair by the window. The old rocker ran a hand through his long, greasy hair. "If me staying here means that you can just come on in anytime you please, then it might do me good to find someplace else to stay."

Elliot cleared his throat. "I was just checking how the single was coming along, man. Wayne told me that you started recording already. You making progress?"

The recording equipment inhabited the far end of the cabin, consisting of a laptop wired to a mixing console that sat on a wooden desk with monitors to either side. Cables snaked from the desk, leading to microphones on stands in the middle of the floor. There were three in total—two for Bill's guitar, and one for his voice. Acoustic foam adorned the walls.

Bill snorted and flicked some dirt from his boot. "Ah, the magic of modern-day recording, eh? Years ago, this would have been a double-digit thousand dollar operation. Now? A laptop, some software, a few decent microphones, presto. Better than any big budget studio. And the single's coming along just fine, Elliot. Just fine. I'd say it's a hit."

"Good. We'll get started on promotion soon. Guaranteed sales."

Bill smirked. "I take it that big house out front wasn't paid for by record sales, though, right? Your parents own this place."

"They did. But they left it to me. I didn't ask them to. It was a family business, running a Bed and Breakfast. I'd give it all back if I could take back their crash."

Bill's smile faded. "You talkin' back to me, kid?"

"Bill, please." Elliot didn't want another argument. They'd happened too often since Bill had arrived. "I've given you this cabin out back and you can stay here as long as you need. I just want to get this single moving."

For once, Bill let the fight go. "Packman Records headquarters, once a B&B. That's pretty Rock 'n' Roll, actually."

"Thanks. Wayne came up with that name, you know. Putting our surnames together. I think most people do that when they're starting a business, but Packman sounded especially good."

"Indeed, indeed, Mr. Truman."

Elliot licked his lips. "Where is Wayne, Bill? You've been gone all night. Not that I need to know what you get up to on your own time, but please be straight with me."

You owe me that for giving you a cabin with a studio, Elliot thought. Now, where's my business partner and producer?

"Wayne lives here, too?" Bill asked.

"I let him and his girlfriend have a room upstairs, yes. His production skills are good to have on hand when we're recording someone. Like now." Elliot cleared his throat again. It'd gone very dry. "Where is he?"

Bill cracked his knuckles. "He's around somewhere, don't worry...Not a bad set up, Elliot. Not bad at all. As I said, the single is moving along just fine. I did a full day today. My voice sounded a little tired after the two shows, but it's all good."

"You did a full day? What about Wayne?"

"I asked Wayne to leave me be for the afternoon, that's all. Wanted to finish up the vocal takes myself. Feel more comfortable recording when I'm alone. I don't have to be so self-conscious if I try something new." He arched an eyebrow. "Speaking of which, I have some final adjustments to make, so..."

"You're asking me to leave?"

"Quick on the draw there, Elliot. That's a good boy."

Heat flooded Elliot's face. "Well, I need to ask you about something, Bill. Other than Wayne."

"Good, because I need to talk to you about something, too, Elliot."

Icy fingers worked their way up Elliot's spine. He wasn't an argumentative person by nature, and Bill could tango with the best of them. "What's that, Bill?"

"You threw this tour together at the last minute. I was playing clubs across the Northwest, and you reached out. You know as well as I do that my Two Smoking Barrels days are over. I couldn't flog albums if my life depended on it. You know the industry these days. I need to know that people will hear this comeback release."

Elliot nodded. "Of course. You're Bill Jennings. Most of the promotion is done by your name alone."

"And what about a bigger show? One in Dublin. I'm tired of these backwoods towns."

"We need to do the backwood towns to get the money for a city show. The Arts Council agreed to finance promotion and the venue if we do a small town circuit first. Part of their Entertainment Outside the City scheme. We have to do it. I told you that when I picked you up from the airport. After we get that money, we can get The Lighthouse in Dublin."

"How big will this release be?" Bill asked. "I've been out of the distribution side of things since the early nineties, and the industry's changed an awful lot since then. I don't like reading contracts, neither, so I expect you to be upfront with me. Give it to me in good ol' plain English, please. I expect international airplay for this release. People are going to lose their minds at the sound of this."

"Well, we'll handle online distribution, Bill. That covers all the major online retailers, with a sizeable PR plan in place for three months once the album goes live. That covers Europe and the United States for advertising, reviews and airplay. Physical distribution will be limited to Irish brick and mortar stores, with a first pressing of five thousand copies. Once they sell out, and I'm sure they will, we'll use that money to go into a second print and get it sold abroad."

"So what you're saying is, people *will* hear this music?"

Elliot arched an eyebrow. "Of course?"

Bill smirked and scratched his stubbly face, making a sound like Velcro. "Well, all right, then. My concerns are laid to rest. I'll take your word for it, Elliot."

Back in the day, when Bill Jennings had fronted Two Smoking Barrels, Elliot had thought of the man as an unsung hero of his generation. After hearing the band's first two records, he'd gone straight out and bought both on vinyl and cassette, listening to them constantly. The vinyl had gotten warped over the years, and one of the tapes had gotten stepped on by Peter Simmons when they were in school, but when Two Smoking Barrels' record label never re-issued the albums to CD, Elliot had grown furious. He managed to get a hold of bootlegs, of course, but without an official CD release, he felt that the later generations had been robbed of one of the greatest forces in Rock 'n' Roll history. He meant to change that. But now, with Bill Jennings on his family property with a bruised face and a bad attitude, he wasn't so sure he'd made the right choice.

Should've left you in the US, Elliot thought. Also—what the hell was that note all about?

Bill shifted his position in the wicker chair, his raspy voice low. "I'm happy to be here," he said. His eyes had gotten a far-away look. "And people are going to hear my music. That's very important."

Elliot tried to agree but couldn't find his voice. Something about the way Bill's mood could switch so fast frightened him. One minute, the old rocker would be completely normal, chatting and shooting the breeze, and the next, he'd spit nails. *Mood swings,* Elliot thought. Something that burdened a lot of rock stars, it seemed. He'd thought that watching Bill Jennings on tape or on stage was intense enough, but being alone in a room with the man, and at nighttime for that matter, downright terrified him.

Finally, Elliot spoke. "People are going to hear this. They'll be dying to hear it once we get a start on the press."

Bill smirked. "You're goddamn right about that."

Ask him about the note, Elliot told himself. Do it.

But Bill spoke first. "How much did this place cost a night when your folks ran it as a Bed and Breakfast?"

"Huh?" Elliot shook his head to concentrate. "Oh, um, one-hundred and fifty euros."

"Then I'm living in luxury, I guess." He crossed his arms behind his head and stretched, his back popping. "Although, Ireland's so damn expensive since the last time I came here that one-hundred and fifty euros probably wouldn't even get you through a day, am I right?"

"Sure."

Ask him about the goddamn note...Just say it.

Instead, he asked, "How did the show go last night?"

Elliot would get to the note. He'd work his way to it. Whoever had written it was clearly delusional, but Elliot had never dealt with an act as big as Bill Jennings. Were these crazy tokens of adoration commonplace? Did people threaten suicide because of a song and blame the performer every day?

"It went all right, by my standards." Bill snorted, spitting into the waste bin by his chair. He removed a carton of cigarettes from his shirt pocket and lit up, the smoke curling towards the ceiling. "Just under a hundred people showed. But still, that's ninety or so in the back ass of Ireland coming to see me. And paying a tenner each, right? So what's that?" He began to mutter the multiplication beneath his breath.

"Nine hundred," Elliot said.

"Right. Just under a grand. After the venue takes their cut, we're left with peanuts. That's great, Elliot. I tell you, I can't wait for these bigger shows. People need to hear the new single I've been working on."

That's it, Elliot thought. *Enough beating around the bush.*

"There's a note on the table," he said, then paused, hoping the old man would take the hint and explain. He didn't.

"Where did it come from?" He pressed on, forcing a smile. "Just a nutcase fan, huh? You get them a lot?"

Bill's face fell. He leaned forward, the wicker chair squeaking. Popping the cigarette into the corner of his mouth, he narrowed his eyes down to slits. Elliot's heart jackhammered. "You know the difference between real music and fake music, kid?"

Elliot remained silent. He shook his head.

"Right. That's because you're a businessman and not an artist. I'm an artist, and I can tell you the difference." He flicked the finished cigarette into the wastebasket and put his hands on his knees. "They say the Blues is the Devil's music, did you know that?"

"I've heard that, yes."

"Well, that's because of the tritone. And the blue notes, of course. People didn't know what to make of blue notes when they first heard 'em."

"Blue notes?"

"Yes. Dissonant sounding things, but that's where the mojo comes from. The quirk of a song. You've heard them before, those little off notes in a Blues lick. The ones that make you think of sex and sin...Those blue notes and the tritone are where the secrets lie."

"What secrets?" He asked quietly.

"The secret of music, my friend."

"What do you mean?"

"Tell me, what was the first record to ever give you gooseflesh? That first time your hair stood on end like soldiers coming to attention, and it felt like your brain was having a goddamn orgasm?"

Elliot blushed. He knew what Bill meant. And he knew the answer, too. "It was AC/DC," he said. "Highway to Hell. I was about eight years old."

"Right. AC/DC. Rock 'n' Roll. And Rock 'n' Roll came from the Blues. You got that feeling, kid, that raw *something*. That energy. Those blue notes and the feeling. It was passed down to that band by whoever it was they were listening to. Chuck Berry, maybe. And do you remember the first time you heard Son House or Etta James? One of those voices. You know what I'm talking about."

"Janis Joplin?"

"Exactly. Janis had it too, sure. That energy. *That*, kid, is what I'm talking about. When you combine those notes, sung by one of those voices, you're getting into an international language that everybody can understand...Because what you're hearing is complete, uncut truth, one that no words in any language could ever explain. You just gotta feel it. What you're hearing, right there, is a person wearing their heart on their sleeve. They are giving you themselves, wholly, unconditionally, and most importantly, with warts and all. It's those warts and imperfections that make the music so goddamn perfect. You ever notice that, huh? That's what gets you, deep down. In *here*." He patted his chest three times. "How relatable that emotion they're showing is, because it's honest...And it works its way through you, doesn't it?" He began tracing his finger around his chest and arms. "It works *all* the way through you...It pours inside you, like honey, and you welcome it and it nourishes you...And you know what? One hundred years from now, and even one hundred years from then, people will hear Joplin, James, Hooker, and it'll *still* bring 'em to tears because they'll know that it's real. That's the heart and soul of music right there, Elliot, and don't you ever forget it."

A tense silence filled the room as Bill stared at Elliot with wide eyes, waiting for a reaction. Then he smiled. "Play me a radio track that's hot at the minute, even five years from now, and I'll bet you my right testicle that when the fad that launched it is over, it's going to sound about as powerful as an old man's fart. That's all it was to begin with, right? A manufactured piece of auto-tuned wholesale garbage in a shiny package for the masses. And at a reasonable price, too."

Outside, the night wind howled. The wood of the cabin creaked, groaning as it settled. Elliot realised he didn't really know Bill Jennings, at all. Sure, he knew the man's musical persona, but not the man behind the mask. And now, with the note, with Wayne gone, with Bill's overnight disappearance, he didn't know what to think. "I still don't see where you're going with this, Bill."

"You asked about that note there on the table." Bill rearranged himself on the chair. "That note was from a fan who came to my show last night in Killdubh."

Elliot had missed the show because he and Wayne had needed to have another meeting with the Arts Council in Dublin. It'd been Bill's second show. At the first, in Ballybriggs, Bill had been on top form, and Elliot had gotten goosebumps all over. He felt safe leaving the second show with no supervision.

Bill lit another cigarette. "You remember that old man who I left with after that first show?"

"Sure. The guy who reminded me of Tommy Chong, yeah. Family friend, right?"

"That's what I told you." Bill blew smoke from his nostrils. "I never met that man before in my life."

Elliot's skin crawled. "Why'd you leave with him?"

"Because that man understood music. He said some things to me at the bar that I haven't heard someone speak so passionately about since I was a very young man." He nodded slowly. "Learn to know your own kin, kid. Learn to recognise them. It will take you far and save you a lot of trouble in life. That said, he was one of mine."

"What happened?"

"We went back to his place and talked music. We had some twenty-year malt, and he told me things I always thought to be true, but never thought possible. Paths have been opened for me, Elliot. Bridges built. I see things in a way now that I could never put clearly into words...But I can play it."

"You guys wrote a song?"

"Calling this creation a song would be like calling the Titanic a rowboat. Nah...Nah, this is something much more than a song, kid. This is energy. Pure and absolute. This is a *gateway*."

Elliot went cold. He wanted to get away from here. Wanted to find Wayne. Suddenly, he was regretting ever contacting Bill Jennings. "What are you getting at? I'm not understanding."

Bill smirked, blowing smoke. "Then let me explain it to you."

Bill Jennings entered Leroy's Lounge in Ballybriggs at eight-thirty with his worn-out Gibson guitar case clutched in his right hand. At thirty-three years, the guitar had been with him longer than most of his friends. The leather handle, in need of repair, creaked with each step. Bill didn't mind. He was used to the sound.

"Bill, it's very nice to have you here." An old man approached, wearing overalls and a greasy baseball cap. A friendly smile spread across his face as he extended his hand for a shake. "You're the biggest name I've ever had come to my bar. I can't thank you enough."

Bill nodded, shaking the man's hand. His palm felt like leather, calloused from years of manual labour, Bill guessed. "Thanks. I take it you're Leroy?"

"In the flesh. Please, Mr. Jennings, if you need anything, just give me a shout. Drinks are on the house."

"Thank you, I'll do that."

Bill left Leroy and looked around the room. He guessed it could comfortably seat perhaps two-hundred patrons, maybe another fifty standing. He'd played places only half as big back in the States. The seats weren't full, but at least half were. Audience members craned their necks to look at him. Some smiled, others stared. Bill waved before making his way to the bar. The place smelled of sawdust and stale beer, but to him, it smelled like the raw stench of live music.

"I'll have a pint and a glass of tap water, please." Bill lowered his guitar and went for his wallet.

"No charge, Mr. Jennings. We're glad to have you. Guinness do you?"

"Sure, thank you."

Bill smiled as the bartender poured his drink. He wasn't used to getting free drinks at shows, not anymore. Back in the days of Two Smoking Barrels, he'd have gotten not only free drinks but full catering and his own changing room. Maybe even a groupie or two. Those had been the days when the music industry had money. Times had changed.

Bill thanked the bartender and took his pint. After a sip, he turned towards the stage as Leroy got to the house mic. "Attention, please, ladies and gentlemen."

The white noise of chatter died down.

"Thank you. My name is Leroy Kava—"

"*Go on, Leroy*!" Someone shouted. The audience chuckled lightly.

"Heh. Yes. I'm Leroy Kavanagh, and I'd like to thank you all for coming out. It is a very special night. When I was a younger man, I enjoyed not Country and Western, like many other people around this village, but Rock 'n' Roll."

The crowd whooped and cheered, stomping their feet and clapping.

"Yes. It's funny how many of you enjoy the same music as myself, but back then, Ballybriggs was a very different place. If you didn't go to mass on a Sunday like a good little boy, and if you didn't listen to the charts like everybody else, then you were *odd.* And they didn't like you." Leroy's face fell serious. "I remember being called names because of my taste in music. One in particular that stuck, because of my lack of weight and fuzzy hair, was *Thin Fizzy.*"

An outburst of laughter.

"Yes, it's funny to laugh about now, but back then, it was very hurtful, indeed. Either way, what I'm trying to say is, isn't it funny how times change? Over the years, those bullies who hated Rock 'n' Roll either kept quiet in their homes or moved away, allowing many of you younger folk to move in, bringing a much-needed piece of culture along with you. We needed culture."

Slow applause swelled.

"Thank you. I don't want to stay up here and ramble, but I will say this...Our community *needs* Rock 'n' Roll. Our community *needs* diversity. Thank you for keeping me in business for as long as you have. I opened this bar with the hopes of having Rock 'n' Roll bands come through on a weekly basis, and ever since nineteen eighty-six, I've done just that. And now, nearly thirty years later, I have the honour of bringing to my bar, one of my all-time favourite vocalists and guitarists. And we're very happy to have him. Ladies and gentlemen, please join me in welcoming, all the way from Seattle, Mister Bill Jennings!"

The crowd stood, cheering and applauding not like seventy-five people, but hundreds. Bill worked his way through the centre aisle, embarrassed by the empty seats at the back.

The audience clapped his shoulders and shouted praise as he passed. Climbing the stage, he nodded to the sound engineer, sitting in a booth out of sight to the audience. The crowd fell silent, watching eagerly. He lowered his guitar case to the floor and knelt beside it, taking out his Gibson.

"You can chat amongst yourselves for a minute," He shouted over his shoulder, very aware that seventy-five people were watching an elderly man squat on a stage with his butt turned. People chuckled. "Going to be a little while here."

After an embarrassing few minutes of back and forth with the sound engineer about cables and microphones (and having to ask the bartender to bring him a stool), Bill was ready.

"Good evening ladies and gentlemen." His voice came clear and crisp over the modest PA. "I'm very happy to be here in Ireland and doing this tour." He began tuning his guitar as he spoke, an old distraction he knew many guitar players used to keep the show moving. "The plan is to put out my first solo album, recorded here in County Wicklow, and have it out in the next couple of months on Packman Records. I'm very honoured that there's still an audience willing to listen, and I thank you for your time. Some of you may remember this one. Two Smoking Barrels recorded it way back in '79. It's called *The Marionette.*"

A polite clap rang out as Bill played the first chord. He closed his eyes and let the notes roll past his lips as he got lost in the music. It always happened that way. He could be doing a show in a full stadium or even in a tiny café—it didn't matter. When the music started, he drifted through the same sonic landscape.

Forty-five minutes later, he thanked the crowd for coming out. They gave a standing ovation and cried for an encore but Bill shook his head and said he hadn't prepared much else. They seemed to understand.

Nodding to Elliot and Wayne (their signal to start packing equipment) he made his way to the bar, the audience hobbling behind like a row of baby ducks after their mother. He signed a total of fifty albums, mostly original 70's vinyl pressings of *Dog Tired* and *The Marionette*, the biggest releases by Two Smoking Barrels. He'd even signed a handful of rare singles that he'd never known existed.

"That's the last photo I'm doing, thank you all very much."

Bill settled at the bar and ordered another pint. An old man sat smiling beside him, drinking what looked to be whiskey. Elliot and Wayne were at the far end of the bar, sorting out the financial side of the night with Leroy Kavanagh.

"Nice playing," the old man said. His voice sounded doughy, as if he'd had one joint too many. His hair reached the middle of his back, tied off in a frizzy ponytail. The bushy beard on his face lifted as he smiled.

"Thanks," Bill said. He pulled up a seat next to the man. "Did you come for the show?"

"Sure, sure. Buy you a drink?"

"I'm covered, thanks. But your next one's on me. Little token of appreciation."

"Much obliged, dude."

Bill cracked his back and thanked the bartender when his Guinness arrived. He took a large mouthful and wiped away the froth stuck to his beard. He thought no place in the world could pull a pint of Guinness as they could in Ireland. "First show out of the States in nearly twenty years," he said. "First show ever here in Ireland, actually. Did you enjoy it?"

"Oh, I thought it was perfect, man."

"Thanks. You got a name?"

"Frank," the old man said. "They call me Frank Carpenter."

"Well, it's a pleasure, Frank. They call me many names, most of them bad, but you can just call me Bill."

"Bill it is."

Frank stared him in the eye as if searching for something. He shifted his position on the stool and cleared his throat. Then he took another sip from his glass.

"There's magic in music, isn't there?" Frank asked, swirling the now nearly-melted ice cubes.

"There sure is."

"Can make your whole body shiver...Make your hair stand on end...Bring you to tears of joy...The entire scope of human emotion, tapped into by one brave enough to do it. You've got power in your hands when you play, Bill Jennings. You've got all the power in the world." He finished his drink and motioned to the bartender for a second. "If you just knew how to release it."

"What do you mean by that?"

Bill's knuckles tightened around his pint glass. His eye twitched. *Who in the world does this man think he is*? Telling *Bill Jennings*, of all people, if he only knew how to release real emotion in music.

"Let's drink up," Frank said. "And then I'll show you. I have many things to show you."

Bill saw something just then, a sort of glow in the old man's eye. It lasted only seconds, then vanished. *Trick of the light*, Bill thought. *For god's sake, drink up.*

Ordinarily, fans didn't spook him, no matter how fanatic or wild they may be, but Bill didn't pin Frank as a typical fan. Bill had been around many famous musicians in his life, and each one seemed to emit some sort of gravitational pull, as if, without even asking, you simply *knew* they were important. Their presence demanded your attention. Frank Carpenter had that very vibe.

"I have a place near here, Bill. Little cabin that I'm renting for the time being. I've acquired something that I'd like to pass along to you, if you'll have it."

At least he's not a crazed fan, Bill thought. *He's not drooling all over me. Besides, I've got at least fifteen years on the guy.*

Bill finished his pint with a gulp. "Okay, you've piqued my curiosity. What is it?"

The old man smiled, showing gnarled and browned teeth. "Come and see, man."

The cabin sat off the main road, tucked away down a narrow country lane. Bill and his new companion had taken a local taxi, free of charge, courtesy of Leroy's Lounge. As the cab taillights disappeared, smoke-like clouds wafted from both men's lips.

"How long have you been here?" Bill asked. He slipped his hands deep inside his pockets and shivered.

"Just the past week, man. Renting it from a very nice couple who own some properties all across Ireland. I mean, it's cheap, it's cosy, and that does me just fine. Know what I'm sayin'?"

"I get you."

Bill observed the house. A claw of weeds crawled up the walls. The stone front had once been painted white but now had faded to a nasty, curdled yellow. Red bricks broke through the shabby paint like sores, and as Bill watched, a spider the size of his fist scuttled along the surface.

"Jesus, that thing was huge!"

"Get them in the winter, man. Looking to find someplace warm, I think. Don't like the cold, they mustn't. Like myself." He chucked, showing crooked teeth that made him look ridiculously goofy. "Hey, never thought I'd have something in common with spiders, did you? Eh?"

"Guess I've never given it much thought."

"Hah. Anyway, let's get inside before we end up like that guy at the end of that movie. Know that one?"

"Sure."

Bill didn't, but he also didn't want to stand outside much longer. The forest looming behind the house gave him the creeps, and after seeing that spider, he didn't want to think about what else might be out there.

Frank spoke as if reading Bill's thoughts. "Ain't nothing out there to worry about." His voice sounded low and thick, his eyes far away. Bill's skin crawled. "Nothing big, I mean. It's Ireland, man. Just some birds, foxes, and maybe the odd newt, you know?"

"Sure."

Bill felt too stunned to ask Frank how he'd known what he'd been thinking. *I gestured with my eyes.* That had to be it. Frank Carpenter could get a good read on people. Those types of people existed in the millions.

Frank clomped through the overgrown plants towards the front door. When he reached it, he gave it a kick. The door swung open.

"Safe to leave it unlocked like that?" Bill asked. He made his way to the doorstep.

"Nobody around here, man. Nobody at all. Wicklow's like Ireland's free-zone. No nothing around here but forests and tiny towns. Being a Yankee like yourself, I like that. Don't you?"

"Sure."

Frank led the way into the hall with a smile. Bill closed the door behind them. The door jammed before it reached the frame and he pushed it with both hands, slamming it shut. Frank apologised, saying that always happened, then clapped his hands. The light bulb overhead, caked in cobwebs, popped to life.

"You've got to be kidding me," Bill muttered, his mouth open. "Clap-activated lights, in *this* place?"

Frank nodded. "That couple who rent it to me are odd, right? Everything's, like, *spooky*, or something."

Bill agreed. He observed the hallway as he followed Frank to the living room. A damp smell drifted in the air, reminiscent of dirty, boggy clothes. Water, Bill guessed, had settled into the strangely painted orange walls. Mould spread from one corner, looking like a Rochester test. They entered the living room.

"Cosy," Bill muttered. But he didn't mean it. The small room had a single couch to one side, looking like the carcass of some unfortunate animal. A small stove sat across from it, rusted and ancient. To the left of that stood an old-fashioned television with a bent antenna. All around were crowded bookshelves.

"It does the job, man. Know what I'm saying? Here, have a seat."

Bill did, and instantly regretted it. The damp, oily material made his body shiver on contact. He forced himself to smile. "Thanks."

Frank laughed. "Dude, you hate this place, right?"

Bill tried to object but Frank waved his hand. "Me, too, don't worry! But we don't have to be here long, so relax. I just want to give you something, that's all."

Bill still couldn't put his finger on why he'd decided to follow this man home, and the more time that went by, the more insane the decision seemed. Frank had absolutely nothing he wanted. In fact, he was quite content with how things were going, so there was nothing he really *needed*. With the tour booked, he had a free place to stay while tracking the album, and once sales took off, he hoped to rent his own place. It wouldn't be a lot, but it would do. So what brought him here?

Frank smiled, his eyes dopey. "You're here because something tells you it feels right, man. And you're correct in thinking that. It's like a calling, isn't it? You just feel it, all deep in your bones and stuff."

"Sure, I do."

"So, let's quench that curiosity, baby."

Frank sidled to the bookshelf, his white ponytail bouncing. His head moved slowly from side to side as he read the spines of the books. "All right," he said slowly. "Here it is."

Pulling one of the books free, he presented it to Bill with a crooked grin. "Ta-da."

Bill exploded with laughter, his side hurting with each breath. "A phonebook? That's what I came all this way for?"

Frank he-hawed, a completely idiotic sound. "It *is* a phonebook, man! How amazing is that? But you know that old saying. Never judge a book by its cover and all that."

Bill wiped a tear from his eye, getting himself under control. "What do you mean?"

"Open it."

Bill tossed Frank a look before working the dusty pages. He had no idea what he was looking for, but he thought he'd know when he found it. He was right. "What in God's name is this?"

Pulling out two sheets, Bill grimaced. The texture felt more like dried out stretches of skin than paper. He held them by the top corner, wrinkling his nose. *Horrendous*, He thought. Terribly old things, awfully filthy, and somehow dreadfully wrong. Faded ink lined both sides of each page in a mismatch of text and symbols.

"Frank, just what the hell am I holding?"

"The secret to the universe, man. At least, a part of it, anyway."

A cold chill worked its way up Bill's spine. "What do you mean?"

"Ever hear of the Necronomicon, dude?"

"You mean that fictional book by that old horror author? Lovecraft, right?"

"Give the man a prize. You're spot on, friend...Only, you got something wrong." He leaned forward, his voice quiet. "*That book's not fictional.*"

Bill stayed silent a moment, trying to find the right words. Part of him, the rational part, wanted to throw these pages at Frank and walk away. The other part, the curious part, kept him rooted to the couch with a tingle of excitement in his lower stomach. *I'm onto something here*, He thought. *Something important...*He itched to find out.

Smiling, Bill laid the pages on the couch next to him. "You almost had me there, Frank."

"Oh yeah?" Frank teased.

"Yeah. I mean, what's even written here? Gibberish from a million years ago?"

"To some, sure. You're partly right. But not if you know how to read it, and know what to do with it."

"One man's trash and all, huh?"

"Exactly. Hand me those puppies, would ya?"

Frank took the pages with a quivering breath that sounded almost sexual. Bill shuddered. The old hippy shuffled the pages about, seeming to look for something in particular.

"You know all about the tritone, I'm sure. Being a musician, right?"

Bill laughed. "The Devil's interval. I'm a rock musician, Frank, so you'd be right about that."

"Give *me* a prize, I say, huh? You know, it was first called that when Guido of Arezzo developed his system of hexachords. Did you know that? They called it *Diabolus in Musica...*"

"The devil in music." Bill nodded. "Handy piece of information to have if I'm ever at another pub quiz."

"On the button, man. And you know *why* they called it that? It's because they were tapping into the root of something great. They knew it, too. They could feel it. Anyone who heard it could feel it, and they didn't need a scientific reason to know why. Some primal part of them just knew that they were hearing something insanely powerful, and evil."

"Which is what?"

"One of the oldest secrets in music, man. A key to open up people's minds, to open up doors."

"Doors? What kind of doors?"

"Doors to places you couldn't even imagine, my friend. *Other worlds.* Worlds that would make you lose your mind even if you only gave them a glance. Places with no water, only sand; others with skies as purple as a bruise; some with spiders the size of school buses. They'd be sure to make the one on the outside of this house like a microbe, right? I'm telling you, there are things living out there that would tear you limb from limb just for *being.* Because they hate your kind."

Bill didn't ask why these creatures hated him, hell, he doubted he could say anything at all at that moment. His mind whirled at a thousand thoughts per second. The excitement building inside him was undeniable, as if he'd bought a brand new sports car but the salesman kept dangling the keys and talking about the amazing features instead of letting him drive the beauty.

Because that's exactly what's happening here, Bill thought. *This crazy bastard's already made up his mind. He's going to give me control. Control of things beyond anything I could ever have imagined.*

"How does this work, Frank?" Bill tried to hide the excitement in his voice, aware that he wasn't doing a very good job. "What do we do?"

Frank nodded slowly, another doped-up smile splitting his face. "We write a song together, you and me. Right here, and right now. I teach you the melody, and we write the words, you dig? For this to be effective, all we need is the right melody. Music is an international language, you know that. You can throw any old words into the melody and it will work—so long as you sing it with conviction. You need to *feel* this melody, deep down inside you, and make other people feel it, too. Think you can do that? Think you can sing this *for real*?"

Bill's mouth became a thin line. "I make a living off of singing from my heart. Don't doubt that. I've never played a single show without giving it every fibre in my body. I don't believe in playing unless I mean it. That's what performing is all about."

"Well then, there's something we can agree on." Frank no longer looked goofy and good-natured. Now, Bill thought, the man looked terribly ancient and deadly serious. "Let's get started, shall we?"

Elliot leaned against the wall, trying his very best to keep down the ball of nerves that threatened to take him over. He'd listened to Bill's tale of Frank Carpenter quietly, without question. Now, he needed answers, but he didn't know where to begin.

"So, we wrote that song," Bill said, lifting his head to look Elliot in the eye. "And I swear, I've never heard anything like it. Frank had an old Guild acoustic in the kitchen, said it was from '87, gorgeous thing, and he gave it to me. He told me what notes to play, how to play 'em. Everything about it was nerve-wracking. I couldn't play one note for too long, because that could cause serious damage, Frank said. I couldn't *bend* a note too much, because even the slightest semi-tone over would render the tune useless. It had to be perfect. And I was determined to make it so."

Leaning back in his chair, Bill Jennings sighed. Something shimmered in his eye and Elliot thought for a moment that the man might cry. "I'll tell you something, kid. Whatever this Frank Carpenter is, wherever he's from...he ain't human. And he certainly ain't of this world."

Elliot waited for Bill to continue, not knowing how to react, while Bill nibbled at his lower lip, his eyes seeing something that Elliot couldn't. He had the look of a man who'd seen the Devil himself.

"We wrote the damn song, man. We did it."

"Why?"

Suddenly, Bill slammed his arms down, making Elliot jump. "Are you a musician? Huh? Are you? Do you know the first thing about being an artist?"

"No?" Elliot said, barely a whisper.

"Over thirty years I've been trying to do one thing. And that's to get people to *understand what I'm about.* I've written songs that made people cry, I've written songs that people've told me have gotten them through the worst times in their whole lives. Soundtracks to better days, even. I've looked out into the eyes of thousands, seen their undivided attention laid upon me like a goddamn *God,* kid...And you know what?"

"What?"

"I haven't seen that for nearly fifteen years."

With a sniffle, Bill fell back into his seat. He wiped his face and crossed his arms over his chest, breathing slowly. "You know what I see when I get up in front of a big crowd now? Let me backtrack a little, actually. First of all, there is no big crowd for me. Not anymore. Can you imagine what that's like? Imagine owning your own *army* of devoted fans, and then, one day, they're all just gone...You have no idea what that *feels* like. To work so hard, build what's in *no way* less than a fucking *empire*, and then see it all dwindle out...Poof...From thousands, to hundreds, and then, just a handful.

"Those handfuls of people, the devoted ones who remember, like the ones I've been playing to here in these small towns—they understand music. They *get* it. And they just want to feel that raw, pure energy I can offer. We agree on that?"

Elliot nodded, not wanting to speak. He was beyond such things. Bill continued.

"So, as I was saying, those big crowds these days, when I do get to play them, are a joke. The only time I get to see a sizeable audience is at a festival. A lower slot on the bill when the place is still just getting busy. A nostalgia act for the older ones who've allowed time to take that feeling away from them. They don't *remember* what music feels like. And now, when I look out onto those crowds, I see blank faces...People talking amongst themselves, drinking beers and dancing to unheard music. Teenagers, I swear to fuck this is true, with their phones out, taking pictures of themselves at the front barrier to prove they were there. Posting it online to their friends who don't even care. Honestly, *no one gives a shit*! We've devalued music so damn much that people just expect you to bleed for free. And why would you do that? Why would you tear your heart out to write the best thing you've ever written when people won't pay attention, and even worse, want it for free?"

"You could do it," Elliot offered, "because you love it?" As soon as the words left his lips, he regretted it.

Bill smirked. "Because you love it? Elliot, kid, listen...I was put here to do the one goddamn thing I'm good at. No, that I'm *perfect* at. Playing music is the hand that God dealt me. I can write music better than most of the human population, and I'm not being big headed when I say that, I'm just stating what I know to be fact. I can play, sing, express, better than most anybody. That's what I got put here to do. Now, imagine what it feels like, when that's your damn trade, and that's what you're the king of doing, and people want it for free. They *demand* it for free. And they won't even listen for more than ten seconds to something you've worked on for months. What else am I supposed to do, huh? Sell coffee or work in a grocery store? When I have so much to give? Can you see where I'm coming from?"

Elliot could. Of course he could. He didn't doubt that the world had swiped the carpet out from beneath every artist's feet in the last decade, leaving them up shit creek without a boat. "I know where you're coming from," he said. "And I agree."

"Thank you…Elliot, we've gone too far, and now there's no turning back. Isn't that the saddest thing you ever heard? There's no way people will pay for music like they used to. The pull factor of being a rock star as a teenager is drying up, and one day, it'll be gone completely. Because every two-bit mongoloid with a laptop and some software thinks they can be a musician. People who have no business being a part of the industry are now taking over. We've gone too far." Bill was silent a moment, seeming to contemplate. "How do you think record sales will be for this release?"

"I think we can get into the thousands within the first week."

"One thousand? Worldwide?"

"One or two, with the right promotion."

Bill laughed. "See, that's what I'm talking about. Back in the day, shit, even in the nineties, you'd be talking over a hundred thousand in the first week for me."

"So, what are you thinking of doing?"

Bill's eyes widened. "Oh, no, see, I've already done it, Elliot. Frank and I have cracked it. We've made something that nobody can resist. If music was a drug, you've only ever heard tobacco and beer. This is China White fuckin' heroin."

"That note," Elliot said. "That was caused by the song?"

"I premiered the new track last night, kid. And I can safely say, it's the greatest thing I've ever written."

"What happened? Tell me, what happened."

"We've gone too far," Bill said with a smile. "And now there's no turning back."

Bill Jennings took to the stage of Patterson's Bar in Killdubh at eight. At nine-fifteen, he thanked the audience and packed the equipment. Nine-twenty, he stood at the bar and ordered his first drink. And at nine-thirty, his first fan approached.

The newcomer wore a pair of horn-rimmed glasses. Bill guessed him to be in his late twenties, with long, greasy hair, and a faded army jacket drooped over his skeletal frame. Admiring the large number of badges adorned to the jacket, Bill smiled and raised his drink.

"Thanks for coming out," he said. "Hope you enjoyed it."

Chatter filled the bar, but something seemed off to Bill. The audience, a measly fifteen people or so, kept shooting Bill strange looks.

"You don't talk? Want me to sign something?"

Bill noticed the man sweated profusely. His moist forehead glistened beneath the dim glow of the bar lights. He licked at his cracked lips.

"What was that?" He asked, his voice like sandpaper. "What in the *world* was that?"

Fear washed over Bill then, making his stomach flutter. "A new song," He mumbled. "Did...Did you like it?"

The entire room fell silent. Bill felt their eyes on him, crawling all over his body, including those of the bartender and other staff members who hadn't paid in tonight. The audience looked closely, their pupils scanning frantically as if looking for something in particular. Bill wanted to be sick.

"I think I should—"

A glass slammed on the bar. Bill looked over his shoulder and saw Frank Carpenter, sitting alone with a smile on his face. The old hippy nodded to Bill. "Tell the boy what it is you played, man."

Nobody seemed to notice Frank as he spoke. Their attention stayed on Bill.

"It was, um...Just a new song, is all. You liked it?"

"I loved it, Bill Jennings." The man spoke slow, as if he'd recently been sedated. He never blinked. "I *more* than loved it...I *felt* it. You touched me."

"And me," a man said from somewhere out of sight. The audience gathered in a semi-circle, blocking Bill in. He suddenly felt very claustrophobic.

"Me, too," another woman agreed. More joined, mumbling like an active beehive.

"Will you play it again?" The first man asked. His eyes vibrated in their sockets.

Bill tipped his head. "I'm packed up, kid. Sorry about that, really."

"Please. Play it again, please...My arms are itching...My heart is racing."

"You...You what?"

"My groin feels all funny," he said. "Oh god, I need to hear it, please..."

A skin-crawling symphony of begging spread throughout the crowd. That noise reminded Bill of the living dead from a movie he'd once seen back in the early seventies. It'd scared him beyond words then and it absolutely petrified him now.

"I..." Bill struggled to talk. It felt like a golf ball had been wedged down his throat.

"He's working on recording it as the new single as we speak, folks." Frank jumped off his stool and stood, smiling. The audience watched him. "I'm his manager, and that's an official press release right there."

"Is it true?" The first man asked. He looked at Bill with something akin to panic.

"Um, yeah...It's the first single for the new album. Should be done real soon."

A large man stepped forward. He trembled slightly, scratching at his rotund belly. "When?"

"Tomorrow?"

"Tomorrow?" The big man broke into tears. "That's *hours* away, Bill! How the hell do you expect us to cope without it for *hours*? I mean, what am I supposed to do? Go home to my wife and tell her that I can't do nothing because I have to wait until the morning to hear Heaven again? Is that what you're expecting? I'd kill her if she spoke, you know that? Her goddamn voice isn't yours...I...I can't do that, Bill. No. You can't make me kill my wife."

"Then how about this," Frank offered. Bill suspected a laugh lurking just behind the man's lips. "I shouldn't *really* be saying anything, not to the public, you know? But you guys have been so great that I'll let you in on a little secret."

All eyes went to Frank now, and the relief lifted like a physical weight from Bill's shoulders.

"There's a second song," Frank said.

The crowd erupted into chatter.

"Quiet down and listen, folks. There ya go...Yeah, there's a second song. And if you thought the one you heard tonight was good, this one's going to blow your goddamn brains out the back of your heads. Imagine what you heard tonight as the appetiser. We're cooking up the main course as we speak."

"Oh God, I just can't wait," A woman yelled. She sounded like she was close to orgasm.

"I'm sure you can't, darling." Frank pushed himself past some of the audience members and made his way to Bill's side. He clasped Bill's shoulder and gave a tight squeeze. "But now, we have to get back to the studio, okay? We're working real hard, day and night, to make it perfect and get it to you as soon as possible."

"All right," a balding man with glasses said. "I guess that's fair."

"It's more than fair. We'll have this new song available to you as soon as we possibly can. Hey, we'll even get it on international radio."

A redheaded woman lifted her hands to her mouth. "Oh thank God," she said, shaking. "Thank fucking Christ."

"Sure, sure. And thank *you* all for coming out tonight, but like I said, we've got to get going now."

Another woman screamed. A man standing beside her told her to shush. The entire audience looked as if they were jacked on coke.

"Please don't go," the redheaded woman said. "Play that song, just one more time?"

The room exploded in agreement. They begged, pleaded, and one man fell to his knees, speaking in tongues, his head tossing back and forth. Another emptied his pockets and began sorting through the contents. He approached Bill.

"Here's forty-seven euros, twenty-three cent. Will you play it, just once more, for that?"

Frank laughed and shook his head. "My Bill will play it all you like once it's released, but you won't care by then, because you'll already own it on your computer-majig, so you can listen to it whenever you please. But just out of interest before we go, how much would you be willing to pay for this new single?"

"I'd give my life." The man who spoke stood easily over six-feet tall, wearing an old tartan shirt and sporting a very thick beard. "My house. My Jeep. My own children. You name it, I'll pay it."

When the others agreed, Bill nearly passed out. He couldn't believe their words. He had known the song held some sort of power over people, but he had no idea how bad it would be until that moment. He'd thought, maybe, they would love it so much that they'd offer to buy it right then and there, or perhaps pre-order the album, forcing Packman Records to go into second pressing immediately.

He had thought they'd love it like no other song they'd ever heard, but he never thought they'd go *insane.*

"Yes, you did," Frank whispered. "You felt it, and it got you giddy, remember? Don't lie to yourself, Bill Jennings. It's not attractive. They're going to worship you again, just like you wanted. You knew this would happen from the beginning. They'll be back, like never before, in their millions."

The long-haired man asked, "What's the name of this new song?"

"I don't know," Frank said, squinting one eye. "Fuck it, call it Brain Dead Blues."

With that, Frank started forward, pushing people aside. They parted like the Red Sea as Bill climbed from his stool with quivering legs. He clutched the bar to stay upright, his knees nearly buckling, and he studied the faces before him.

"I love you, Bill Jennings," a man spoke. He looked to be in his sixties, his wife hanging on his arm. The wife cried, smiling at Bill. "Me too," she said. "I love you, too."

"I love him more." This came from the large bearded man. His face grew red. "Don't you dare touch him, none of you! I love him *more*!"

"Okay, folks." Bill's voice sounded far away to his own ears. "I'll see you all at the next show, and we'll get this new single online tomorrow, that's a promise."

One man jumped from foot to foot, squeezing his groin as if it pained. *"I just can't fucking wait, man!"* Spittle flew from his lips. "Be careful, all right? Don't let anything happen to you before tomorrow. If you die before finishing that song, the fucking world will end. There would be no reason to live! For anybody!"

"Don't die, Bill! Please, don't die!"

Bill assured the crowd that he wouldn't as he pushed his way to the front door. Every shoulder he brushed off, every arm or leg, made his skin crawl. Then someone said something that made him pause.

"Did you just threaten Bill Jennings?"

It was the large, bearded man again, and he was snaking his way towards the crotch-squeezer.

"Why in god's name would I threaten him? I love him!"

"*Not like I do*!"

The bearded man threw a punch so hard that the crotch-squeezer didn't have time to react. It sounded like a baseball bat smacking steak. The crotch-squeezer went down immediately. Then all hell broke loose.

Bill tried to force his way outdoors as the fight began. A woman smashed against him, pushed, and they both sprawled to the ground. His ankle got caught beneath her and he struggled to pull it free. Pain crept through his leg. He heard his name called over the screams and smacks, and then Frank appeared.

"Still wasting time here? We need to get going, Bill. Stop fooling around. Not getting any younger."

Frank reached out and Bill took his dry, calloused hand. With a grunt, Frank pulled him to his feet and held open the front door. "Come on, now, dude. Let's make a move."

A winded gasp could be heard as one man gut-punched another. The victim doubled over and fell about. Bill jumped to the side to avoid him but wasn't quick enough. His face smacked the wall. Pain blossomed immediately and he cursed, rubbing the spot.

"You hurt Bill Jennings, you stupid sonofabitch!"

A woman scuttled towards the doubled-over man with a pint glass held above her head. Bill got out the door just before he heard the smash. Nobody came after him. Nobody called out. The whole crowd was far too busy drawing blood to even notice he'd left.

"Come on," Frank said. He lit a cigarette, a smile on his face. "Get in the taxi. We're going back to your place this time."

Bill and Frank made it to Elliot's Bed and Breakfast just after midnight. No lights were on in the main house, letting Bill know that Elliot wasn't home. *Still at the meeting in Dublin*, He thought. *Good.*

"My cabin's around back," he said. "Come on."

Bill led the way around the house, the freezing night air chilling his face. He shivered, pulling his jacket tighter around him.

"Down here," he said. "Nice little place."

"And it's all in there? The recording equipment?"

"All there, and all set up, ready to go."

"Good."

Bill removed the keys from his pocket and opened the door. When he stepped inside, he shuddered at the change in temperature. Frank followed him and closed the door behind.

"Cosy in here," Frank said. "Real nice digs, man."

"Does well enough for my needs. Come on, here's the setup."

Bill led the way to the other side of the cabin where the laptop and mixing console sat. He tapped the laptop keys, waking the monitor and recording program.

"Digital recording software," he said. "Been a long time since I saw some tape used in a studio. In fact, it's been a while since I saw a proper studio, at all. Last album I did was a DIY job just like this, and in all honesty, the thing sounded just as good as or better than any big budget studio I ever used."

"You talking to stall, man?"

"Probably."

Bill swallowed. He'd be lying if he said he wasn't nervous, but he was sure Frank already knew that. Running a hand through his hair, he sighed. "Look, Frank, what happened back there?"

"You know exactly what happened."

"I know that I played the new song we wrote, but after that, I don't."

"You do, Bill. Don't lie to me, man, don't even think you can."

Bill stayed quiet, waiting for Frank to explain.

"You knew exactly what you were dealing with. You knew the power it possessed because you could feel it. I could see it in your eyes when you played, man. You could see the effect it was having on them, how they squirmed in their seats, how their eyes glazed over like they were in a trance. *You knew.* And you *liked* it."

Bill didn't even hesitate. "I did," he said.

"We have the power to make something incredible out of you. A God, Bill Jennings. A mother-fucking God. But we need to work fast because those Crazies are going to be getting restless. And then they're going to come looking for you. Some might get depressed and end their lives from withdrawal, already, but the others? The ones with their brains melted and rage on their minds? Who knows."

"They might try and find me?"

"Wouldn't you, man? You saw exactly what's happening to them. Their brains are frying like eggs, and it's driving them crazy! You're the only thing that they can think of, and the idea of that song to them is like the idea of the last smack in the world to a junkie. They'll be sniffing about for it, soon, so stop fucking around. Let's get this recorded and make history."

The note, slid beneath the cabin door almost three hours later, went unnoticed.

To Bill, the process felt less like a recording than it did documentation. They never touched the first song they'd written. Frank said they had much bigger matters to tend to. Instead, they worked on the second song. The important piece.

The procedure went like this: Frank would call out a phrase and tell Bill the melody, line by line. Bill would play it, and once Frank was satisfied that Bill had it absolutely perfect, they'd hit the red button. Bill would play it twice, then they'd listen back and pick the best take. They'd dragged that take to a master track on the recording interface and then start with the next line. They never recorded two lines in a row, and Frank was very stern about that. He said they couldn't play the arrangement from start to finish until the time came. He never said when that would be, only that Bill would know.

Each time Bill got a line right, he felt nauseous. Something about the melody got under his skin, wriggled about like a maggot, infecting him. He vomited three times. Twice, he stopped playing to dry-heave, but after some water, he could continue. Each time it happened, Frank laughed so hard that his face reddened.

Five hours passed before they finished. The entire song, Bill counted, clocked in at one minute and seven seconds. And now, with the sun beginning to rise, he strolled to the window and looked out at the garden, bathing in twilight. He faintly heard early birds, tweeting their morning song. The plants were mildewed and still.

"That's it," Frank said, his voice harsh and raspy. "It's done."

Bill yawned and scratched his face. His eyes stung from lack of sleep. "What have we done exactly, Frank?"

"You're damn excited about this, aren't you? I can see it in your eyes. No, don't worry, you've got every reason to be because this is the big one, man. This track is going to blow people away." Frank's eyes suddenly widened. "Well, well, what have we got here?"

Bill watched as Frank bent slowly, coming back up with a piece of paper in his hand and a smile on his face. "They've found us," he said, shaking the note.

"Who?"

Frank read the note like a love letter from a secret admirer. He chuckled and snorted, pointing out sentences that gave him a tickle. Bill turned cold with each word. When he was finished reading it, Frank wiped at his eyes and tried to catch his breath.

"Somebody came here?" Bill asked. He worried he might pass out. "They're going to kill themselves? Because of me?"

"Oh, Billy-boy. You didn't mind when they were busting each other up back at the bar for you, so why worry now?"

"I did mind, of course—"

Frank interrupted him by raising a hand. “Stop. Now you’re insulting me. One more lie out of you and I’ll show you things that would make your brain seep out your ears like stew.”

Bill didn’t doubt that for a moment. Everything Frank had said so far, no matter how bizarre or surreal, had been the truth. Bill had seen too much to question it.

The cabin door creaked open.

“Hey, I saw the lights on, you guys working on something?” Wayne Truman stepped inside. He wore a nightgown and his hair stood up at crazy angles from sleep. He had on a pair of glasses, and stubble darkened his cheeks. “What’s going on?” He asked.

“Wayne? I thought you were at the meeting with Elliot?” Bill said.

Wayne smiled. “It’s six in the morning, man. Meetings don’t usually last half a day.”

Frank arched his eyebrows at Bill before turning to Wayne. “You boys have got a hit on your hands with this one, son, believe me. Why don’t we go talk business and leave ol’ Bill here to catch some rest, huh?”

Wayne smiled politely. “Um, sure. Just...Who are you?”

“I’m Bill Jennings’ new manager and co-writer, and I’m pleased to meet you. Hope you guessed my name.”

With that, Frank clicked his fingers and Wayne fell still. The smile slid from the man’s face as his shoulders drooped, looking like a bad magician’s trick. But deep down, Bill knew this wasn’t a trick.

“I’m going to take ol’ Wayne here back to the house, and you’re going to get some sleep, hear me?”

Bill nodded, speechless.

“Hey, hey...How you holding up, dude?”

“Someone’s about to kill themselves because of me...We have to stop them, don’t we?”

"You know you have absolutely no intention of doing that. And believe me, by the time this song gets aired, many, many more people will have died. They'll be the lucky ones. But you already know that, because you can feel it. And you're not going to try and stop it, are you?"

Bill's mind slopped like a soupy mess. He couldn't collect his thoughts, no matter how hard he tried. "I guess not..."

"You guess right." Frank smiled then, his face a frightening mask in the cold light of dawn. "You did good work, Bill. Be proud. I'm going to leave now, you understand? And you're going to catch a nod."

"Okay, I guess I'll—"

His eyelids began to droop, heavy as lead. His vision blurred and doubled, and he struggled to fight it. "Frank, I can't keep my..."

Where Frank should have been, a figure stood—a figure not entirely human. A large mass of wriggling bits and eyes slopped from former arms and legs, and Bill screamed. Then the world turned black.

"So that song is on the laptop right now?" Elliot asked. He needed to sit down, but he couldn't move. His chest felt constricted and he wanted his inhaler, but something kept him rooted to the spot.

"It's right there, Elliot. And it's calling me."

"Why? Why would you play it? There's people dead because of this! How could you do such a thing?"

"*Because I want people to listen*!" Bill slammed his hands down and stood, stalking towards Elliot. "There's no power in the *world* that could help me resist what that man was offering. None! People have forgotten the true value of music, and I'm here to remind them. I'm here to give it to them like they've never had it before."

"Bill. Back away."

For the briefest instant, Elliot caught sight of something in Bill's expression. He thought it might've been remorse, but it disappeared too soon to tell.

"I think they'll be here soon," Bill said, nodding towards the door.

"Who?"

"The Crazies...They're hunting me like a pack of wolves. I dreamed about it. Their brains are melted into a stew. One even has a chainsaw, I saw it. They want me. They want this song."

"You're really frightening me. I'm serious, I'm fucking terrified right now."

"Me too, kid...But isn't it a good kind of fear? Like a rush or something?"

Elliot shook his head, still unable to move.

"Come on, it is. These Crazies will come, foaming at the fucking mouth for this track, and they'll stop at nothing for it, and I'm going to play it to them when they arrive. They're my fans, forever. Unconditionally. My music's all they live for. And isn't that all anybody could ever want? To be recognised as a true artist, for people to *get* what they do?"

"But you're already a recognised artist, Bill. You had your moment in the spotlight back when Two Smoking Barrels were big. Even now, you've got enough of a following to make a comfortable living out of this new album, and with sales and tour dates, isn't that enough?"

"You don't walk in Heaven just to return to Earth, kid. I'm *special.* My music is the reason for these people's existence, and you want me to just live *comfortably*?" Bill's face fell. "I'm a God, Elliot."

"You didn't even write that song...Frank told you what to do."

"*You little sonofabitch—*"

Bill came fast, but Elliot moved quicker. He darted to the right just as Bill's fist cracked the cabin wall. Stumbling back, Bill glared at him, cradling his hand. His voice bellowed throughout the room. "This is *my* song! This is *my* legacy! And—"

He paused then, looking out the cabin window. A smile spread across his face. Elliot got chills.

"And these are *my* people," he said.

Elliot rushed to the window beside him, wiping condensation from the glass. Outside, darkness stretched in all directions, the only light source coming from the house. And in that light...

Elliot watched as three figures stalked across the back lawn while more shuffled around the side of the house. Their mouths hung open stupidly, and they lurched as if they'd been in an accident. Elliot supposed they had, in a way. Their brains had fried.

Bill's vision had come true. One of them carried a chainsaw.

Elliot found it hard to breathe. His knuckles turned white from gripping the windowsill. His eyes wouldn't move from the figure with the saw. He dragged it like a dead carcass, the blade leaving a gash in the earth. "Why have they got weapons, Bill?" Elliot asked.

"Because they can't exactly chance somebody getting in the way of them hearing my song, can they?"

Bill watched as five more people rounded the house. Three women and two men. One of the women carried a garden rake, another a knife, and the third held a hand trowel. The man in front had a large rock that came to a frighteningly sharp tip. The second held what looked to be an iron.

Elliot nearly burst into hysterics right then and there but managed to hold back. He couldn't take it. An iron? His brain wouldn't register the sight out the window as reality.

"That man has an iron," he said. "Would you look at that."

Bill chuckled. "He sure does...He sure does."

Pushing himself from the window ledge, Bill smiled to Elliot. "Out of my way, kid. I need to get to the laptop. It's not very polite to be unprepared when guests arrive. And as you can see, they're almost here."

"They're going to kill me, aren't they?"

"Why would they do that? Unless you plan on getting in their way, that is?"

"I don't want to hear that song, Bill. I don't want to become one of them."

Bill shook his head. "It won't make you one of them. From what I saw in my dream, this track will do things much more powerful than you or I could ever imagine. Something much different to brain melting. So, please, step aside. And don't be rude to my guests. They've come a long way. Besides, you were a fan first, weren't you? Aren't you curious to hear the new single?"

Elliot wanted to punch Bill, wanted to knock him out. But he didn't. Terror had left him a quivering mess, and, instead, he stood aside.

"Thank you, Elliot." A smile touched Bill's lips. "That's a good boy. And look, our audience is here to witness the premier."

Faces of utter maniacs pressed against the cabin windows. Bulging eyes stared into the room. Some brought up their hands, their fists smacking against the glass as if trying to grab at Bill and not understanding the obstacle in their way. Their sagging mouths bobbed open and closed like fish out of water gasping for oxygen.

They're brain dead, Elliot thought. *They're going to tear me limb from limb.*

"Bill!" One of them yelled. The voice sent shivers down Elliot's spine. It sounded dopey and slurred. "I love you, Bill!"

"I love you, too!" Bill tapped the laptop, waking the monitor to show the recording program. "Love you a whole bunch."

Then a noise that made Elliot want to faint ripped through the night. A chainsaw.

Wood flew across the room as the saw teeth chewed through the cabin door. The deafening noise made Elliot smack against the wall and he willed himself to fall through it. The blade hacked away, slipping in and out of the hole as easily as a heated spoon through lard. The opening grew larger by the second.

Then the chainsaw stopped.

Somebody was screaming. It took Elliot a moment to realise it was him.

A bearded head popped through the hole in the door, crazy-eyed and covered in sweat. Elliot realised it must be the man Bill had spoken of before. The one who'd been at the second show.

"Coming in," the man declared. His expression was that of an absolute lunatic. "We can't wait for this."

Before Elliot could stop himself, he shouted out. "Wait!"

Silence. Bill arched an eyebrow and looked to Elliot, a smirk lifting his left cheek.

"I...I haven't cleaned up in here. You can't come in. You'll be able to hear the song just fine from outside."

Ridiculous. No way in hell would a dozen Crazies armed to the teeth stay outside because of an unclean cabin. Elliot knew that, but he also banked on the fact that they were fucking insane.

Bill chucked softly, a look of admiration on his face. He nodded, clearly impressed with the improvisation. "You know what, guys? The kid's right. Ain't no reason to hear the new track in such a dirty environment. It's a beautiful night out there, perfect setting for this new song. And as he said, you'll hear it just fine from outside."

"Okay, Bill," one of the women replied. "We don't want to do anything to upset you, don't worry. But please make sure it's up very loud!"

"I will, darling." Then Bill whispered, "Besides, this song isn't for them, Elliot. This one's for me. My reward."

Elliot kept his voice down, too. "You don't have to do this. Please, listen to me. Whatever is going to happen can't be worth ruining people's lives."

"The future of music has been ruined, don't you see that? There's no going back to a time when it had value. We've raped it for all it's worth, and now all we're left with is fake audible turds that don't deserve the title of a song. The real artists, the real musicians, they're left working in coffee shops and garages across the globe for next to nothing, and soon enough, they're all going to say, 'fuck it. What's the point?' And they're right to. They get no respect, why should we get theirs? This is the ultimate Rock 'n' Roll middle finger to the Universe for being so unkind to me and mine, kid. I'm going to tear a hole in its fuckin' ass."

"Don't do it, Bill, please. Don't punish the entire world for a mistake."

"Looks like we're all out of options, kid. We've gone too far. Do you propose an alternative? One in which artists are paid for their hard labour of putting words to the human condition and bottling the psyche? One in which songs about an ex-partner aren't saturating the airwaves and ass-shaking ain't a topic? Do you?"

Elliot wasn't surprised to hear the pleading in his voice. His bottom lip quivered. "I don't know."

"No...And that's just the problem, isn't it? No one knows. But I do. We're finished with music, so turn out the lights. Remember that song? It's over. Rock 'n' Roll's dead. We've killed it. Now let's give the whole damn universe the greatest *fuck you* for doin' it."

With that, Bill clicked a button on the laptop. The speakers began hissing white noise as the milliseconds on the recording program sped along, heading towards the first bar of the track.

Elliot groaned. Clutching his stomach, he fell to his knees. His eyes began to burn and his bladder tightened. His bones began to ache as if made of glass. He hadn't even noticed that the song had begun to play. He tried paying attention to it to keep his mind off the pain, but the sound only made it worse.

The tune, if it could even be called that, was incomprehensible. The chords weren't something Elliot had ever heard, perhaps because their purpose wasn't to sound musical, at all. He knew their real reason; to open a door. Listening to the song, Elliot thought it sounded like hearing a mathematical equation, if that could be at all possible. The guitar had been tuned erratically, octaves and half-notes spread across the sonic spectrum. Spaces between those notes were timed out to be very precise. The entire thing, to Elliot, came across as extremely complex. And yet, throughout all this chaotic dissonance, he *did* hear a melody.

Snaking through the disorder like a lurking predator, the melody bent and twisted to find its way. Elliot's brain thrummed when he caught it, like a rusted needle prodding the soft and fleshy meat.

Outside, Bill Jennings's faithful followers moaned in ecstasy. Their weapons dropped to the porch with dull thumps. Another bang came as one of them fell over and began to spasm on the ground. They screamed in pleasure, their voices shrill and hair-raising. And through it all, Bill Jennings stood motionless.

Elliot watched him from the floor, unable to move with the pain. At the edge of his vision, the room throbbed and pulsed, but Bill appeared unaffected. If anything, he looked to be enjoying himself.

Bill's mouth fell open and his eyes slid shut. He raised his hands, like a prophet receiving an order from a higher power, his head tilted back.

"Can't you feel it?" He yelled above the noise coming from the speakers. "It's happening...The whole world is about to feel the power of my music."

With that, something very strange happened. No loud pop or bang accompanied his words as Elliot expected, but *something* materialised in the corner of the room.

A rectangular section of shimmering air, not unlike a heatwave, bobbed and swayed, and through it, the cabin warped as though it'd gone underwater. The rectangle reached nearly to the roof and was as wide as a couch. Elliot didn't have to be told what it was.

He looked at the gateway to the Otherworld. And screamed.

The mirage-like effect had stopped, replaced by a clear view into an alien landscape. It happened suddenly and without warning, like a television set popping to life.

In the gateway, Elliot watched as dark clouds lulled along a rolling red sky. Something flew between those clouds, something too large to be a bird, and from this distance, the only thing Elliot could liken it to was a pterodactyl.

"You see it, too?" Bill shouted. "There it is, Elliot! The Otherworld! Another reality, another existence! The other side..."

Bill slowly crossed the room, cautiously inching closer and closer towards the hole in the world. He emitted a sound, fast and airy, like a child getting too close to his favourite movie star. Then he began to cry.

"It's so *beautiful*, isn't it?"

Something deep inside Elliot knew this gateway wasn't meant for human eyes, a secret not to be understood by the average being.

"I see a great land," Bill said. "It's magnificent...Stretching for miles, kid. Not touched by mankind. The earth looks dry, cracked, but there's a lake beside it. And there's something in it."

Elliot wanted to slam his own face into the cabin floorboards, smash his skull in until everything disappeared and he got to slip into the big sleep. But he couldn't resist the pull of curiosity that tugged like a fish hook somewhere deep in his mind. He began to cry.

"What's in the lake, Bill? For the love of God, what's in the lake?"

"There's structures down there," Bill said. "Tall things. They reach almost to the surface. If I had to guess, I'd say that this lake is drying up. They're...They're buildings, Elliot. I think I'm looking at a city. A city beneath the water."

Bill turned to face Elliot then, a bizarre cocktail of fear and hope on his face. "What do you suppose lives in a city beneath the water?" He asked.

Elliot screamed as something long and thick, like an engorged snake, slithered through the gateway from the Otherworld.

A tentacle! Dear god!

The tentacle flung about the room, smashing into the far wall before whipping back in the opposite direction. It found Bill, grasping his midsection, curling fast. A gasp forced its way from the rocker's lips, the sound a deflating tire would make. Bill smashed his fists down hard, but under that thick, oily skin lay nothing but muscle, and lots of it.

Bill's feet lifted from the ground, his legs thrashing while Elliot watched on in shock, shaking his head from side to side.

No, he told to himself. *No, no, no...*

Then the smell hit—a rotten, thick stench that forced him to breathe through his mouth. Elliot imagined a school of dead fish, baking in the sun. He wiped his watering eyes, just as what made the source of the smell appeared. A mass of black skin rose to blot out the red sky of the Otherworld. An eye filled the gateway, jet black and caked in mucus. It moved painfully slow, peering into the room, and when the eye landed on Elliot, he froze. He stared into the darkness. And that darkness stared back.

It's a God, Elliot thought. *I'm looking at a God.*

The cabin began to rumble. The head in the doorway slowly slipped away, back down to the unseen depths of the lake. The awful red sky reappeared, and the tentacle receded, pulling along the carcass of Bill Jennings. The rock star's head lulled from side to side, his long grey hair falling into his face. His mouth hung open, blood leaking and spattering the floorboards. Elliot winced as Bill's legs snapped, pressed beneath the weight of the tentacle. Then Bill disappeared, gone through the gateway of the Otherworld.

The song played on.

Summoning what little strength he could manage, Elliot stood. He stumbled towards the laptop, chancing a glimpse over his shoulder in case any of the brainsick had gotten inside. They hadn't, not yet. But Elliot knew they would soon. He could hear them clamouring as they scooped up their weapons from the porch. The chainsaw once again roared to life, making him yelp.

Elliot reached the laptop just as the horde of Crazies broke through the door, falling inside. Their attempts to stand were impeded by the bearded chainsaw-wielder who swung the blade in careless arcs, slicing into his companions. They didn't seem to mind. One man's arm severed at the elbow, spraying the rest with blood. The severed arm thumped to the ground, still clutching his weapon.

Elliot reached for Bill's guitar without thinking. He needed a weapon, anything, and swinging it over his head, he brought the instrument down as hard as he could on the laptop. A crash rang out as the computer shattered, the dreadful music abruptly cutting out. Elliot turned to face Bill Jennings' followers.

The man with the chainsaw screamed. He dropped his weapon, grabbing at his head as his eyes began to bleed. One by one, the Crazies fell to the floor. The woman with the rake slipped onto the still-running blade of the chainsaw. She howled as it ripped into her back with a sickening sound, jerking her body. Beneath her, smoke ebbed and curled, black and rotten. The chainsaw died with her, the noise slipping away and the body settling down. Silence followed.

Elliot allowed the guitar to slip from his hands and clatter to the ground. He looked to the people on the floor, wiping a hand through his hair. He whimpered. A dozen bodies lay inside his cabin.

He turned, stomach cartwheeling at what he might see, but the gateway had disappeared. Then he collapsed to his knees, cradling his face in his hands. He wept, something Bill Jennings had said earlier looping in his mind.

"We've gone too far, and now there's no turning back."

CRITTER

"WHAT ARE YOU?"

Angela stared at the tiny creature beneath her bed. It sat hunched in the corner, hugging itself. The little, piggish nose worked hard as it breathed, the skin on its face the texture of aged leather. No bigger than her forearm, the thing's body was covered in thick, dark hair. Its eyes glistened in the harsh light of Angela's torch. At nine years old, Angela had come to accept that there were no such things as monsters in the real world. Her father had told her so. And he had also told her that there were none, specifically, under her bed. Her father had been wrong.

"I'm not going to hurt you," Angela whispered. Stepping forward, she raised an eyebrow. "I swear. I'm nice. You can come out."

The creature looked back at her, shaking.

"My name's Angela. What's yours?"

No reply.

"Are you hungry? Do you want some food?"

The creature remained planted, eyes wide.

Angela had always wanted a puppy, but her father said they were too messy, and too much of a hassle to keep. She said she'd walk it every day, and never forget to feed it, but her father had still said no. A cat was out of the question too. They were sneaky and strange, and they freaked him out. In the end, they'd gotten two goldfish. They'd named them Goldie and Locks.

Angela hated Goldie and Locks. They were silly pets. Not even *real* pets, like David's dog Russ, or Mary's parrot, Jasper. Those were good animals. Proper pets. Goldie and Locks just swam about in their bowl, their mouths hanging open stupidly and sometimes with a trail of poop stringing out of their bottoms. Sometimes they'd even bang into the glass of their fishbowl. Still, she did enjoy feeding them. At least then, they *did* something.

A smile spread across Angela's face.

"Give me a second, hold on."

On her bedside table, there was a chocolate bar she'd stashed in her bag after school. She'd brushed her teeth by this time, so if her father knew about it, he'd put it in the cupboard until tomorrow. Angela had bought the chocolate bar as a comfort snack after Kathy Hogan from across the street had set her terrier on her again.

The small dog had yapped and snapped and chased her all the way home. She hated Kathy Hogan. Kathy didn't deserve to have a pet, but somehow, she always had everything she wanted. Not like Angela. At the very least, she deserved a secret chocolate bar.

Plucking the bar from the table, she unwrapped it carefully. The crinkle of the foil sounded very loud in the quiet house. Her father was still awake, talking softly on the phone in the next room. If he heard the wrapper, he'd be in like a shot. Angela held her breath and quickly wrestled the chocolate free of its confines. The sweet scent teased her and made her mouth water, but she wouldn't eat any of it. This bar was for the creature.

Getting slowly to her knees, Angela snapped the chocolate bar in two and placed one half under the edge of the bed. She scooted back to the middle of the room and waited. Her heart beat heavily inside her chest.

Angela gasped as the creature scurried from its hiding spot. It looked between her and the chocolate, its tiny bean-shaped nostrils twitching.

"It's okay. You can eat it. Go on."

The creature picked up the bar using both of its tiny, leathery hands. It opened its mouth and Angela's stomach fluttered.

Inside its mouth were small needle-like teeth poking from pale gums. It sank them into the chocolate then swallowed the piece whole. The creature's gaze fell upon the second half in Angela's sweaty hand. Then it started to move towards her.

Angela screamed.

Her father, panting and red-faced, burst into the room. His chest heaved beneath his white pyjamas, the phone still clutched in his hand.

"What is it, sweetheart? What's wrong, huh?"

"There's a monster under my bed, Daddy!"

Angela's father brought the phone to his ear. "I'll have to call you back, Rodger. There's a monster situation here that I need to solve, pronto...Yeah, sure. Talk soon." He put the phone into his pocket and lowered himself to the floor beside her, his knees popping as he went. He rubbed her back and chuckled. "Angie, there are no such thing as monsters."

"You're lying! There are! He's under there—*look!*"

Angela's father nodded to the chocolate in her hand. "And what's this, little lady?"

"It's chocolate. I gave him a piece and he wanted the rest, but his teeth were so *sharp,* they made me scream..."

"Sounds like you've had too much sugar, sugar. You know

you're not supposed to have chocolate this late. Is that the only one?"

Angela groaned. Parents always seemed to ask the dumbest questions. "Of course it is. You need to get the monster, Daddy!"

Her father sighed. "Okay, okay. I'll get the monster but then you're brushing your teeth, understand?"

"Yes."

"Good."

Angela's father crawled to the bed. He lowered his head and picked up Angela's torch, swiping it back and forth.

"...Oh my god..."

"What? What is it? Do you see it?"

"My Beatles records, Angie. What are they doing under here?"

"...I liked the pictures."

Angela's father sat back up with three vinyl records in his arms. Angela had taken them from the living room a week ago to read the liner notes and the lyrics. She liked The Beatles. She had just forgotten to put them back.

"There's no monster besides a record snatcher in here. That's you, kid. Now come on, time to brush your teeth."

"It's still under there, Daddy. I can't sleep in here tonight. I can't, I *won't*."

Angela's father placed his hands on his hips. "Okay, look. You can sleep in my room, but only for tonight, got it? Can't make a habit out of it again. You're a big girl now."

"Thanks, Daddy."

She slept restlessly that night, tossing and turning to the sound of her father's ceaseless snoring. The idea of the creature in the next room never left her mind. Still, after some time, she drifted off.

She dreamed of monsters.

In the morning, Angela's father made her favourite breakfast of bacon and eggs. She ate the eggs, but only picked at the bacon. The idea of eating meat turned her stomach after what she'd seen in her dreams.

"Nightmares," Angela said. "They weren't dreams. They were nightmares."

"Huh? Honey, is everything all right?"

"No, everything is not all right. There's a monster under my bed. He has sharp little teeth and a face like a pig. Nothing's going to be all right until I can get rid of him."

Shaking his head, Angela's father cleared their dishes. "Look, I have to get to work. I'm really sorry about this, honey, but Tammy isn't free to look after you today. Can you entertain yourself, like a big girl?"

Angela nodded. Inside, she was delighted. She loved being home alone. Being by herself meant doing *anything* she pleased. She could put make-up on her dolls, watch hours of TV, use her father's laptop, dress up in anything she liked, eat ice-cream...Even wander the forest out back, the one that her father hated being so close by. Kids always seemed to go missing in forests, he had once said.

"I'll call Harriet when I get to work," her father added, talking more to himself. "She might be available. Hopefully."

"Harriet? But Harriet smells of cabbage and she just sleeps all day. I hate her."

Angela's father laughed. "Yeah, that will happen when you get old. Listen. Do this for me, all right? I'm trying my best."

"Okay, sure."

"Everything will be better when I get home. I promise."

"Okay..."

Angela's father kissed her on the forehead and made to leave. He called out a goodbye as he stepped outside and she waited for the noise of the car engine to disappear before she got up and went to the front door.

Her father hated her being outside when there was no one at home to look out for her. It stemmed from the time he'd found her building a hut in the forest. There'd been a snake hole nearby that she'd never noticed. Her father had cried when he'd discovered her and made her promise that she'd never go into the forest alone again.

But *she* still wanted to go out. And besides, if Harriet *did* come by, she would be asleep on the couch all afternoon, so what difference did it make? It was too nice a day to miss. The sun was high, and it was a Saturday. Angela went outside.

"Get her, Preston!"

Angela's stomach lurched as the little yapping terrier raced towards her. Its jewel-encrusted collar gleamed in the bright sun. The dog made it to the other side of the road and onto the yard in a matter of seconds. Across the street, Kathy Hogan watched on in delight from her porch.

Angela scrambled with the front door handle, her hands slick with sweat. Something smacked against her leg. Then bit.

"Ow!"

Angela managed to get the door open, viciously shaking her leg. The tiny terrier yelped and flew through the air, landing on its back on the porch and scrambling to its feet. It bolted for her again, but she got the door closed just in time. The terrier barked and scratched on the other side of the door. Panting, Angela slid down to the floor and cried. She looked at her leg through blurred vision. Preston had bitten right through her favourite pair of tights.

"Little *shit*!" Angela shouted. It felt good to use bad words when her father wasn't around. "How dare you, you *bastard*!"

Kathy Hogan's voice came from outside, muffled by the door. "You hurt my Preston! I'll get you for this, Angela!"

Dabbing her eyes on her arm, Angela shuffled to the kitchen, her shoulders hunched. Kathy Hogan didn't deserve to have a dog. She just trained it to be mean and bite people so they would be afraid of her. Angela hated her. And she hated that dog, too. If only she could—

Angela's breath caught in her chest. The garbage bin was moving.

"You're in there, aren't you?"

The bag inside the bin stopped rustling.

"Come out. I'm not like Kathy Hogan. I wouldn't hurt you. I'm not mean. I promise."

Angela sniffled and crept towards the bin. She wasn't afraid. If she could face Preston, then she could face a piggy, little thing like this. She reached out, inching closer.

The creature sat on top of the rubbish, more terrifying than she remembered. Its furry little back shuddered as its large mouth worked open and closed, those tiny fish-hook teeth tearing through that morning's leftover bacon. It caught sight of her and screamed.

The noise was like a tea kettle on the boil, high and sharp. Angela screamed, too.

When they stopped, the critter trembled. Taking a deep breath, Angela shook her head. "It's okay. You're just like a spider, aren't you? My father says that they're just as afraid of you as you are of them."

Cautiously, the critter went back to chewing on the bacon. Its eyes darted to Angela now and again, but she got the impression it was becoming more comfortable in her presence. It ate slowly.

"You're a hungry little fella, aren't you?"

"Awwaga geeww..."

Angela's chest lurched. Had that thing tried to copy her sentence? Could it talk? "Can you say *you*?"

"*Geeuu...*"

"Oh my god...You're much better than *any* dog!"

With newfound courage, Angela hurried to the bin. The tiny critter made a high sound, like a growl, and she stopped.

"It's all right. I know what will make you trust me. I have more bacon in the refrigerator. Would you like some of that?"

"*Ggaaattth...*"

"I bet you would. Wait right here."

Angela took a raw slice of bacon from the fridge and returned to the bin. The bacon felt cold and slimy in her hand.

"I don't think you'd mind it raw, would you? I would never eat it raw, never, ever. But you might like it."

The creature swallowed the last of its bacon before looking to the fresh slice wiggling in Angela's hand. Its eyes widened, glistening in the morning light.

"Don't!" Angela warned. "Don't come at me like you did last night, okay? I'll hand it to you...and then you're going outside with me. It's a nice day. We'll go into the backyard and enjoy it. Understand?"

The creature gave no indication if it did or not, it simply kept its eyes trained on the raw bacon. Angela inched closer towards the bin as a thin line of saliva dripped from the creature's fatty lips onto the garbage. She slowly lowered the bacon, watching it curl onto the rubbish like a sleeping snake. When she removed her hand, the creature lurched for it, making her yelp. It finished it in seconds.

"Okay, now I'm going to pick you up. Don't be bold."

Angela slowly reached for the critter, her hands trembling. It eyed her, studying her curiously. It made a low, mewling sound the closer she got. But it never tried to bite her. Angela let out a shaking breath and wrapped her hands around it.

It felt fluffy and oily, like unwashed hair. The smell of onions and wet dog invaded her nostrils and she grimaced.

"Phew, you're a stinky one. That's it. Don't bite. Please..."

The creature sniffed at her palms, its nostrils flexing. It continued to make that cat-like sound, and she could feel it vibrate between her hands, but it didn't try to nip her.

With the creature held safely, Angela shuffled to the back door and stepped out into the bright sunlight.

"Here we are. I'm going to put you down, okay?"

Angela lowered the critter to the porch then slowly sat beside it, not wanting to frighten it. It sniffed at the wood, interested in the new environment. A spider scuttled past, and the creature lapped it into its mouth with great speed. It crunched on the insect and purred. Two of the spider's legs jittered from between its lips.

"Do you have a family?" Angela asked. "Did they leave you here? Or maybe you got lost? Do you have a mommy and a daddy? I just have a daddy. His name's Philip. My mommy died when I was five. She had a brain aneurysm in the car park of a cinema one night. I don't remember her much, but I have photos and she was very pretty."

The creature looked at her with interest. It continued to purr.

"Kathy Hogan has a terrier named Preston. I hate them both. She bullies me at school because I'm not pretty like her. The boys call me Sicko too, because one time I had an upset stomach and still had to go to school, because my dad couldn't leave me at home by myself. He had to work and Tammy wasn't free to look after me. She's in college and I want to be like her when I grow up."

Angela reached towards the critter. She kept her palm open and lay it beside the thing. She knew from watching videos online that if you reached for an animal too quickly, or in the wrong fashion, it could perceive it as a threat. So instead, she laid her hand down, hoping the creature would make the first move. It sniffed at her palm, then licked it with a tongue as rough as sandpaper.

Angela giggled. "Eww! That's disgusting. Still, you're much better than any dog, you know that? You're unique. That's what my dad says about me, too. There's no one else in the whole wide world like me. And my crooked teeth, my freckles, all make me who I am. They make me perfect. So now, I like them. I like you too. Do you like me?"

The critter continued to purr. It sniffed at the wood beneath its clawed feet and moved around in circles, exploring.

"Kathy Hogan makes my life hell. Daddy says not to pay her any attention. But she *makes* me pay attention. It's hard to ignore a backpack in your face, or a slap on the back of your head in class. Daddy said she's spoilt, because her mommy is a rich person who got left loads of money. Her daddy is a drunk who sleeps most the time, so my dad says Kathy's mom *overcompensates* by buying Kathy anything she wants. Including that poopyhead, Preston."

There was banging on the front door, loud and hard.

"Does anybody know you're here? Are they going to take you away?"

The critter's interest remained on the floorboards.

"Philip!" a voice called from the other side of the house. "Come out here, right now!"

"Oh no, that's Kathy's father. You wait right here, okay? Don't go anywhere."

Angela went to the front door, taking a deep breath before opening it. She peered up at Richard Hogan. The smell of beer poured from the man in a wave, making Angela's nose twitch. His bald head shone in the bright light. Around his dirty work boots, Preston sniffed and wandered.

"Where's your father, girl?"

"My daddy's not home. He's at work."

Richard smirked. "You kick my dog, did you?"

"No, sir."

"Then you calling my Kathy a liar? Huh? Because she says she saw you kick my dog."

"No, sir. Your dog bit me, so I shook it off. That's what happened, honest."

"Not the way my Kathy tells it. She says you kicked our dog, so it bit you. Serves you right, you know. Should never kick someone else's pet."

Preston wandered away from the porch and inspected the flowerbeds along the top of the yard. Angela's head whirled with a single sentence: *Please don't go around to the backyard. Please don't go around to the backyard...*

"How would you like it if someone kicked you, huh?" Richard Hogan asked.

Angela's bladder threatened to let go. She looked up at Richard and her body trembled. "Please...I'll tell my daddy to stop by later."

Angela tried to close the door, but Richard put a dirty work boot in its path. It bounced back open.

"You shouldn't close a door in a grown-up's face, you little *bitch.* It ain't polite."

He grabbed Angela by the scruff of the neck and shoved her. Angela balked and fell three paces but managed to keep her balance. Her body shook. She stared at Richard Hogan, her eyes wet. After a moment of silence, Richard sighed. "Don't you ever touch my dog again, hear? Or I'll be back. You can bet on it."

Richard turned and strutted back across the street, leaving Angela with her stomach in knots. Had a grown-up just laid his hands on her? Could they do that? Grown-ups were meant to be the ones to confide in when someone bullied you. But who were you supposed to tell when the adult was the bully?

Angela closed the front door, her face scrunched in pain and confusion. She felt scared and shaken.

Where did Preston go?

"Oh, no..."

Scrambling to the backyard, Angela took the kitchen in three strides. She burst out onto the porch, scanning left and right. What if Preston got to her new pet? That terrier would tear the tiny creature limb from limb.

Angela's breath caught in her throat.

Ahead, Preston's collar lay in the grass. It looked slick with blood. Beyond that, Angela's new pet sniffed at what looked like a pile of carpet that had been run through a blender with inners. A lot of inners. The whole world seemed to spin, and Angela grabbed the porch railing to stay upright. Her legs were like jackhammers. The tiny critter chewed on one of Preston's legs. It sucked the meat clean off as if it were a spare-rib. It still made that low, purring sound.

"Oh, no. *No, no, no...*"

The critter's head snapped in her direction. Its leathery face was stained a shining brown. Its eyes lit up, and it dropped the half-eaten leg. It waddled quickly towards her through the grass, looking like the world's strangest wind-up toy.

"Ow, ow, ow," it said, copying Angela's words. "*Owwwww...*"

Was it trying to smile? Angela thought it was. It stopped just short of her and sniffed at her torn tights. Its tiny nostrils flared, sucking in her scent. The purring noise it was making became louder. It liked her. It definitely liked her.

"You ate Preston," Angela said, pointing to the terrier's remains. The creature looked at her, happily. "You ate a dog!"

Then Angela began to laugh. It crept up from her stomach like a ticklish snake, boiling over until she couldn't take it. She giggled hysterically. The creature's smile grew wider.

"You *ate* Preston! You *ate* Kathy Hogan's dog! Good boy!"

She reached down to pat its head. The creature mewled at first, the hair on its back standing up straight, then it relaxed. Angela's palm came away red. She wiped it on her torn tights.

"A grown-up hurt me today. He came over and said that I kicked Preston. But I didn't. Kathy Hogan is the liar, not me. Then he *pushed* me. He grabbed my clothes and pushed me. He's nothing but a big bully."

The creature's eyes kept darting back to the dead terrier, but it seemed to enjoy being with Angela. It looked to like the attention. Its stomach gurgled.

"You're still hungry, aren't you?"

The creature whimpered. Saliva dribbled from its lips.

"I don't like when people bully me," Angela said. She pouted and folded her arms across her chest. "I've had it with bullies. You wouldn't know what it's like, because you've got sharp teeth and claws. But I'm going to fight back and show them that I won't take it anymore. No one will mess with Angela Hughes ever again." She smirked. "You wait right here. I'll bring you something good."

Angela started towards the side of the house. She expected the critter to follow her, like a puppy, but it appeared that food was more important to it. It hopped through the grass back to its buffet of shredded flesh, bone and fur. Angela didn't mind. She hated that dog, anyway. Her insides danced with excitement.

After three knocks, Richard Hogan finally answered the door. Angela had waited until there was no one else around to cross the street to his house. She had heard Kathy Hogan and her mother on the next block over, shouting Preston's name, but other than that, the street was empty. Good. No one was watching.

"What do you want?" Richard asked, arching an eyebrow.

"My daddy's at home now, Mr. Hogan. He'd like to speak with you."

Richard's face fell. "Now you listen here..." He bent to one knee, pointing a finger in Angela's face. "You kicked my dog, so I put you in your place, understand? Now, I'm an adult, I'm bigger than you, so you don't ask me no questions. That's just the way it is. I punished you for hurting my Preston, and that's what happened. Don't you tell your daddy 'cause *that's just the way it is.*"

"Oh, but I already did, Mr. Hogan. And he's mad. He's very, very mad."

The colour drained from Richard's face. Angela continued while a laugh threatened to spill out of her.

"He said that he's *fucking pissed.* I don't know what that means, but I know that he's angry, for sure. He's in the backyard and he wants to see you right away. He said if you don't come over, then he'll come over here. He also asked me to ask you if you *understood*?"

Richard swallowed. It looked like a stone had caught in his throat. "Y-yeah, I understand, Angela. I'm...I'm coming."

Angela smiled. "Okay!"

She turned and skipped across the street, scanning it in both directions as she went. Still no sign of anybody around.

She shouted back over her shoulder. "He's in the backyard, Mr. Hogan! He's waiting for you."

Angela led the way around the side of the house, Richard following close behind. She looked to her torn tights as anger washed her over. *How dare that family bully me,* she thought. *Who do they think they are?*

When she reached the grass, she spun and smiled. "Ta-da!"

Richard Hogan's mouth dropped open. He gasped.

"What in the Lord's name?"

Running to the mess of animal on the lawn, he cried out. Angela giggled and covered her mouth.

Richard fell to his knees, an unintelligible noise escaping his throat. He scooped up the pile of what used to be Preston's head and trembled.

"What did you do? What in God's name did you do? You little...you little *bitch*!"

Behind him, Angela's critter waddled through the grass towards Richard. Its hair stood up on its back, like a threatened dog. It made a low mewling noise. Another living thing sat at its food, Angela realised. She watched the two of them, her heart beating faster in anticipation.

"I never liked your dog, Mr. Hogan. And I never liked you, either. I absolutely *hate* Kathy, as well. So you can blame her. She started it."

With that, the creature bit down on Richard's leg. He yelped and thrashed about on the grass, kicking out blindly to try and dislodge the beast. Angela's excitement began to devolve into distress.

What if somebody heard him? Richard was making an awful lot of noise, after all. If someone knew that he was here, then they'd know she had something to do with him going missing. That's what was going to happen, right? Richard Hogan was going to be eaten alive. Angela Hughes was going to be responsible.

The critter tore through Richard's jeans in a matter of seconds. It gnashed its pointy little teeth again and again, working its way down to Richard's hairy leg. Then it went to work on the fatty meat there.

Richard fell to the grass, his skin smeared in sweat and blood. He grated his teeth together as he looked down to the source of the pain.

"What the hell is that thing? Get it off me!"

But Angela had no intention of removing the monster. Instead, she'd scooped up her father's garden trowel from the ground and stalked towards Richard.

"What in God's name is this?" Richard grabbed for the critter in panicked lunges, but it was too quick. It continued to feast. The creature reminded Angela of a piranha, using its fishhook teeth to tear the man's ankle to ribbons. "Angela, *help me*!"

Angela shook her head. The whole world seemed to have transformed into a twisted dream. Her body felt light as a balloon as she glided across the grass, the garden trowel clutched tightly in her small hand.

Then she stopped. Her eyes grew wide.

"What's happening?" Tears streamed down Richard's scrunched face. By now, the creature had devoured most of his calf, that purring noise mixed with hungry whines.

Angela had stopped because a dark shadow had fallen over the man, one that made her bowels threaten to go loose and finish destroying her tights.

Two creatures stood behind Richard, both looking almost like her new pet, only much larger. They had come out of the forest at the end of the yard, undetected. They were easily each over six foot in height, their thick brown hair oily and reeking of decay. Their leathery faces were haggard and wrinkled. As they watched Richard Hogan, their black eyes shining and excited, their nostrils quivered, attracted by the scent of blood and flesh. Their extraordinarily long arms came down to below their bent kneecaps, ending in sharp, black nails. They had come to feed.

Angela dropped her trowel and ran for the house. She could hear the monsters join their companion in the feast. Perhaps they were her new pet's parents, brought forth from the depths of the forest by the notion of fresh meat.

Richard Hogan's shrieks only lasted seconds, drowned out by terrible, slopping sounds. Something ripped, like Velcro, and Angela tried hard not to vomit.

Was that his leg? Her mind was frantic. Or his head? Oh god, please don't say that it was his *head*.

Slamming the door behind her, Angela gawked out of the window. She stood on her tiptoes to see clearly, her breath heavy. She trembled as she saw the source of that godawful ripping noise.

It had been Richard Hogan's head, after all.

The two larger creatures lapped at his body with sickeningly large, black, slug-like tongues. The blood dribbled from their mouths, soaking into the dirty fur of their chests. One of them had Richard Hogan's head clasped in its claws. There was a strange clicking noise as its jaw dislocated and its mouth fell open to a nauseating size. Sharp rows of teeth, like shards of glass, lined its lips. It inserted Richard's head and bit down. A repulsive crunch rang out across the yard.

Angela moaned. Now that she could see the creatures more clearly and from a safe distance, she noticed the difference between the two. The one who had eaten Richard's head had breasts. Her chest was much larger than the one on the right. Besides, Angela thought, the one on the right was *definitely* a male. The sight of that thing made her want to scream.

The male creature mercifully began to drag Richard's carcass towards the thicket of the forest. Angela's pet was still on Richard, now taking mouthfuls from his thigh. The bushes rustled as the critters passed through, birds taking flight in all directions. The grass in the yard was painted in gore. Then the garden fell still.

Angela waited for an hour to pass, giving the creatures plenty of time to get far away from her house. She didn't want to go out there and have them see her. If they did, they were sure to devour her. Yes, she had taken care of what she guessed was their child, but still, she wasn't stupid. They were animals, after all. Angela knew animals couldn't be reasoned with – especially ones who had an appetite for human flesh.

The mess of innards and blood had been easier to wash away from the grass than Angela had expected. The creatures had left little evidence behind other than a shredded piece of what must have been muscle. Besides that, there was only blood – a lot of blood. It had washed away easily with the garden hose, foaming like a red river. Angela inspected the yard before returning to the house. It was all gone. Everything. The garden was back to the same way it always had been.

The next morning, Angela woke to her father's voice from downstairs.

The day before had been strange. Angela felt as if she had the word *guilty* tattooed across her forehead. When her father came home, every glance he gave her made her stomach lurch. He had asked if she was feeling okay and said that she looked a little ill. Angela had agreed with him, suggesting that maybe it was something she had eaten. He'd put her to bed early and stayed up later than usual, on account of Richard Hogan's disappearance. Angela had heard him on the phone with his best friend, Rodger. He said that Richard Hogan was an alcoholic, and he'd always expected the man to up and leave his family. He was just surprised it had taken so long to finally happen. After that, a phone call from a very distressed Linda Hogan, Kathy's mother, had come in. Angela's father had tried to reassure her that Richard would show up eventually. He'd suggested that maybe Richard just needed some time to himself. He was sure Preston would also be back very soon. Dogs do wander off, after all.

"What's up, Daddy?" Angela stretched and scratched her hair as she made her way down the stairs. She felt better after a good night's sleep.

"Look at this." Her father pointed to the open front door, where scratch marks streaked across the wood. They only reached knee-height and looked deep. Something had desperately tried to get in while they slept. "Looks like that little terrier came back to town, after all. Must have been scared and confused being out at night, came to the wrong house. At least that's one mystery solved."

Angela smiled. "Sure. Must have been Preston trying to get in, all right. Or maybe another wild animal? Something that wanted to be *my* pet?"

Angela's father cocked his head and chuckled. "You're a strange one, Missy."

CORDYCEPS

"ANNIE LEE? WHAT'S she doing out and about?"

Sam cut the bandsaw. "What'd you say, Leonard?"

The air was thick with floating sawdust. It drifted out of the gloomy garage that served as the Grey Wood Carpentry workspace and into the bright sunlight of Mayfair Street. The screeching saw settled as Sam lowered his protective goggles and exhaled. It was too hot of a day to be cutting timber.

"Annie Lee just walked by. Haven't seen her in months. Ain't she got cancer?"

Sam nodded. "Last I heard, yeah. I need to get some air, come on. Smoke break."

Stepping out of the clammy garage, Sam squinted from the bright glare of the day. All along Mayfair Street, the carbon copy homes were bathed in sunlight. It seemed as if Leonard's Garage was the only building in town that sat in the shadow of Harrison, the mountain that made up this side of the valley. The Harrison Trail was the only draw the small town had, and each year during the summer months, families flocked there to walk the twelve miles to the top of the mountain and back. Why in the world that passed as recreation to them, Sam wasn't sure.

Leonard pointed up the street, his old, weather-worn hand shaking. "See? Annie Lee. She's outside."

Sam was more concerned about the shaking in Leonard's hands. He worried about how much time they had left to run the garage together. At sixty-nine, Leonard should, by all means, have stayed in retirement and left the shop to Sam, who still had a good twenty years before he threw in the towel. But Leonard was stubborn, and hard times called for desperate measures, he said. They'd play it by ear until they couldn't anymore. Sam was thankful either way, because without Leonard, he'd still be unemployed and trying to find life's answers at the bottom of a bottle.

Sam fished a cigarette from his pocket and sat on a cinder block by the garage door. "She's going for a walk. What's the big deal?"

"She hasn't been out in months, Sammy. I'm telling you, it's strange. Lillian, her caretaker? She pops by now and then to chew the fat with me, and I just saw her last week. Said that old Annie was just about ready to kick the bucket. Couldn't even get out of bed anymore. It's just peculiar. Don't you find that peculiar?"

Sam lit his cigarette. "Things might have taken a turn for the better, who knows?"

"Yeah. Yeah, maybe."

Folding his arms, Leonard watched Annie shuffle further down the street. His liver-spotted brow wrinkled in concentration. "It's curious, all right. I mean, it looks like she's going for the Harrison Trail. That's a twelve-mile hike up and back. What's she thinking?" He shifted his weight to his other foot. "Do you mind if I pop over to Lillian to see what the deal is?"

"We're due for a lunch break anyway. I'll come with you."

Flicking his cigarette butt into the yard, Sam stood and

slipped his dirty baseball cap onto his sweat-slicked hair. He remembered when that cap used to be red, but now it was so oil-stained it was nearly jet black. No point to try and clean it at this stage either, he thought. It would only be black again within a month due to the many hours that he and Leonard were putting in lately. Grey Wood Carpentry was the gift that just kept on giving, Sam joked to himself. But in all honesty, he couldn't complain.

Following Leonard down Mayfair Street, Sam lit another cigarette. They passed by the quiet, prefab houses, all identical except for the colour of their front doors. Air as thick as soup hung heavy yet fresh, as it always was in this part of North Carolina. That reason alone was enough for Sam to move here from Seattle two years ago. He'd grown weary of city life, and since the factory let him go, he'd needed a change of scenery. Back to his family roots in North Carolina seemed as good a place as any. Leonard had welcomed him to town with open arms and a new job. Sam was forever grateful.

They climbed Annie's porch and Leonard rapped the door melodically as Sam flicked away his second smoke.

The door slowly opened on its own but no one appeared to be in the house.

"Lillian?" Sam pushed the door open wide. "You here?"

No reply. Somewhere out on the street, a dog barked relentlessly.

"She's not here, Leo. We can always phone her."

"Just a minute." Leonard stepped into the house, his index finger raised. "I just need to make sure everything's okay."

Sam stayed on the porch. A cold turkey sandwich waited for him back at the garage and his stomach called for it angrily. Missing breakfast had been a mistake but he'd overslept and had to rush. A nice tall glass of cold water wouldn't be a bad idea either, now that he thought about it.

"Oh, Jesus!"

Sam had never heard Leonard's voice sound like that before. Fear licked across his stomach in a cold wave. He made his way into the shadows of the house, his boot heels clicking on the hardwood. His heart punched at his ribcage. "Leo? Where are you?"

"Kitchen."

Sam pushed open the swing door and stopped in his tracks.

The thing that lay on the kitchen floor had once been Lillian Palmer...the thick, wavy brunette hair gave that away. Apart from that, she was wholly unrecognisable. She was a horror show.

Thick white cords that looked like bone sprouted from her pink blouse, the fabric left shredded. They spiralled upward from her chest to neck-height, like crooked tree branches. At the root they were a deep red, fading to the purest white by the tip.

The largest one grew from Lillian's forehead. The skin around it lay in tattered ribbons.

The older man's voice croaked, "Oh sweet Jesus, Sam. What's happened here?"

The room spun, and Sam held onto the counter for support. The bizarre sight was unlike anything he'd ever seen. The mushroom scent of decay hung in the air, the odour churning his stomach.

How long had she been here? And what in God's name were those bone-like appendages spiking through her flesh?

Sam couldn't speak.

"Should I call Dr. Philips? I should, shouldn't I?" Leonard rubbed his hands together nervously.

Sam finally found his voice. "Yeah. That would be a good idea. Call Dr. Philips, and if he's not available, call 911."

As Leonard pulled his phone from his pocket, Sam leaned against the counter and tried to control his breathing. His legs wobbled as he made his way to the kitchen sink for a glass of water. His skin quivered at the very idea of having his back turned to the abomination that lay on the floor, but he needed to do something to calm down. He hoped the water would help.

Sam stopped.

A brown paper bag lay open beside the kitchen sink. White powder glistened inside. Sam lifted the bag gingerly, cringing at the weight. There must have been kilos of the stuff. The bag crinkled as he turned it over in his hands, some of the contents spilling.

Someone had hand-written on the side of the bag. It read:
Cordyceps

The words seemed a childish scrawl, as if a five-year-old had written it. Or somebody very old, Sam thought.

Leonard peered over Sam's shoulder into the open bag. "Cordyceps?"

"Yeah," Sam said. "What is it?"

"It's a fungus. Some people think it's a kind of medicine."

"How the hell do you know that?"

"I pay attention to things. I know pharmaceutical companies sell it all over, like supplements in tablet form and powders and so forth, all FDA approved, you know?"

Sam turned the bag over. The childish scrawl fell into view. "Well, this one is hardly FDA approved now, is it? Leo, is it ever used to treat cancer?"

"Maybe."

They looked at the body on the floor, though now it hardly even appeared human. The arrangement of spiky bones looked like a miniature forest growing from her torso.

"Disgusting."

A knock at the door startled Sam, and Leonard called, "Dr. Philips, come in. We're in the kitchen."

Terry Philips entered the kitchen. He was a quiet man at the best of times, a characteristic that most folks in town seemed to like. The doctor's knees popped as he knelt beside the body. He unzipped his bag and muttered something to Leonard that Sam couldn't hear.

Sam's heartbeat drummed in his ears as silence fell around them. A clock ticked away somewhere in the house. Then something smashed that silence.

One time, when Sam was fifteen, he'd slashed the car tires of a man he knew to be sleeping with his mother. He knew his dad knew nothing of the affair. The oxygen bled from the tires in an airy gust. The sound he heard now sounded an awful lot like that.

"Out!" Dr. Philips commanded. Sam didn't need to be told twice.

The three men raced together to the front lawn of Annie Lee's house, looking back at the home like it was a snarling wild animal. Sam swallowed. A lump the size of a tennis ball seemed lodged in his throat. He eyed Dr. Philips up and down. The man was caked in a white powder.

Terry Philips spluttered and pulled at his clothes, sending the dust away in a dancing white cloud. He blinked quickly, getting it off of his eyes.

Fear crawled up Sam's spine. "What happened?"

"She exploded." The doctor's wide eyes reflected the panic in his voice. "No one goes back inside that house. Understood?"

The doctor ripped his tweed overcoat from his back and threw it. It hit the lawn with a puff of dust. The wind carried the cloud away down the street. Sam watched it drift away up into the air until it disappeared.

"I need to get to the hospital," Dr. Philips said. "Call an ambulance."

Sam was stunned, but Leonard said, "I know what Cordyceps is. I know it infects ants. Imagine it infected a single ant. Which it has done, by the way, many, many times. It's a parasite. Once infected, that ant's mind then belongs to the fungi. Its infected mind makes the ant climb upwards, and if any of the other ants in the colony spot any signs of odd behaviour, they'll carry that infected ant far away. As quick as possible..."

"Why do they do that?"

"Because..." Leonard looked uncomfortable. "The Cordyceps needs to grow...it erupts from the host ant...when it grows to its full height, those deadly spores will burst from its tip and infect more ants. Ants know this somehow and remove the infected member. Otherwise, the infected ant will climb high enough so that the spores will rain down upon the colony and infect them all."

Sam felt lightheaded. His brain wouldn't allow him to process what he heard. "Can it infect human beings?"

"Well, you saw Lillian..." Leonard's voice trailed off as he punched 911 into his cell phone.

Suddenly Dr. Phillips spoke. "Yes." The doctor's voice sounded dreamy.

Sam's stomach dropped at the sudden change in the man. Like someone had flicked a switch, the doctor now appeared to be as high as a kite. "Excuse me, gentleman. I need to go," the doctor said.

"Go?" Sam asked. "You mean, when the ambulance arrives?"

The doctor ignored him. "Up," he said. "I'll go up. It seems so much nicer up there, don't you think? It's a beautiful day for a walk up the Harrison trail."

The doctor lurched down Mayfair Street, his eyes glazed and a smile splitting his lips. Sam and Leonard watched him go without a word. Sam was too afraid to move, and too afraid to stop the man. Instead, he turned to Leonard. "You don't think...you don't think he's acting like those ants you talked about, do you?"

They turned their heads upwards to the handrail at the top of Harrison's trail. Annie Lee rounded the corner. From the main road, she looked tiny. Her hunched gait told Sam who it was.

Annie stumbled towards the wooden handrail, admiring the tiny town from her beautiful vantage point. On any other day, it would have been a wonderful sight to see. But now it made Sam's heart flutter and his stomach lurch. He knew why she stood there. She had climbed up high, just as infected ants did. If she'd done that much, she'd do the rest.

Soon enough, the Cordyceps would register that she was up high enough, and then it would grow from her skin. It would burst from its host shell like something on the set of a science fiction movie. It would grow and grow, until it couldn't grow anymore. And then it would explode.

It would rain down onto Mayfair Street.

It would infect the colony.

Sam's legs turned to jelly. He kept his eyes on the old woman, perched up high. He half-ran, half-lurched down the street, trying to find his voice. Eventually, he managed to speak. "Leo, come on...we can't wait for the ambulance. Run!"

"I can't run, I'm old."

"I'll help you." They made their way for their workspace. "We need to get inside the garage."

Sam kept his eyes on Annie as he spoke, her figure silhouetted by the high sun behind her. It sat in the sky above the mountain like a raging white ball. Annie Lee was a black outline, and for now, a normal person from afar. But that soon changed.

From Annie's head grew a long, thin appendage. It moved with unnatural speed. It reminded Sam of stop-motion animation. The thing looked like a curling, spindly tree branch. It continued to grow, twisting as it went.

Sam bolted for the garage, pulling Leonard behind him.

Entering the garage, Sam made for the protective masks. He threw one back to Leonard without a word and quickly fastened another onto his own face. His breathing was amplified inside of it, and it smelled like sawdust. But if it kept him alive, he'd never take it off again.

"Do we have any more of these?" Leonard's voice was a muffle.

"Just our two. Never saw a need to buy more." Sam thought it over. They couldn't stay in the garage forever. And if the masks were going to work, they'd know soon enough. There was no way of finding out other than to go back outside. Another idea hit him.

"Look, I think we need to get up the Harrison trail. I need to know if..." Sam swallowed. "If what you told us about the ants is happening here."

Leonard nodded, his eyes glistening. "I'm really scared, Sammy. But I need to know, too."

"Good. Then let's not waste any more time. Come on."

Outside, they saw Mr. and Mrs. Roberts making their way up Mayfair Street. Sam stopped on the lawn. The couple wasn't walking, they were shuffling. The sight of them gave Sam the chills.

"Come on," Sam spoke from inside his mask, "let's catch up to them."

They called to the couple, but the Roberts never turned. Instead, they lumbered slowly onward. Sam moved in front of them and looked at their faces. His stomach dropped. Their mouths drooped. Their eyes stared, glazed and unfocused. Their legs seemed to carry the rest of their body's dead weight.

More figures approached from further down the street. The sound of doors opening up and down Mayfair filled the air. The residents emerged and made their way towards Harrison Mountain.

"We need to get up there, Leo. Come on. If one of them bursts, we're going to get it for sure. We need to get up higher so we don't catch the spores."

Leonard nodded. His head swung from person to person as they shuffled up Mayfair Street. Sam knew that since Leonard had lived here for the past twenty years, he considered these people his neighbours, his friends. "That's Donny Edmond," he said. "and Earl Jones. And there's Mrs. Fetcher."

Sam shook his head. "I'm sorry, but they're different now."

He began to jog slowly, turning every so often to make sure Leonard was keeping up. The old man cried, but kept up the pace. For a man in his sixties, Leonard did very well. Sam quickened his speed.

They made their way up the dirt trail, passing beneath the branches of tall pine that rustled in the wind. Hearing birds chirp from their nests, Sam wondered if the animals would be infected as well...just how bad could it be?

At least half an hour would pass before they reached Annie Lee. They didn't stop for a break once, even though a stitch gnawed at Sam's side and the mask made him sweat profusely. He needed water badly. Although he wondered how Leonard fared, he didn't take the time to look.

They rounded a corner and Sam pointed. "Look, there!"

Dr. Philips stood beside Annie Lee, looking out over their picturesque town. They looked like a pair of grotesque statues. Their eyes drooped and their mouths hung wide open. Dr. Philips acted as if he had been lobotomised. They looked like a couple enjoying a break on their evening stroll—if it weren't for the thing that grew from Annie Lee.

"Higher!" Sam shouted, grabbing Leonard. "We need to climb above her!"

Pulling his friend by the jacket sleeve, Sam raced up the trail. He had to watch his footing to make sure he wouldn't trip over a rock or root. Finally he felt high enough to stop, turn around...and look.

The Cordyceps had broken through Annie's forehead, a bony spear reaching nearly five feet in length. A wave of nausea rolled up Sam's stomach and he fought to keep it down.

Leonard gasped. "Oh sweet Jesus H. Christ!"

He didn't need to say anything else. Sam could see for himself.

They came from the city like an inky wave, moving ever so slowly. The townspeople made their way to the foot of Harrison, where they disappeared into the sea of pines below, hundreds of them, and they were making their way to the top of the mountain.

A ripping sound drew Sam's attention back to Annie Lee, just as she exploded.

IN THE WOODS, WE WAIT

MY NAME IS Teddy McEvoy, I'm seventy years old, and last night I lost my wife. I'll soon go and join her, myself, of that I'm quite sure. In the last twenty-four hours, my life's changed dramatically...It's funny how that can happen in such a short time. I can't afford to sidetrack here, so I apologise if I do, but I'm just so tired. I'm so very tired...

My arthritis is setting in something fierce, so I need to get this down quick.

Before I go back out there, I need you to understand a few things. First of all, I'm certain the tragic deaths of Theodore and Ellie McEvoy will be announced on the local news tomorrow. The reporters might say that in my old age I succumbed to Alzheimer's or maybe even dementia from the loss of my wife, only twenty-four hours before me. Every word you hear will be a lie. And if you're reading this, I'm happy that someone will know the truth, and that I didn't write this all down in vain. I left a note downstairs for Sheriff White to apologise about his son.

The second thing I need to tell you is that her comb's on the bed. The white one, the one she used on her hair every morning. It wasn't there a moment ago. I should know, I made the bed when I got back this morning, after my shower. I make that bed every day. Force of habit, you know? I was caked in mud and god knows what else. My joints were killing me, I needed that hot water bad, and when I finished, her comb was there. Even now, I can see it reflected in Ellie's mirror, right behind me. I'm sitting at her vanity table.

That's why I decided to write this down, not just about what I saw in the woods, but all of it, even the comb and what I believe to be other hallucinations. It's probably due to the bite, an infection, perhaps, but it's on my left arm, and thankfully, I'm right-handed. I cleaned the wound in the shower with peroxide and bandaged it. All around, the skin was a deep pink. Agonising to clean. My arm's still killing me. But enough of that. I need to stop rambling and get down to the point.

This morning, I woke up in Brian's field. That's the other side of Pure Mile Road. I must have fainted after the gunshots.

Ellie didn't respond when I'd shouted her name. She stayed about ten feet ahead of me at all times, and I just couldn't keep up. God, I screamed my throat hoarse shouting her name. She never even acknowledged me. I cried at being ignored after a while. My legs hurt, and I'd left in such a hurry that I'd forgotten a flashlight. She didn't bring one, either. But, once again, I'm getting ahead of myself here. I need to start at the beginning.

She'd been in the garden only a few hours before. I could see her through the kitchen window. We'd been talking about getting a dishwasher, and I'd said I'd do the dishes after we ate if she drove me to the hardware store the following day (that would have been today), to pick one out. I never did learn to drive, and I guess I never will. I depended on her so much. I miss her with all my heart, and I just hope this is all over soon, so that I don't have to hurt much longer. I need the pain to go away, both mentally and psychically. I think I need to get a glass of water and calm down.

Okay, let me start again. She was out in the garden, her back to me. She stood and said she heard something. Of course I was curious. The valley in Calico is surrounded by woodland, hundreds of acres of it, so strange noises are nothing to worry about. Usually it's just the trees creaking, hunters shooting in and out of season, or some other such nonsense. But she said she heard singing.

"It sounds so beautiful, such a sad melody," she said. I chuckled and asked if she'd come back inside, but she said she wanted to hear the rest of it first.

"You can still hear it?" I asked.

She looked at me with faraway eyes. "Can't you?"

That's when I became frightened. Ellie and I were by no means spring chickens. I'd reached the big seven-zero last February, three years Ellie's senior. We had talked about dementia after Greg, her brother, succumbed to it last year. Although, we came to the conclusion that it wasn't something either of us thought we'd ever have to worry about. We both did plenty to keep our minds active, and had always loved our Scrabble Sundays. We had more wit between us than most of the folks half our age. But at that moment, I wasn't so sure.

I said I honestly couldn't hear anyone singing, but I strained my ears anyway, hoping I would catch the melody. I still heard nothing. She had said, "oh", all drawn out, more a breath than a word. Then she'd turned and started towards Pure Mile Road.

I called to her, thinking she was playing a trick, as she had an odd sense of humour...I just noticed I wrote 'had' instead of 'has'...I better find her soon, because I can't take another minute of this. I didn't understand what she was doing, so when she reached the end of the street and didn't turn back,

I power-walked after her, calling her name. A smile twitched my lips, I remember. A nervous one. I was still waiting for the prank to happen. When she reached the start of Pure Mile, I got scared. I called for help, but no one came.

So, I ran after her.

Pure Mile runs parallel to the main road. It's a dirt-packed path used by walkers and hikers that leads through the forest. Large pines loom overhead, blocking out the sun. The far end opens out onto a natural lake, and further on past the lake is what's known as the Miner's Village. It's a barren landscape that used to be a mine back in the fifties. I hadn't been up that way in years on account of how steep of a walk it is, and as I followed Ellie, I thought I'd have another heart attack. My ticker pounded my ribcage and I could hardly catch a breath.

To say I was terrified would be an understatement. I'd never seen her act remotely peculiar before. After chasing her for what seemed like hours, my mind wandering to the worst conclusions, she veered to the left—off the pathway and up into the woods. She moved so gracefully, as if her age was of no significance. Mine was. I lost sight of her. I heard her glide under tree branches and hop over rocks as if she'd done this a thousand times before. The thick pines snapped me in the face. I tripped more than a dozen times and had to keep taking breaks to catch my breath. All the while, I still wheezed her name.

I don't mind telling you, as I sat there crying, trying to breathe, I felt very old, very alone, and very scared. Then, when I was about to keep going, something caught my attention. I could hear footsteps, fast feet hitting packed dirt. It wasn't coming from Ellie's direction. Someone was coming up Pure Mile.

The owner of those feet called my name. I shouted to them, letting them know where I was. I sat slightly up the mountain in the thicket of the woods to their left. I had managed to find my voice, but it was very weak.

Light shone through the trees, making silhouettes.

"Teddy?" It was a man, and he sounded worried. Working his way up through the thick clump of trees, I realised it was Bob White, Sheriff White's son. Also a police officer. When he broke through the last few trees, he looked out of breath, and just as scared as I was.

"Teddy." He sounded relieved. "What's happened? I heard you calling from my place. Thank god I found you. What's happened?"

I told him all about Ellie, my throat hurting from the lump in it as I spoke.

"I'll go find her," Bob said, like a dog owner telling his pet to stay. "You wait here."

I got very angry at the young son-of-a-bitch just then. His stupid moustache made me want to punch his lights out all the more.

"She's my wife, and I'm coming. I'm not going to slow you down." I didn't know if that was true or not, but I was determined to find out.

I kept my head down, letting Bob's torch light the way ahead. In the glow, I could make out the carpet of pines beneath my feet, and I did my best not to slip. All the while, I worried where my wife had gone. My chest tightened every time I pictured her face.

Eventually, we reached a plateau, a clearing in the woods about the length of a football field. No trees grew there. Instead, they surrounded it, as if on guard. The earth looked clear of pine needles, the ground spoiled and dark. Bob asked if I'd ever seen this place and I told him I hadn't. Then he bent and scooped up a handful of dirt, letting it slide back through his fingers.

"Soil's ruined. Nothing's growing."

Captain fucking obvious, I know. God forgive me, I wanted to hit him bad.

A branch snapped on the far side of the clearing, in the woods, making my breath hitch in my throat. Bob swivelled his light towards the sound, bathing the wall of trees in a soft glow.

"Not strong enough at this distance."

"Bob, maybe you shouldn't..."

But he'd already started across the clearing, his neck stretched forth as if a few more inches allowed him to see better.

Bob made it about halfway when the second branch snapped. Louder this time. He paused with a gasp, then called Ellie's name.

That's when things got very strange.

A figure slowly emerged from of the darkness at the far end of the clearing. Bob called Ellie's name again, and I stood frozen, my heart pounding. My palms began to sweat and my lips dried up. My legs turned to rubber as I walked towards Bob and started calling her name, too.

A rustling came from just beyond the tree line.

Bob's light focused on the thing shuffling forward. It let out a moan, low and ominous, sending ice-fingers up my spine. I could hear my own heart beating very loud. Stepping into the clearing, I squinted to see better.

"What in God's name?"

It would have looked like a person if the thing's arms weren't so unbelievably long. They reached nearly to its kneecaps. I'd never seen or heard of anything like it. The head was a joke of a human's. It had no hair and a long face, and its features were *melted*. It's what I imagine a person's face would look like if they'd gotten radiation sickness. The thing's skin looked dark grey and it wore what were formerly clothes. I know they were formerly clothes because the remains of a sneaker clung to its left foot. The rest was unrecognisable shreds of cloth, caked in dirt.

Hoisting its freakishly long arms above its head, the thing shambled towards us. In the moonlight I could see liquid glistening and dripping from its mouth. It seemed to be salivating.

"Stop moving!" Bob cried out, removing his gun from its holster. His hands shook as he levelled it. "I-I'm warning you, stop!"

My hands were balled up so tight I think my nails drew blood.

A sharp smell hit me. Bob had pissed his pants. I'd been wrong about the kid. He whimpered like a dog, sure, but he never ran.

The thing plodded closer.

At this distance, I could make out its eyes. Milky white, no pupils. It got within fifteen feet when Bob warned it again. At ten feet, he fired the first round.

I jerked, my heart bashing through my chest. The shot echoed through the clearing and my own skull. The bullet left a gaping hole in the monster's chest, one as big as a coin. From it slopped a dark, sludgy substance. A rancid, fishy odour followed. I gagged.

The thing didn't seem to notice the injury. Instead, it just kept shuffling forward, its creepy arms still raised. The mouth gaped open and closed like a fish out of water, saliva smacking and dribbling. Bob fired another few rounds, but, once again, the thing didn't respond. Then it was on us.

Looking back, I don't know why we didn't run. It just didn't occur to us, I guess. People act funny when they're terrified.

The thing's arms smashed down on Bob White's hands,

knocking the gun away. Letting out another moan, the monster sounded annoyed more than anything.

Then it spun on me. I had no time to react. Before I could even register what was happening, it had lifted my arm to its mouth, tearing away a chunk of flesh. The pain was like nothing I'd ever experienced. I whipped my arm back, screaming, and ran for the woods, back towards Pure Mile, towards home. I could hear Bob right behind me, yelling his throat raw.

My eyes watered, blind spots dancing in front of me. When the pain started to dull, I realised I was slowing down. Not intentionally. And that's where my memory starts to fade.

I have a brief recollection of the ground rushing towards my face. Then of Bob White's muffled, far away voice saying that the thing wasn't following us anymore. I think I let out an involuntary sound the whole time. I remember hands rolling me to my side, and then hearing cloth rip. I remember the bobbing sensation of being carried.

A gunshot came soon after, followed by Bob yelling, leading the creature away. I silently wished him luck. Then, nothing.

I opened my eyes to a grey sky. It had to be hours later. My face felt damp from the dew on the grass. I was nauseous. Sitting up slowly, I winced as agony shot through my arm. I tapped the bite wound lightly with my fingertip. Tender, and a little numb. Bob had tied it off with his shirt. A dark crimson stain blossomed beneath the fabric. Flexing my fingers caused me to suck air through my teeth.

The birds were singing, but it was still dark out. I put it to be about four or five in the morning. I lay in Brian Randolph's field. I could tell because of the white horse in the little stable, eyeing me from the far end, and because the field sloped upwards, with Pure Mile at the top. I stood and started towards the path.

I felt lightheaded, and walked very slowly, concentrating on putting one foot in front of the other. I tried to piece together what was happening but struggled to absorb it. Why had my wife gone out towards that thing? Were there others? How had she known where to go? Are they being changed by something lurking in the trees at the clearing? Something that calls them? Too many questions, too few answers. I can't accept this as reality...Maybe I *have* gone senile, after all. Perhaps I'm in some hospital right now, muttering in an easy chair. I hope so.

The nearly hour-long walk back home felt like the longest stretch of time in my life. My thoughts were empty, I was surprised at that, but at the time I wanted nothing more than to get home. I concentrated on getting the scenery past me, one tree at a time.

When I got inside the house, as I said, I showered, did up my bandages, and surprisingly, ate. That was about two hours ago.

Then I stopped to write this.

I know in my heart that Bob White is dead, and I feel bad for wanting to hit him before, especially after seeing how courageous he acted. But I said I'd write down the whole truth, and nothing but. Well, at least, what I understand to be the truth. Don't ask me how I know he's dead. I just have a feeling. After the gunshot, before I fainted, there's something else, just out of reach.

They'll be looking for him by now, I bet. No one could have seen me come home, at least, so no one will come knocking. It was far too early when I got back into town. But leaving? They'll see me leave. It's hard to ignore an old man with a shotgun.

I'm going to wrap this up now because I need to go and find my wife. I doubt what I find will be what I want, I'm no fool, but I need to know.

I just hope she's not one of them. One of those *creeps*.

I don't know how that's even possible, but something's telling me she very well could be. Maybe it's the damn bite screwing with my head.

God, it hurts.

All I know is that I'm going to put this pen down now, grab my shotgun, and head back out to the clearing. Before the pain becomes too much. This time, I'm not going to run away.

PS—I can hear that singing now, Ellie. And you were right. It sounds so beautiful.

MEETING GREGORY

I WAS ELEVEN years old when I met the boy who haunts me. I came back to Carbhin for my class reunion yesterday and couldn't get over how small the place looked now. The bus dropped me at The Brook and took off with a honk, leaving me standing at the 'welcome' sign by the old bridge. Tall pines waved overhead, and I smiled.

As a kid, I remember the river beneath the old bridge as a vast, mile-long monster, snaking through packed, dry earth. It's really nothing more than about eight feet wide, if that. Leading down to it stood a wall of ferns that tickled at your skin as you skidded down a steep slope to the open, flat clearing. Going down that slope as a child was like smashing through a dark, primal jungle. I felt like a real adventurer. Yesterday, those ferns only reached my stomach, and that decline was a few simple steps. I went down with ease.

But when you're a child, those small, hidden paths can seem like gateways to other worlds. And sometimes, that's exactly what they were.

The Brook, as it was known to the locals in town, was where I'd met the boy. There were many rivers that made their way through the surrounding woodlands, but for some reason, that particular run of water got the title of The Brook, even though it was actually a river. People in Carbhin weren't the most imaginative when it came to naming things.

The reruns of Bugs Bunny cartoons were starting to get on my nerves on that particular Saturday morning in 1996.

I'd watched them every weekend on the dodgy aerial television in the living room, curled up in my Thunder Cats blanket while I ate cereal. As usual, I'd been the only one awake in the house. My brother, six years older than me at seventeen, wouldn't usually pop his head out until noon on the weekends. Being that age, he drank with his friends in the field behind our house until all hours of the night. My Mom knew, but there wasn't much she could do because she worked...*A lot.*

Weekdays were spent at the local shop *'Up the Town'*, as locals liked to say. Saturdays and Sundays meant the mushroom farm in the next town over, an hour trip by bus, which she'd make every morning at six a.m. I'd get up at the same time as her to see her out. My father'd been long out of the picture by then, just an alcoholic sperm donor, more or less.

I'd discovered the Green Road about a month before that Saturday while out with my best friend Alan.

Alan had heard that if you cross through the school (which was right next door to my house at the end of the housing estate), pass the cemetery, and head towards the old sawmill at the entrance to town, there lay a spot where the teenagers used to go about a decade before us. Supposedly, it'd been abandoned for ages before we came along. Alan said those teenager's names were carved on trunks, and some of those names were still legible, so, naturally, we wanted to see. Besides, at that age, weekends were notorious for those kinds of adventures.

New discoveries along the way constantly grabbed our attention, stretching the ten-minute walk to the bridge by about a half hour. At the back of the school (somewhere we were never allowed to go during school hours), we found a black sludge swamp, hidden behind the pines that lined the right-hand side of the building. One of the trees sprouted a branch that looked thick enough for hopping, and we did, screaming and holding on for dear life, trying not to fall into the murky slush. Thinking back, I'm pretty sure the puddle had come from a burst septic tank. Good thing neither of us fell in.

We were terrified of being on school grounds when we weren't meant to be. To play basketball on the front courtyard would most likely cause some cranky old git to yell '*get-the-fuck-out*'.

Anyway, we passed the cemetery, and I will always remember laughing at Alan for making the sign of the cross. Most of the locals did that, my family probably being the only exception. Rural towns in Ireland tended to be very religious at that time, and my family's lax attitude towards the Church was best kept a secret.

Making our way past the cemetery, Alan and I noticed the road beginning to change. The potholes became more frequent and the footpath ended, forcing us to walk with our backs pressed to the thick bushes behind us. A single careless car coming too fast around a corner would mean the end of us, and it nearly happened a handful of times—not that we noticed the seriousness of it back then. Our attention lay solely on getting to The Brook.

The sound of babbling water grew stronger with each step. Then, a low brick wall lined the road to either side, and we knew we were standing on the bridge we'd been looking for. The stonework of those walls looked cracked and dilapidated even back then.

I clearly remembered the tall trees blocking the sun overhead and the overgrown ferns that kept the clearing from view of the road. I know most adults would walk that bridge and continue on, not sparing a thought to the goldmine of hidden playgrounds all around. But we were kids, and we knew better.

Alan and I stayed on our side of the bridge, listening for any approaching vehicles. We didn't want to be caught making our way off the road. People in Carbhin liked to talk, and if we were spotted, that meant an end to our adventure. We strained our ears for cars. There weren't any.

Racing to the ferns, we pushed the first wave aside, revealing a forest of the fuckers hiding behind. We ran through them, down that steep dirt hill, until we made it to the clearing. I'll always remember that fresh green smell that carried with us every time we broke through. It smelt of Summer. Of Freedom.

My baseball cap had the magical ability to stay on my head back then, no matter what I was doing. Thinking about it now, it must've been too small for me. I remember taking it off my head to wipe sweat from my brow as I looked about the clearing, trying to catch my breath. My jeans were wet and green at the knees, and I loved it. We smiled when we saw the markings on the tree trunks, and we recognised one or two of the names. Mrs. Browne, the nice lady who owned the apple orchard on the other side of the school, apparently used to date Kenny Porter, the local postman. It seems they were IN LUV 4EVR. Alan claimed to know all the names, but I knew he was lying. He lied an awful lot.

After reading the names and having a giggle, we sat at the edge of the river, kicking off our shoes and lowering our bare feet into the cool, dark water.

We'd gone there to see a new place in town, and that had been the real reason. *That* excited us. The names on the trees were just an excuse, and we both knew it.

The water, pitch black in the shadow of overhead pines, didn't scare us. We never planned on getting in. I never knew how to swim, and still don't. We sat there for almost an hour, listening to the birds call from the trees, to the gurgling of the slowly passing water, and to the punch of air that the odd passing car threw. We talked about starting school again in September, about stories we heard from our other friends, few as they may have been, and about the latest Nintendo games, which we played almost every afternoon. Alan talked about trucks, too, because his father drove them, but I had no interest. We splashed our bare feet about in that cool water, simply listening, talking, and enjoying the silence of being away from town. I know Alan appreciated it.

Alan came from a family of four brothers, of which he was the youngest. The other three had an infamous temper that many local kids had the unfortunate luck of seeing. The Porter household was considered one of the poorest in town, and the local kids let them know it. Of course, those kids would never say it to any of the brother's faces. To do that would lead to a burst lip or broken nose. The Porters were like rabid dogs. You didn't want to be alone with one of them, or even make eye contact in a crowded place. Their house always stunk to high heaven of sweaty socks. That I remember clearly. It's strange how a scent can stick in your memory, long after you've left a place.

Their parents were alcoholics, I know that now, but back then I didn't understand. Their dad drove a big, white Globe-Trotter truck on weekends, and what little money he made was what they lived on. Still, the whole town was dirt poor, so I never understood why the Porters were gossip targets. Everyone needs to feel a little better about themselves, I suppose, and even people with little will try and shit on the ones with nothing, so's they don't feel like the bottom of the barrel, themselves. *Hey, we might not have much, but at least we're not as bad as the Porters.*

After our chat, Alan and I went home. We planned on coming back the following weekend to fish. Some older kids told us that if you broke off a piece of cheddar cheese and rolled it into a ball, you couldn't fail. We thought we'd try that. The water looked deep enough and we knew Rodger's general store '*Up The Town*' stocked cheap rods and nets. I'd built up some allowance from previous weeks so I offered to pay for them. I paid for most everything with Alan, but I didn't mind. He was a good friend.

On the walk home, both of us absorbed the day's heat and said very little. I needed to get back and put some dinner on for my brother or I doubted he'd ever eat. He wasn't the most *together* teenager. When I reached that age, I'd turn out much the same, but that summer I was doing just fine. Alan and I said our goodbyes at the entrance to the housing estate and went our separate ways. My mom left some frozen dinners to microwave (same as every weekend), and I put them to heat. After dinner, I spent the night playing video games.

The following week dragged by. With our other friends gone on holidays, and with Alan having to stay at home to do chores pretty much twenty-four hours a day, I stayed home and kept myself busy. I read my comics from morning to night, watched the occasional movie with my brother when he finally bothered to wake up, and tried to teach myself the harmonica.

When Alan didn't call that Saturday morning, I knew that his dad had forced him to come and help him on the truck. It didn't happen often, but now was one of those times, and the day I had been looking forward to all week looked like it wasn't going to happen. I decided to make it happen anyway. I didn't mind spending time alone.

I walked to Rodger's at half past eight in the morning and picked up a net and some candy bars to keep me content while I tried to snag some fish. I had no idea how to fish, but I liked the idea of figuring it out for myself. It was another scorcher, and my baseball cap helped against the intense heat. Being pale as a maggot, I always seemed to burn if I didn't have some form of protection.

The walk to The Brook was beautiful and quiet. The air sat thick, and only the occasional fresh breeze soothed my skin from the baking sun. I passed through the school grounds, not stopping at the sludge pit this time. It wasn't as much fun by myself. I went by the cemetery and continued down the road until it became riddled with potholes. Once again, the ferns grew larger and the pines grew taller, encasing the road and telling me I'd reached the bridge. I broke through the embankment and fell out into the clearing, making my way to the riverside to eat my first chocolate bar. That's when I heard him.

There was a hooting, like an owl, but that was impossible because I knew owls were nocturnal, and it was only nine in the morning according to my wristwatch. It sounded different too—deeper. A human voice. A boy.

As far as I knew, I was familiar with every kid in town, and none lived out this far. I won't deny that I got a little scared. No kid I knew came out here. And who the hell hooted, for Christ's sake?

A rustling in the ferns grabbed my attention and I sat, paralysed. I remember my breath tearing through my nostrils and the ringing in my ears. I wasn't afraid of logical dangers—kids never are. It never crossed my mind that it could be a kidnapper or something like that. I was thinking more along the lines of werewolves and zombies. *That* shit scared me.

When he fell through the bank of ferns, I let out a yelp. My skin burst with sweat and I wanted to run but my legs wouldn't move.

He looked about my age, maybe a year or two younger, with sandy blonde hair and dirty glasses crooked on the bridge of his nose. A snot bubble hung from his left nostril and he fought to keep it inside. He had a goofy smile, and that made me relax.

That was the first time I met Gregory. Only then I didn't know his name.

He made his way over to his side of the river and stood, looking at me with excitement. My heart still pounded but I cleared my throat and spoke. "Hi."

That's all I could manage. He stayed silent, studying me, his little hands flexing in and out of weak fists. I noticed he was slightly cross-eyed.

He called out to me, his speech slurred. "Ghost."

I could tell then that he was mentally disabled. You could always tell by the voice. We had a few of them around town, and I know now that it was due to inbreeding, and that's no joke. Small towns without a lot of visitation and even less public transportation meant that there were quite a number of people who 'kept it in the family'. I knew three or four of them on a first name basis.

He started across the river with his attention still on me. Splashing into the waist-high water, he slogged across, dragging his body through the slow currant. I stood and contemplated running, but part of me remained interested. I thought I knew just about everyone in this town, at least by sight. I mean, who was this kid? Where did he come from? I decided to stay.

I stood, took a few steps back without turning, and waited for him to get across. He moved with ease, as if he did this all the time, and when he climbed up the embankment on my side, his white shirt clung to his wet skin. He pulled it from his flesh and let it flap back absently, eyes still trained on me behind those dirty frames.

He called out to me again. “Ghost.” Strange.

I spoke slow and steady. “Ghost? What do you mean? My name’s Owen. What’s yours?”

“Ghost.”

Funny name. I knew it wasn’t his real name, but I decided to play along. “Nice to meet you, Ghost.”

I extended my hand as he approached. Once again, fear crept through me, but I held my ground. I shivered as he took my hand in both of his and pumped my fist a good three times. His palms were wet and cold from the river.

“Is Ghost. Good.”

“It’s good to meet you, too.”

“Trees,” he said, dragging the word out. “Is nice trees.”

“They are nice trees. Do you come here a lot?”

He didn’t answer me. Instead, he made his way to a large pine that stood by itself in the centre of the clearing. All the other trees created a circle around the area, but this large one stood alone. My new friend waddled over to it, sniffling up that troublesome snot, and fell to his knees. I winced at how hard he plopped down, but he didn’t seem to notice. His head rolled around on the skinny stalk of his neck as his eyes scanned the packed earth. He began digging like a wild dog, his hands working the dirt into a frenzy, causing it to spray out behind him in clumps.

“What are you doing that for? Something down there?”

He looked at me, his mouth hanging open, and without a word, he returned to his work.

“Okay then.” I folded my arms and watched. After a good minute of this, he finally reached inside the fresh hole and rooted about. I could smell the turned earth from where I stood.

"Is good, Ghost," he said. "Is good tree."

"Yes, it is."

I had no other answer for him. He came up with something in his hands, and it took me a second to recognise it. A filthy and torn comic book. Then the name clicked.

"Ghost," I said. "I get it now."

It was *Casper The Friendly Ghost.* On the cover, a shocked Casper had just walked through a painted fence, coming away with the paint stuck to him. It said *Look For Me On TV* along the top, the text hardly decipherable anymore. It also stated that it cost 12c. I nodded to my new friend to show him that I understood.

"Ghost. It is good. Do you like *Casper*?"

"Ghost, good. Is..."

He trailed off as he opened the pages and smacked them aside, transfixed by the pictures. He slammed his index into some of them and looked to me to make sure that I saw them, too. I nodded and smiled to show him that I did. I winced again as he walked to the edge of the water and fell to the packed earth, once again not seeming to notice the pain. Picking up my rod, I made my way over to sit by him and start my fishing.

He watched, interested, as I opened the packet of cheddar that I pulled from my pocket. I didn't know if using the cheese to fish would work, but I wanted to try. My new friend began to drool as I broke off a corner and began to ball it between my thumb and index finger, preparing it for the hook. The sharp smell was out of place with the fresh green scent of the clearing.

"You want some?"

I broke off a good-sized piece and handed it to him. He took it without a word and held it to his glasses for inspection before popping it into his mouth. As his jaw worked, his breathing became noisy.

"Good, huh?" I asked.

I tried a piece myself as I pulled up my rod and skewered the ball of cheese onto the hook. When it looked secure, I released the line and cast into the slow, black currant. Then I placed the rod down and fixed the catch to hold the line in place. I almost looked like I knew what I was doing.

"Good," my new friend said, a trickle of spit working its way down his chin. "Is good. And, look, Ghost!"

He threw up the comic, the pages flinging out dry dirt. "Ghost so good." "Yes, Ghost is good."

We stayed that way for a while, and I shared one of my chocolate bars with him. He ate it greedily as he swatted through the *Casper* comic for the tenth time already. When the day got too hot and the glaring sun became too much, I made my way home. I said goodbye to my new friend but I don't think he understood. His brow furrowed and his head cocked to the side.

Then, when I got up to leave, he tried to follow me. That worried me. I said not to do it, that I would be back tomorrow, and he seemed to get that, at least a little. Standing there by the river, he watched me make my way back up through the ferns. I could feel his eyes dig into my back the whole way. I didn't look back but I shouted goodbye over my shoulder. I never got a response.

"A retard?"

Alan stared at me with an idiot look on his face. "A *real* retard? Our age?"

"Stop it."

"Stop what?"

"He seems nice, stop calling him that."

"Well, that's what he is right?"

Alan could be a dick.

He was right, of course, and he was just acting his age, but I didn't like to hear it out loud. His curiosity and excitement were what I had expected when I told him, but I still didn't have to like it.

Alan had told me what'd happened with his dad that Saturday. The old man had been too hung-over to carry out his work deliveries, confirming what I'd already expected, so he'd gotten Alan to go along and unpack the goods at the stores while he sat in the cab, his cap pulled over his eyes as he tried not to vomit.

Alan called to my house at eight in the morning, his freckled face cooked from the baking sun. We watched a couple of cartoons as I told him about my new friend.

"We're going there today, yeah?"

"Of course. Just be nice to him."

Alan snickered. I had a bad feeling about this. I knew that deep down he was a good kid, but his brothers had a way of rubbing off on him when he was around them for too long. It sounds cocky, I know, but sometimes I think without me as a friend, Alan would have been a bastard of a child, just like his brothers.

"And his name's Ghost?" he asked.

"That's what he said, and he seems to like it. So yeah, his name's Ghost."

We set out at ten. The day wasn't too hot yet, but I had lathered myself with sun cream, expecting the worst. The light smell the cream gave off always made the day seem undeniably like summer. I still love that smell. We stopped at the sludge marsh out behind the school and had a couple of hops on the low pine branch, but getting to The Brook was the real adventure that day, and we quickly abandoned the sludge to make tracks. The real reason for the trip had become settling our burning curiosity about my new discovery. *The new kid in town.*

We practically fell through the slope of ferns and out into the clearing. A startled animal smashed into the oily river and scattered away beneath the bridge, leaving a trail through the black water. I watched it go, its tiny legs kicking beneath the surface. Shouting after it, amazed, I wondered what in the world it could be. Alan told me it was an otter. That was the first time I'd ever seen one.

"Where is he?" Alan asked, growing impatient.

"We just have to wait and see."

"Imagine he was really a ghost. Like, actually imagine. You were out here and he came to you, and he didn't really exist. How cool would that be?"

The idea had come to me that week, actually, but cool wasn't how I'd describe it. I imagined the kid finding me and haunting me, like in the many horror novels I'd read that summer. I could see myself entering the bathroom for a piss late at night, only to find Ghost standing behind the door with his mouth lolling open and a vacant look in his eyes.

Pushing the image from my mind, I made my way to the lonely pine and searched for the scattered earth pile that Ghost had dug. It didn't take me long because he hadn't bothered to pack it back in all too well. I spotted the corner of the *Casper* comic poking out and pulled it from its grave.

"See? His comic. He does exist."

"Is that *Casper*?"

"Yeah."

We sat at the river edge and flicked through the book, not really interested in the story, but doing something to pass the time. After about ten minutes we began to talk louder, trying to get Ghost's attention if he lived nearby. We threw big stones into the water and whooped when they cracked off others beneath the surface with a satisfying thunk. Then there came a hooting, a happy sound.

Alan tensed. "He's not *weird*, is he?"

"He's fine," I told him. "Relax."

My new friend came hopping through the ferns on the far side of the river, his arms flapping at his sides. He had on the same white shirt that he'd worn the week before, only now it was filthy from exploring outdoors. He saw us, and his face lit up.

"How's he going to—" Alan's question got cut short as Ghost splashed into the water and wadded across. He didn't seem to be bothered by the change from land to water. Working his way over, the water rippled and lapped at the embankment with each step he made.

Ghost shouted out, a ticklish laugh beneath his voice. "Ghost!"

I laughed too, and as he slogged up the bank on our side of the river, I handed him his comic book. He took it absentmindedly and without breaking stride. He had his eyes set on Alan.

Making his way over, Ghost stood face to face with my friend, his nostrils labouring heavily. That string of troublesome snot came again but Ghost snorted it back like a pro. Water dripped from his clothes.

"Hi," Alan said. "My name's Alan."

"Alan..." Ghost's mouth stayed open. "Is good."

Alan laughed. "You know you're a retard, right?"

I couldn't believe it. "Alan!"

"What? I'm only asking." He turned back to Ghost. "Like, you know what that means? That you're retarded?"

Ghost's face scrunched tight. If he was annoyed or upset, I couldn't tell.

"Cats," he said. Alan howled and clapped his hands together. "Cats, he said! Cats!" I could feel the anger getting ready to burst out of me like a coke that just had a mint dropped inside of it. My fists clenched, and I shook. The words came out before I had time to stop them. "Shut the fuck up, you absolute idiot!"

My throat went raw from that, and my voice echoed throughout the clearing. "You're the fucking retard here, you know that?"

Alan paled. Ghost stood aside, his face unreadable. I'd scared them both. In truth, I'd scared myself.

"I'm, I'm sorry," Alan said. "Honestly."

My heart punched my ribcage, my chest heaving. The adrenaline in my body made me a little sick. "Say it to him then. Not to me."

"I'm sorry."

Ghost seemed to understand, his face lighting up again. That made me happy to see, and the sudden change of mood made the outburst I'd had seem silly.

"Is good," Ghost said. "Alan."

We stood in awkward silence as the babbling river continued undisturbed.

Alan broke the tension. "Come on. I've got an idea."

He took a penknife from his pocket and my urge to vomit returned. My voice sounded very far away to my own ears. "What are you doing?" I asked.

A look of shock spilled across Alan's face. "You're not serious, are you? It's for the tree, dumbass. I want to carve our names in it."

The relief that washed through me felt better than pissing on a full bladder. I laughed, loud and nervous. I knew Alan was a good friend, but still, when I hadn't seen him for a while and I knew he'd been hanging out with his brothers. It always took him a while to come back down to my level. Thankfully, he seemed his normal self again.

"The single one," he said, pointing with the closed knife at the lonely pine in the clearing. "I didn't see any names on that one."

"It looks smaller than the rest," I said. "Maybe it was only tiny when those teenagers used to come here."

"Maybe. Still, looks like a good place for *our* names."

Alan made his way to the pine and Ghost and I followed. I tried to read my new friend's face but it wasn't possible. I hoped he felt comfortable with us, even with the knife out.

We stopped at the trunk and Alan popped the blade from the hilt. The metal gleamed as the sun crossed it, blinding me for a split second. Ghost looked amused, his eyes large. I'd seen it hundreds of times before. Alan began to work on the trunk. He clasped the penknife hard in both hands and slammed it into the bark with a dull thud. He'd done it a little harder than I'd expected and his face went red and ugly.

"You all right?" I asked.

"Yup."

Dragging the knife down diagonally, Alan sent splinters of wood to the carpet of pine needles by our feet. He pulled the knife free and slammed it in a second time, this time going down in the opposite direction. He sliced cleanly across after that, finishing the first letter of his name. I grew a little worried at how much he seemed to enjoy stabbing the tree. Ghost watched silently.

It took Alan a long time to finish his name, but he worked restlessly on getting it done. Had Ghost and I left, I doubt he would've even noticed. I think he'd have stayed there all day, stabbing that tree until someone came looking for him.

When he finished, he stood back and folded the blade into itself. He panted, sweat beading and slipping down his red face. "What'chu think?"

The carving in the tree read: ALAN - OWEN - GHOST.

The writing belted around the bark, coming full circle, and we walked around it, reading the three names over and over. I don't think Ghost knew what it read but he seemed amused, anyway. For some reason, I just knew that Ghost rarely got new experiences. It was written on his face and stamped in his reactions.

"It's great," I said, and I meant it, too. The letters were bold and clear and deep. "Well done."

"Thanks."

Muted footsteps clomped the tarmac up on the road. More than one pair of feet, by the sound of it. A bad feeling washed over me right away, my stomach fluttering uneasily and my mind reeling through possibilities of who it might be. Ghost called out, not a word, just a sound, and I shushed him by holding up my hand. My mouth went dry.

I looked to Alan, eyes alert. I whispered, "Your brothers?"

He shook his head in response, jerking his shoulders. "Alan!" The call echoed out, startling a rook from the foliage overhead. It sounded like an older kid, maybe thirteen or so, judging by the depth of the voice. One of Alan's brothers, for sure. My friend's name got called again.

Stepping forward, Alan sighed. "What?" He shouted. I shot him a look. "What?" he said. "What do you want me to do? They're going to find me anyway." There came a rustling from the ferns as the newcomer pushed his way through to our clearing. More rustling followed, making my legs turn to jelly. I had been right, there were two of them.

Alan's older brothers Jerry and Lenard fell into the clearing, smirking and looking stupid. I took a step back. Ghost did, too.

"What are you faggots doing here?" Jerry said. He had a white T-shirt and jeans on, like someone transported from the Rock 'n' Roll fifties instead of the mid-nineties. Lenard stood behind his brother with his hands stuffed deep into his pockets. He was a brick of a kid, fifteen years old and going on thirty. A beer gut bulged from his too-small shirt that could match his father's. Jerry continued, "Found the old spot, huh? S'nice down here. Quiet and stuff. No one to hear much at all." He shot Lenard a knowing look and they both laughed. "And who's this?"

Jerry made his way forward, arms swinging. He looked like the biggest prick to ever strut the face of the earth.

He studied Ghost's face. "You retarded, are you?"

Ghost stared at him. His lower lip began to quiver and it made something inside my chest go tight. The reason he'd met these assholes seemed like my fault.

"Can he not speak or something?"

"Is ghost...Alan," Ghost said. "Is good."

"*What the actual fuck*?" Jerry and Lenard doubled over, smacking their knees as if they'd just heard the funniest joke on the planet. Their faces turned red, and I wanted to be able to sink through the dirt.

"Where are you from, kid?"

Once again, Ghost could only look at Jerry, not knowing what to do. His mouth moved but no sound came. His eyes began to water behind those dirty frames.

My voice came from nowhere, and I was surprised to hear it myself. "Oh just fuck off, you asshole."

They turned on me.

Jerry went into mock-shock, lifting a hand to his chest and fanning his face. "My, my, Alan," he cried. "Your friends aren't very nice. And who do we have here? His boyfriend?"

I didn't respond. I couldn't. I felt scared and angry and lightheaded.

"I'll get you to answer, you little shit."

Jerry's arm shot out before I could even register what happened and Ghost went down like a sack of potatoes. He'd smacked the kid on the forehead, sending his glasses flying.

Ghost's head thumped the dry dirt, his blonde hair fanning out. His glasses lay by his feet. I screamed and ran to his side, skidding through the dirt and falling to my knees. And that's when I got kicked. *Hard.*

The air shot out of me as Jerry's work boot connected with my stomach. Hard leather smacked soft flesh, and I went over. Winded, I gasped for air, blind spots dancing across my vision. I panicked when I couldn't catch my breath.

The sounds of the world faded away from me, replaced by the blood thrumming in my ears. I thought I had to be a goner at that point. A good twenty seconds passed before my stomach stopped tensing and I finally managed to suck down some oxygen. I got control of myself and shook my head to clear it. My clothes were filthy and covered in pine needles from flailing back and forth in the dirt. I hadn't even realised I'd been rolling around. My mind must have been concentrating on simply trying to breathe. I looked beside me and Ghost sat up straight, his face housing a mixture of terror and hurt.

I looked to Jerry, who now had a cigarette lit between his lips. He puffed out grey smoke that swirled into the hot day and grinned. One eye squinted against the smoke, and he looked to Ghost, who stared at the lighter with fascination. Jerry flicked his silver Zippo and sparked the wheel, igniting a fat, healthy flame. He clicked it shut and did it again, eyes trained on Ghost.

"The retard is hypnotised by the flame. Look."

I watched Alan, who stood by the lonely pine, not meeting anyone else's eye. I could tell he felt ashamed. And I felt angry. I knew he couldn't have told his brothers about our plans to come here because I'd only told him about Ghost earlier that morning. They must have followed us, looking for some fun.

"You like it, huh?" Jerry asked. He tossed the Zippo at Ghost. It skidded in the dirt and hit off the bottom of the kid's trainer. Slowly, Ghost scooped it up and examined it, turning it over in his hands. It seemed to calm him down. He appeared happy again.

"Now, you," Jerry said, pointing a finger at me. "Speak to me that way again and you'll lose your fucking teeth. Understand?"

At that moment I wanted to charge him, and fuck the consequences. But I knew not to. It wouldn't have done anyone any good. So instead, I nodded, because I knew that would at least make them leave, and at that moment, that's all I wanted.

"Good." Jerry hocked a spit by his boots. "Now you faggots know that when I ask you a question, you give me an answer. That right?" He waited and I nodded.

"Good. We'll see you girls around."

They strutted back through the ferns. Jerry only stopped long enough to flick the butt of his cigarette in Alan's direction. It missed him by a mile, but the message was clear. After that, the two brothers disappeared through the foliage and left us in stunned silence. It felt like a physical weight had been lifted from my shoulders.

I wish I'd seen Ghost pocket that lighter. I'd been too busy watching the Porter brothers leave and hadn't even considered he might do it. Too many other thoughts were running through my head. *Had* I saw it, I would have stopped him, of course. But I didn't. To this day I hate myself for that.

Coming over like a timid dog, Alan helped me to my feet. I took his hand without a word and we both helped up Ghost. His forehead looked a little red, but otherwise he seemed okay.

I took his dirty glasses from the ground and wiped them on my shirt before handing them back to him. I'd wanted to clear those lenses since I met him. He popped them on, a little crooked as they'd been before, and smiled at me.

"Is good," he said. "Is good."

I laughed. "It's all good."

We slogged towards the river edge and sat for a moment, waiting for the adrenaline to wash out of our systems. I still shook and needed to calm down. The sound of the river helped. I watched the ripples of the water as it rushed by, not thinking about anything in particular, just letting my brain process what'd happened. Eventually, my body relaxed.

Ghost made a noise and Alan and I looked to him. He pointed at the tree, his lips curled into a smile.

"Good," he said. "Tree, good."

I laughed, which made Ghost laugh. Alan stayed quiet, but he smiled, at least. It seemed his brothers couldn't ruin us completely. We sat and talked for the rest of the morning, Ghost chiming in now and again with his usual, limited vocabulary, and when the sun got too high, once more we said our goodbyes. Alan and I needed to go home and get lunch, and I assume Ghost did, too. I still didn't know where he lived, but I knew that there must be some grown-up waiting for him to come back.

I went to shake Ghost's hand and he surprised me with a hug. Alan laughed, but I didn't. Instead, I hugged him back.

Then he hugged Alan, just as enthusiastically, and it made me happy to see Alan return the kind gesture. Without a word, Ghost walked to the edge of the water, and once again, without pause, he began to wade across. We watched him go before leaving too.

"Is good," Ghost called without looking back. "Is good Ghost." That was the last time I ever saw him.

The next morning, my mother shook me awake. Sweat shone on her face and she still wore her nightgown. The sun was on the rise outside my window, and I placed it to be about half-six in the morning.

"Come on, get up," she said.

"What's going on?"

"House on fire, down the Green Road. The Thompson's place. Fire trucks and police cars are everywhere."

"Who are the Thompsons?"

To see my mother so excited shocked me, until I became an adult myself and discovered that *any* piece of action in a small town attracted people like flies to shit. She bolted down the staircase and I heard her feet pat on the wooden steps before smacking the linoleum of the downstairs landing. Pushing my blanket aside, I slipped on my jeans and rushed after her.

We ran outside and I caught the tail end of a truck, heading past the school, past the cemetery, and down the Green Road.

I felt stupid that it hadn't clicked with me sooner. And when it finally did, it hit me like a punch to the stomach.

"Mom, who are the Thompsons?"

"*Weird* family. Glad you never got to meet them. The Dad, George, was a local, he must be in his sixties or seventies by now, but he was a barfly at Monroe's for many years. Always smelled like piss and cigarettes." She shuddered. "Creepy old man. No one knows what happened to his wife, but he had a daughter with him in the house, I know that much. I've even heard people say that he and she were..." She shivered and laughed. "You're too young for that."

I was, and wasn't. I knew what she meant. Sex. I didn't know how it was done, but playground jokes had at least taught me enough to know about it. And I knew what such things were capable of leading to. I'd heard jokes from older kids about babies being born with retardation because of the couple *keeping it in the family*. And I felt, not for the first time that summer, like puking my ring up.

"You're very pale, are you okay?" She put her arm around me. "Hey, it's all right, honey. I doubt anyone's dead or anything like that. I'm sure he just left a cigarette lit or something silly. He's a very stupid old man."

My voice seemed to come from somewhere else. "Did anyone else live there? In that house?"

Mom laughed. "No one, baby. I mean, people joked that they had a kid together because they're filthy, dirty people, but it's just a laugh. Only the two of them live there. I'm sure they're fine."

I hoped she was right. But deep down, I knew she wasn't. Something inside me twisted and turned, telling me what I already suspected. The Thompsons did have a son. And two hours later, as we waited for the official word like the rest of the town, I got proven right.

The house had burned to cinders.

The Thompson's place was an old, decrepit home, tucked far in the woods on the other side of The Brook. Two bodies were found in the ashes, both burned. Another body, that of a child, was found in the basement. The official diagnosis came as suffocation. My friend had choked on the smoke.

I remember the smell around town that day, the sharp and bitter stench of ash that stung my nose. Little black specs floated all around, landing on the streets and the cars. I remember wondering if that could be wood ash, or perhaps the cremated bodies of one of Ghost's parents. Or Ghost, himself.

I stayed in my room all day that day. My mom asked if I felt okay and I lied, telling her I felt ill and just wanted to play video games.

I cried a lot.

It was the first time I had lost someone, and I wasn't prepared. How could I have been? I was eleven years old. I couldn't confide in anyone besides Alan, but to get to him would have meant leaving my room, and I wasn't prepared to do that. Besides, if I'd seen Jerry, I'd most likely have tried to kill him.

I blamed myself for bringing it all into Ghost's life and for not dealing with Alan's brothers better. But mostly, I blamed myself for not paying more attention to that damn lighter.

I don't think I ate all day. My mom said I was pale as a ghost, and even that had made me burst into tears. She took care of me that day, not knowing the real reason I felt down, but sensing something the same way all mothers do. I couldn't bring myself to tell her, but the results were the same. She really helped. I hardly slept that night, but the next day, I felt good enough to look for Alan.

When I knocked at his door, his mother told me that he didn't want to see me. That was the first time that had ever happened. My stomach knotted at the thought, and I went back home, rejected. Guards were still milling about the town, and that's all people spoke about. That, and the backwoods family of three that were dead on the Green Road.

Two days later, the body of the young boy was identified. His name was Gregory Thompson. He was twelve years old.

The whole town seemed genuinely shocked. Stories that had spread at late night bars about George and Margaret Thompson were funny to tell, but no one really believed them. Just another way to poke fun at those less fortunate. "Old George Thompson," they'd say when the beer got flowing. "The filthy old creep, out there in his dirty little house in the woods, fiddling around with his broken daughter. And you know they even have a handicapped kid together, right?"

Every story has a grain of truth, though. And on this occasion, it turned out they were right.

No one knew what the deal with Margaret was. My own theory is that George messed her head up so much that she didn't know her up from down or her left from right. Didn't have a single free-willed thought of her own or question her situation. A depressing thing to imagine, even to an eleven-year-old.

The shock at the discovery of Gregory's body didn't affect me because I had expected it. Apart from Alan, his brothers and me, I don't think anyone else in town knew he existed before that. When they had found the basement, word got out it was where they had kept him locked up. Someone said he had a waste bucket sitting in the corner, a shabby mattress, a couple of spare changes of clothes thrown about the floor, and not a whole lot else. Pre-internet days meant everything traveled like Chinese-whispers, but still, I believed it. I couldn't *not* believe it. Even though small towns had a tendency to exaggerate any kind of scandal, this seemed to fit what I'd seen.

The Thompson family name stayed on people's lips for the next month or so. It'd surfaced that a cigarette lighter had been the tool used to start the fire. The lighter had been found in the basement, at the top of the stairs. People said the house had been old, and must've gone up at record pace. Some speculated that old George couldn't live with himself, too many secrets, and had tossed the lighter into the basement to bring it all with him. But I knew the real reason.

I still wonder if Ghost knew what he was doing. And I still can't find the answer.

Alan and I never spoke again, and when I saw him back at school that September in 1996, he never even made eye contact. Whether he didn't want to or simply couldn't, I don't know. I'd like to think it's because he felt bad, more than bad, and needed to allow the tension inside him to rest. Some things never get closure, and that's something important I began to learn that year.

That whole story took place twenty odd years ago.

I came back to town for my school reunion yesterday, but I couldn't resist going to The Brook. The place hadn't changed, and unsurprisingly, a lot of the people hadn't, either. That came as a sad realisation. Alan hadn't come to the reunion, so I had asked around, and word was after school he'd gotten a job at the sawmill. Most of the men in town went that route. I thought about trying to visit, but decided against it. If he wanted to forget about our friendship I thought perhaps I should let him.

I stood in the clearing where my world had changed back in 1996, and just as before, I listened to the river. No hooting came from the other side. No noise whatsoever, save for the rush of water.

I missed my friend.

Making my way to the single pine, I smiled at how it still stood tall and proud, only now it looked a lot bigger. My heart stung at the sight of the three names carved in a belt around the bark, still visible, even after all those years.

ALAN - OWEN - GHOST.

It'd been a good thing Alan went so deep with his pocketknife, after all.

I got to my knees, dug at the ground, and didn't stop until I found what I came for. My fingers grazed against paper, and I pulled the comic free. Mouldy and rotten, but definitely the same book I'd seen all those years ago. I looked at Casper, noting how the pages had faded, the text blotted and the paper hardened. The paint-smeared ghost on the cover had faded, but I could still make him out. I sat and read the comic then, pulling the pages apart while trying not to rip them. The whole time, a troublesome snot tried escaping my nose, but of course, I sucked it back in like a pro. I'd learned from the best.

I missed my friend more than ever at that moment.

The world had real monsters, and they weren't the tropes you expected as a child. That long-gone summer, I'd stopped believing in movie monsters, and started fearing the real kind...But ghosts? I believe in ghosts. In fact, one still haunts me to this day. He might have been Gregory to the rest of the world, but to me, he was my Ghost. And even friendly ghosts, it seems, still haunt.

THAT'S THE PRICE YOU PAY

THE SECOND TIME he came into my shop, I knew that he was definitely one of them. He'd aged by at least a decade.

Even the first time he came by, I knew he had to be one. You see, he had that benchmark look I've grown to associate with his type. That youthful, but off-coloured skin, the darkness around the eyes, the fingers of a pianist, but most of all, his staggering good looks. I hate all of them for that. They seem to be very handsome or very pretty, but *seem to be* is the important part of that sentence. When people of his association change, you'd prefer your eyes were gouged out with a rusty spoon than admit that what you were looking at could be real. That kind of thing messes with your head.

I asked him his name and he told me. James. James Lewis.

He had nothing to hide, and telling me that information wouldn't make a difference to anything. After all, I was a man in my fifties who ran an antique shop in downtown Seattle. What damage could I possibly do to him or his reputation?

James Lewis was a vampire.

Sure, you might think, dream on, old man. But I'm telling you, they're as real as mumps and measles. They're like both of those things, too, in a way. They're dangerous to humans, but only if you let them get out of control and don't understand them. Thankfully, after a lot of time to digest the information, I do understand them. In fact, more so than a lot of the recently turned understand themselves. That's some PC bullshit right there, huh? 'Recently turned'. Anyway, a vast number of them can't accept what's happened, and because of that, there's a large suicide rate among the newly undead. It's understandable. I mean, think about it. Their whole lives have been forever changed in an incomprehensible manner. They're forced to live off the blood of the living, and to stay indoors for the most part. Sunlight doesn't kill them, that's exaggerated like most myths, but it *does* hurt them. Something to do with the pigmentation of their skin, or something like that. And besides their youthful appearance, they have an air of sickness about them, like the disease has crawled onto the surface for everyone to see. In some sense, I pity them. Once they understand, most normal people do.

From the stories I've heard, a lot of vampires confide in their loved ones, who, once they see with undeniable evidence that the victim is telling the truth, accept them. A lot of these loved ones will buy hypodermic needles and stock up their fridges with pints of their own blood to keep undead friends and partners happy. The vampires need that blood to survive. That part of the myths you've heard is true. Tragically.

At first, many of them can't control themselves. Did you ever get so aggravated that your brain scrambles and all you see is red? You just want to hurt someone, and nothing else matters. One of the poor bastards told me it's like that but amplified to an unbearable degree. After a while, if they decide to live with themselves, they learn to get it under control. Those who can't come to me. Because I'm the doctor. I'll get back to that.

The garlic bit you've heard about is pure bullshit. The wooden stake through the heart? I'm not so sure. I've never personally tried it, and as far as I'm aware, there's no *Buffy* around to confirm it. Holy water? Once again, never tried, never will. I have something that works much better.

I have a mirror.

And a vampire cannot see its own reflection. Unless of course it's my mirror that you're talking about.

My shop sits at the harbour, just under the Viaduct at the bottom of town. I've run the place for twenty-three years now. They say an underground city lies beneath Seattle, did you know that? I have a theory about that city and the vampires, but it's not relevant to what I'm trying to tell you, so we'll save it for another day.

I've always had a fixation for vintage collectibles, especially those of the exotic variety. The stranger the item, the more interest I tend to have towards it. Once, when a local circus went out of business, I approached the owner about buying most of his freak show display.

He was a friendly man, but when I spoke to him, something in his eyes countered the good-humour vibe. A fear lingered in those eyes, one I'd never seen before, or since. And, comically so, he looked like every ringmaster you've ever seen or heard of. He had a pot-belly, a dark waxed moustache, the works. But those eyes...

He sold me a foetus in a jar, said to be a daemon's love child. Looked like a putty-made baby floating in formaldehyde to me. Sold it to a lovely young couple from Japan for one hundred dollars. Hell, I only paid fifteen, myself. I got facial hair in a ziplock bag said to belong to a bearded lady. That got snapped up on eBay from an international buyer for three-hundred. An extra five for postage. Luckily, I had a certificate of authentication and a photograph of the woman to go with it.

There was a taxidermy two-headed duckling, too. That one made me laugh. Looked like Norman Bates had a little too much to drink before getting to work. Still, got me a solid one-fifty. A whole trailer full of this stuff waited, and I took it all, gratefully. I stocked up a new section in the shop for a niche market, and I planned on making a mint.

What I didn't plan on was getting the mirror.

It really was a thing of beauty. A thick black wooden frame held it, adorned with symbols carved deep into the grain.

Riccardo. That's the ringmaster's name. Just remembered.

He told me he'd come across the mirror while traveling somewhere in Southeastern Europe. Bulgaria, I believe. Said it to be a local superstition that if any mirrors were left uncovered in the wake of a death, a gateway to the Otherworld would be opened, and evil spirits could cross through at will. Hence, the locals would cover all mirrors in their homes until a suitable time had passed. The only thing I know to be fact is that a Bulgarian woodworker made the frame. He'd carved his name on the inside. *Nikola Daskalov.* Where the glass got forged? No idea.

You know how some people describe the surface of a lake to be glassy? I never knew what they meant until I saw this mirror. And, in fact, I'd go the opposite and say that this glass looked *lakey*. Bear with me here. When you look at it, and I mean truly pay attention, sometimes I swear you can see something lurking just beneath the surface. Like some sea creature is prowling below the water, waiting to pounce. I'm convinced that just like beneath the surface of the ocean lies an underworld, beneath this glass waits an Otherworld.

Riccardo had informed me he was done with the mirror. The thing brought too much trouble, especially when word got around it was in his possession and in the United States.

He wanted to be upfront with me and have no secrets. He needed it off his hands. He gave it to me for free.

And I took it.

He told me that the vampires called him the Doctor, and that I needed to get used to the name. Did I believe him? You've got to be kidding me. However, I knew a funny attraction like that mirror would drive business, so I took it with a smile, despite his warnings. I set it up in the back room which used to serve as storage. Pinned some dark silk drapes to the walls. Got a low wattage bulb for the overhead light. Place looked gothic and tacky as shit.

I hung a sandwich board outside reading: VAMPIRES! WE'VE GOT JUST WHAT YOU'RE LOOKING FOR: YOU! COME INSIDE AND SEE YOUR REFLECTION FOR THE VERY FIRST TIME! NO CHARGE!

The customers would have to pass by the Oddities stand to get to the back room, you see. So by the time they came out of the Vampire room, giggling and shaking their heads, they'd pause at the freak show items, and why not grab a souvenir? They were already in the shop, after all. Location, location, location, folks.

And it all went fine until the first undead sonofabitch showed up.

His name was Patrick Kennedy. Looked to be nothing more than a mid-thirties junkie. This was Seattle, after all. I'm used to the stoners, junkies and freaks.

Patrick asked to see the mirror, and I pointed him to the back room with a smile. When he returned, a couple of minutes later, he'd aged a few decades. I can tell you, I nearly passed out from fright. The small wrinkles around his eyes, mouth, and on his forehead had deepened. His hair had gone from a deep, rich brown to streaky grey. He looked old.

Patrick slowly approached the counter, reaching into the inside pocket of his overcoat. As he did, I reached for the pistol I kept for protection beneath the counter. I stopped when he removed a letter and handed it to me with a sad grin.

He asked me to post it to the address written on it for him *when the job was done.* I didn't know what he meant, but something in his eyes made me take it. That's something else I forgot to mention: His type are very persuasive. I still don't know if that's a technique they acquire on account of their transformation, or it's just how sad and vulnerable they always seem. Either way, I took the note and told him that I'd post it *when the job was done.*

Patrick told me that he'd be back when he felt ready, perhaps before Sunday. I'd no idea what he meant by that, but I'd said, "fine", and watched him leave.

I wanted to open that letter, badly. But instead, I waited until Sunday. As I said, I deal in oddities. And Patrick Kennedy had to be the biggest oddity to ever enter my shop.

On Sunday, he arrived. In the middle of finishing off a BLT, I welcomed him with a smile. He asked if the mirror still sat in the back room and if I'd kept the letter. I answered yes to both. He thanked me and nodded. He also called me Doc.

Patrick entered the old storeroom and closed the door behind him. Silence followed. I waited. I'd lost my appetite so I packed away my sandwich and listened. A couple of minutes passed, then five, then ten. After that, I decided to check on him.

I knocked on the door cautiously, but to no answer. With a deep breath, I told him I was coming in.

I opened the door and stopped on the threshold, my head reeling. In all my fifty-six years on this earth, I thought I'd seen everything. I'd seen a dead body, belonging to a homeless person who didn't make it through a particularly cold night.

I'd been through a divorce, and I'd lost a best friend to cancer. I'd worked shitty job after shitty job to make ends meet until I started my own business. I thought I'd had it all figured out until that moment.

On the floor lay a pile of ashes. The room stunk of singed hair and burnt flesh. I made for the front door like a man in a dream and locked it, the room spinning around me. Turning over my sign on the window from *open* to *closed*, I stood there, trying to think.

I have no idea how much time passed, but it had begun to rain outside and had gotten dark. I remember moving like a zombie, grabbing a sweeping brush and an old coffee jar. I went back to the room and swept up Patrick Kennedy's remains. After that, I tore a page from my notebook on the counter and taped it to the jar. I took a pen and wrote VAMPIRE REMAINS on it, and then I laughed. Hysterically. I couldn't stop.

When I finally got myself under control, I tore open the letter he'd given me. I couldn't help it. I decided I'd copy down the address on the front of the envelope and buy a new one to post later. Let me tell you, I must have read that letter three or four times. A suicide note. As I'd expected.

It had all the usual stuff—*I'm sorry. I hope you understand. I couldn't live with myself anymore. I'm sorry for what I did to Poppy, the dog.*

Well, to be honest, the last part threw me. I figured he must have lost control and sucked the poor canine dry of its blood, but still, I couldn't stop laughing at the absurdity. I don't think anyone would want their last words to be *I'm sorry for what I did to the dog.*

Finished with the note, I placed Patrick Kennedy's remains onto my Oddities shelf and went home. I didn't know what else to do. No sleep came to me that night.

Did I consider the police? Of course. I stood by the phone for at least an hour, contemplating what to say. But what could I say? That someone turned to ash in my storeroom? Sure I had a note written by him, but besides giving it to whoever Patrick intended, what use could it be in an investigation? I decided not to call them. Instead, I went back to work the next day.

I sent the letter on the following Tuesday. That Friday, another freak came by.

The bell chimed over the door and I looked up to see a woman in the store. Just like Patrick, she had that young-but-tragic air about her. Her beautiful, dark eyes gave her away as one of them.

She asked about the mirror.

I stopped her there, asked her what this all meant. I couldn't take it anymore, and besides, what did I have to lose? She knew about the mirror, so she had to know more. If she didn't believe me, and I'd been wrong about her, fine, it would make me a senile old man who ran an antique store, big deal. But I took a gamble and told her everything. I told her about the mirror, and about what I'd seen. I told her about the ashes and the note. I asked her if I could be losing my mind, or if that man, Patrick Kennedy, really was a vampire. That's when she told me about the suicide rate among the recently turned. My mirror, she said, was a vampire in itself.

She told me that legend of the mirror, in their community, became reality when Riccardo brought it to American soil. After all, imagine somebody offering you a vision of yourself for the first time in god knows how long. Wouldn't you be curious? All that time, forever youthful, but never knowing how you look. Then, out of the blue comes a magic mirror. But there's a price. There's always a price.

I realise now that the longer these beautiful creatures stare into the thing in my storeroom, the more years it takes from them. How much of your youth would you be willing to sacrifice to look yourself in the eye again? From what I've seen, apparently a lot. They know the mirror will eat them alive. They know it will drain them until there's nothing but a pile of ash on the floor. All of their legends tell them so. And still, they come. They come to see the vampire in my storeroom.

I allowed the young lady to go and see for herself. She left no note for me to send. As with Patrick, I locked the door to the shop, and then I waited. After five minutes, I knocked. She never opened. Entering the room, I once again found nothing but a pile of ash on the floor.

A second coffee jar was purchased, and a second label made. It also read VAMPIRE REMAINS. It too went on my Oddities shelf. I didn't know where else to put them.

A young couple came by that afternoon and had a laugh at my two jars. They opened one and sniffed the contents, laughing and pretending to throw it at one another. I watched them, interested, feeling as if the whole world had gone crazy. Then the lady asked me how much I wanted for it. That's when an idea struck. I told her twenty. She said they'd take it. Then she asked where I'd found teeth to mix in with the ash, and what animal they came from. I told her the truth. They were vampire teeth, I said, and the ashes belonged to a burned up vampire. I told her about the mirror, about its power. She laughed, amused. Her boyfriend laughed.

I laughed.

I sold the second jar of remains to a preppy young guy who had a great time looking at himself in the mirror. He listened to my story of the vampires with great enthusiasm. I realised people would always be amused by my tale, but none would believe it. Hell, would you? What else could I do besides go with the flow? With the forty bucks I made from those remains, I went and bought some containers that looked like urns. Found them in a Save N' Shop for five apiece. Nice ones, black and slim.

One time, when an off-duty police officer came by to browse the store, he saw my three new urns on the Oddities shelf. They had all come in that week. The officer chuckled and said he should have me arrested for selling the remains of the dead. He looked in the mirror and thanked God he wasn't a vampire. I told him the story about the mirror, and what it did to vampires and how I got the ashes. Then he bought an urn.

So far, my vampire suicide booth has earned me a solid five hundred and thirty dollars. The shelf has a good stock of new remains, and it continues to grow every week. They sell like hotcakes. I tell everybody who comes the truth. They all laugh. And some even buy ashes.

Most of the vampires pay no attention to the urns on the Oddities shelf when they come by. They're too lost in their own world at the prospect of ending it all. They usually drift by the shelf without a word, but one or two stop and have a giggle. It seems everybody laughs at my shelf.

But James Lewis didn't laugh.

He went into the storeroom without asking if the mirror could be real or not, if I had any customers around, or if I had a particular way of doing things. He just wandered back there like a man in a dream, and five minutes later, he turned to ash. I swept him up about three hours ago.

A half-hour ago, I sold him.

HUNGER PAINS

MARY-ANN LOOKED BEAUTIFUL, even covered in blood. Blocking the glare of the high Memphis sun, Henry called her name.

Mary-Ann stumbled across the field that separated the family farms. The rough, dry dirt caused her to sway.

Wiping his forehead, Henry called again. "Mary-Ann, you all right?"

An aggravated crow cawed, taking flight from the line of trees out by the barn. Henry wanted to run to Mary-Ann, wanted to help, but his bad shape held him back.

Oh, come off it, He told himself. *You're scared shitless. The girl's covered in blood!*

He licked his lips. "I'm going to go call someone, all right, Mary-Ann? An ambulance, maybe. Do you think you need one?"

She got closer. Henry could make out more details now. The blood, dry and brown, looked as if it'd been there for some time. Her familiar smooth skin had turned colourless and waxy, her eyes the shade of curdled milk.

Her mouth fell open.

"You say something, Mary-Ann?"

A moment passed, then she let out a winded gasp. Henry's arm hair prickled and his crotch tightened.

"What in God's name is wrong?"

Mary-Ann's pace quickened. She fell forward, clomping her legs like a drunk trying to walk a straight line. She let out another clogged wheeze.

Henry whimpered and balled his fists. "Ah, fuck...I'm coming, hold on."

Panting, he heaved his three hundred pounds across his father's field, cursing the old man for leaving him with nothing more than his mother to take care of. His mother, pretty much useless after the death of his father, had retired permanently on the living room couch. She got up to piss and shit, that's about it. Sometimes, not even then. But Henry wasn't going to let his father's farm go to waste. He wanted to keep things running smoothly. When Momma finally kicked the bucket, he'd have the place to himself. Then he'd get the house, too. He would find a nice gal like Mary-Ann, maybe even start a family.

But now Mary-Ann was, well, Henry didn't know what the hell she was.

Henry stopped swinging his weight to catch his breath, blind spots blooming in his vision. Planting his meaty hands onto his kneecaps, he sucked air. A stitch started gnawing at his side. He held up an index finger to Mary-Ann and wheezed. "One...Minute..."

Mary-Ann groaned. She raised her arms out, reaching for him, her hands dangling with each step.

Pushing himself upright, Henry began to jog again, his heart thrumming in his ears. He made it five steps before stopping dead in his tracks. Had Mary-Ann said...

"Brains...*Brains.*"

"What?" Fear licked Henry's spine. "Okay, I'm calling an ambulance."

He'd left his phone in his jacket pocket in the loft. Turning, he heaved himself towards the barn. Fresh sweat oozed from every pore, dripping into his eyes. He scrunched his face in disgust. What the hell was wrong with Mary-Ann? Had she been hit by a car?

Looking back, he noticed the girl heading for the house. "My phone's in the barn, Annie," he called. "Just sit down and let me bring you some water. Don't bother Momma. That dodgy step broke this morning, and I don't want you twisting your ankle."

Mary-Ann ignored him, causing Henry's stomach to tighten. He didn't want her to see the state of the house, not with his mother nearly fused to the fabric of the couch. And that stench...Today, it was mostly bacon grease and piss. Mary-Ann could *not* go in there.

He called her name again but got no response. Instead, she began to climb the porch steps, the wood sagging beneath her waxy legs. Her yellow, stained sundress swayed as she briefly lost her balance, quickly correcting herself. Then she lurched towards the front door. A dull thump came as her face connected with the wood.

"*Henry!*"

"Momma!" The word, a ball of ice, caught in his throat. "It's Mary-Ann, Momma. Something's wrong. Don't let her inside, okay? I'm calling an ambulance. She's covered in blood."

"Say what?"

"*I said she's covered in blood!*"

Reeling back, Mary-Ann slammed into the door again. She let out a noise, sounding as if her tongue had swollen from too many bee stings. As she came away, a splatter of brown stained the wood where her head had made contact.

Momma sounded panicked, her words hard to distinguish from inside the house.

Henry stomped his foot. "Mary-Ann, stop that!"

"What's she doing, Henry?"

Mary-Ann slogged forward again, and this time, the door gave. The rotted wood groaned as it fell open, and Mary-Ann flopped inside. A muted thump followed as she hit the hardwood floor, out of sight.

"Oh, sweet Jesus..."

Henry rushed forward, then stopped. He tried again. Stopped again.

"Oh, come on...You can do this." He huffed a breath, planting his hands on his hips. His bladder threatened to let loose. "Just go. For God's sake, you pussy. *Go.*"

After a moment, he squealed with frustration. He ran his fingers through his hair and pulled, his scalp screaming. "Just fucking *go*!"

A shout from inside the house. "*Henry*! Help me!"

The peach fuzz on the back of Henry's neck stood and he slogged forward, the dry dirt crunching beneath his feet. He reached the porch and looked past the limp, hanging door into the hallway.

Too dark to see.

He shouted, "Momma? You okay?"

A shadow, darker than the rest of the hall, appeared at the doorway. Mary-Ann. Chewing something.

Henry backed away, his mouth moving soundlessly, the taste of bile filling his throat. "W-What's that in your hands, Mary-Ann? What're you holding?"

Standing on the porch, Mary-Ann's skin looked pale as a corpse's. Her eyes were dry and scabby. Fresh gore dripped down the front of her sundress, some catching on the material. The rest splattered on the wood by her feet. She took a bite of what she held, making wet, squelching sounds.

"Momma!" Henry screamed. "Momma! Speak to me!"

No reply.

Mary-Ann lowered her cupped hands and began lurching forward. The gooey crimson mess, wet and glistening, fell from her fingers.

"What have you done to Momma, Mary-Ann?"

The girl reached the porch steps—and fell.

Her left leg buckled on the top plank, sending her sprawling to the dirt. A sharp crack echoed out and Henry winced. Mary-Ann smacked to the ground with a wheeze, her hair spread around her in a cloud of dust. Bone jutted from the grey skin of her ankle.

"I'm calling for help," Henry said, slogging towards the barn. He needed to call the hospital, the police, *anybody*.

Behind him, Mary-Ann moaned.

Henry reached the double doors of the barn and forced them open. The rotting lumber groaned as it caught on some weeds. Cursing, he forced his weight against the door, pushing it over the tuft. It popped free with a creak and flew open.

The familiar scent of hay filled his nose, and the shade cooled his skin. Dust particles danced in the shafts of light. A wooden ladder to the loft stood on the far side and Henry forced his aching feet towards it. His shirt clung to his chest and he pulled at it, puffing a gust of heat towards his face.

Henry placed his foot on the lower step and heaved his himself up with a grunt. The wood creaked but held. He paused halfway to wipe the sweat from his brow.

The second floor wobbled on its support beams as Henry heaved himself up. He hadn't been to the loft since childhood, but the planks needed replacing so he'd gone up that morning to inspect the damage. Besides his father, no one had been in the loft for over a decade. Looking around, he remembered being up there as a kid. One summer, he'd tied a blue polypropylene rope from the loft to the door of the barn, then, wrapping a shirt around the rope, he'd leaped, gliding down and dropping midway onto a bale of hay. That same rope now sat in the far corner, curled up like a dead snake. Beside it lay his jacket and phone.

Henry snatched his phone and dialled emergency services. After a while, a robotic voice told him that all lines were currently busy. Whining, he tried again. No use.

Shards of light seeped through holes in the wall, and Henry ran to one, needing to see through to the yard. Pushing his eye against the wood, he squinted. He could make out the trees at the far side of the farm, but not much else. Moving around, he tried to get a better angle. Something clinked off his foot. Frowning, Henry peered down at a dirty metallic lunchbox.

He swiped the lunchbox from the floor and rammed it against the wood. A loud crack shot through the barn. The wood began to splinter, so he tried again. This time, the plank broke through. The resistance of the wall disappeared as the lunchbox plummeted to the ground outside, landing with a clank. The loft suddenly filled with glaring light, and Henry lifted his arms to shield his eyes.

Another moan came from somewhere outside. This one didn't sound like Mary-Ann.

Blinking, Henry poked his head out, hating the heat on his already hot skin. His eyes throbbed in rhythm with his heartbeat as he scanned the yard. Something moved to his right but by the time he looked, it'd disappeared. Something else moved on the porch of the house.

Henry screamed.

Momma was crawling down the porch steps like a salamander. Her caved-in head leaked as if a pipe had burst, soaking the wood around her. Her grey slacks slid further and further down her legs as she moved, revealing flabby, pale flesh. She didn't seem to notice.

"Momma! Can you hear me?"

"Braaaainss."

Henry's skin turned to ice. He jumped when Mary-Ann moaned from behind.

The girl stood in the barn doorway, silhouetted. Her body slumped forward, her head lulling to her chest. Her arms drooped by her side and her left foot dragged at an odd angle. She made her way inside.

The Ladder! Can she climb?

By the looks of her, no. Her limbs dangled like floppy roadkill. Henry ran to the ladder and heaved it up, just in case. Mary-Ann whined in response.

"Shut up!"

Lying the ladder flat on the loft, Henry listened to Mary-Ann shuffle about below. He scooted to the edge and peered down. The girl's head fell back and she looked up at him, her mouth agape. Henry grimaced and returned to the hole in the wall, wanting to see where Momma had gone. The lunchbox lay on the ground outside, broken from the impact, its contents spilled.

"Chocolate?" Henry couldn't suppress the nervous laughter. "Well, found your stash, Pop."

His stomach grumbled. How could he be thinking of food now, with this all happening? Besides, the chocolate had to be out of date.

It's not like I'd go down there and get it, anyway. Mary-Ann's dangerous.

Lifting his eyes, he saw Momma pull herself towards the barn on her stomach. Her slacks had slipped and caught around her ankles in a clump. As he watched, she threw an arm out, digging her fingers into the dirt and heaving herself another few inches. She left a flattened, bloody trail from the house.

Something rustled in the trees at the far side of the yard, followed by more moaning.

"Oh, Christ, no." Henry lifted a shaking hand to his mouth. "Not more, please."

It has to be a virus, He thought. *Just like one of those old movies about the zombies in black and white! Except...They never asked for* brains.

Two men fell from the trees into the yard. Their bodies sagged, their legs carrying dead weight. They walked like drunkards, staggering with each step. Both their scalps had been cracked open, same as Momma. A mess of flesh hung and swayed from their foreheads, oozing down their faces.

Henry recognised one of them as Lenny Appleton, the man who ran the grocery store. The other was James Kirkland, the in-house Elvis impersonator at the Rock-A-Hula. He was still in costume.

The two men stumbled towards the barn, catching up with Momma's dragging body.

Then, more exited the tree line. Much more.

Henry's stomach cartwheeled as all around, the farm came to life. They came from the trees, from the fields, from the road, from behind the house. All of them moaned for the same thing—Henry's *brains*.

Some of their heads lifted, their glazed-over eyes finding him. Henry pushed himself away from the hole in the wall, trying to hide. His legs buckled and he fell to the floor, panting. Streams of hot tears slithered down his face. He gripped his hair with both hands and squeezed. "*What the hell is happening*?" Then, to Mary-Ann, "*You ate Momma's brain! How can you walk around without a brain?*"

Henry was disgusted at himself as his stomach rumbled a second time. He placed a hand across his midsection and moaned. From outside, the approaching hoard of the dead sounded like an agitated swarm of wasps.

Henry scurried to the edge of the loft and looked down. The dead knocked against the side of the barn as they lurched towards the open door. Slivers of light lined the floor, and as the dead passed, their shadows made a strobe light of the sun. Then the first of the hoard reached the door.

Hunched over, the man's arms swung. His shadow stretched out ahead to amplify his form. The form of Elvis Presley. James Kirkland's dead eyes found Henry as he fell inside. The rest followed.

Whimpering, Henry scurried on all fours to the wall. He pressed his back to it and willed himself to disappear. Lightheadedness set in. Sickness. The groans and cries from below blended together in a soup of skin-crawling white noise. Henry whimpered. The overwhelming heat and the toxic stench of decay seemed to be increasing. Henry tried breathing through his mouth, but the thought of what he'd suck in disgusted him. He shifted uncomfortably, squeezing his eyes shut, trembling. He didn't want to see anymore. Besides, the cries of the stinking dead didn't seem so loud. Had they gone away?

As blind spots danced around his vision, Henry listened to the fading noise of the dead. Then he blacked out.

Henry woke with a start, gasping for breath. The air hung heavy with the stench of spoilt meat. He wiped his eyes, his head muzzy, his heart jackhammering.

A steady vocalised hum filled the dark barn. On his hands and knees, Henry went to the edge of the loft and peeked down. The floor moved like an ant hill. Body to body, the dead fell about, their arms grasping as if he was the Saviour. Sandpaper voices called out for brains.

Warm sweat rolled down his forehead and Henry wiped it away, his eyes puffy from crying. *Everybody's down there,* He thought. *The whole town. Dead.*

A sniffle stirred a vocal response from below. Henry ignored it and made his way to the hole in the wall, looking out. A few lonesome town-folk fell about in the dry fields. The sky above them showed the first sign of dawn, the farm bathed in silver light. A soft mist hung low to the ground. As Henry watched, one of the dead tripped, thumping face down soundlessly.

Henry pushed himself away from the hole and shook his head. He wiped his running nose on his sleeve and made his way to the edge of the loft.

Below, the dead reached up, their fingers flexing like plump, white worms. Their mouths slopped opened, some drooling. Each of them, Henry noticed, had a cracked head.

"*Brains*!"

Henry studied the sea of faces. There stood Mary-Ann. Beside her, Justin Kenny. There, Patrick and Fiona White. Richard Ingram, the bartender. Momma.

Momma had finally stood at some point. Her grey slacks pooled around her ankles. Her milky eyes looked just like the rest. Henry knew she wanted his brains as much as the next.

I could jump, Henry thought. *Just taking a step forward and end it. It'd be easy.* He chuckled. *Right. Too afraid to live, but too frightened to jump.*

His stomach grumbled, a cramp spreading through his midsection. He needed to eat.

"You want a piece of me, huh? Need to eat? Not the only ones, you know."

He spotted the dead face of Charlie Harris. Charlie had always made fun of him. Charlie who'd hopped into the air every time Henry took a step in the schoolyard, crying, "*Earthquake, Earthquake!*", always getting a laugh from the other kids. Henry locked eyes with him. "Big, fat-ass Henry outran the end of the world. Didn't see that one coming, did you, Charles?"

Charlie didn't reply, but Henry's stomach did. He rubbed it. "How about I eat one of you? How would you like *that*?" Butterflies began fluttering inside his chest. *I'm giddy,* He thought. *I'm losing it.*

"That'd be good, wouldn't it? Ol' fat Henry, just couldn't stop eating, not even at the end."

Charlie stared back with glassy eyes, his mouth moving silently.

Then Henry's face scrunched. He fell silent for a moment. *Well, why not? Why not eat the bastard? Poetic justice and all that. I'm a dead man, either way. Why not go out with a bang?*

"Last Supper."

*And what if it doesn't kill me? What if...*Henry giggled. *What if, after chewing on the last bone of dear old Charlie Harris, I survive? I could build up my strength. Concentrate better. Start to plan a way out of this mess, make for the next town and see how far things have spread. Maybe even find others.*

Henry cocked his head. "How am I going to get you, Charlie? Huh? How am I meant to get you up here so's I can eat you?"

The response seemed to be *brains.*

"You're all useless, you know that? Fine. I'll think of something myself."

Henry pushed himself up, his eyes landing on the hole in the wall. Could he jump? No. It was too far and the ground was much too hard. He'd snap his ankle and be an easy target. Spotting the blue polypropylene rope in the corner, Henry smiled.

"Gonna lasso you, Charlie Harris. Wring your damned neck."

Henry swiped the rope from the floor. He began tying a Honda knot, something he'd done since childhood, back when they had horses. He started by making an overhand in the end of the rope, passing the tail back through. He tied a stopper at the end of the tail for more durability. Wiping his face, he inspected his work. Good.

Henry made his way to the edge of the loft. "Like fish in a damn barrel."

The swaying sea of faces pushed forward, each trying to get below him. Their stench wafted. Gagging, Henry waited for Charlie to get into position before he began to lower the rope.

"Come on now, don't move."

Charlie didn't. The noose fell loosely around his head, and the dead man opened his mouth, biting as it passed.

"Stop that," Henry said. "Need to get this around your dumb neck. There we go."

The rope flopped on Charlie's shoulders. Henry smiled and gave it a yank. The rope tightened. Charlie's brain-calling cut as his vocal cords squeezed.

"All right, then. Come to me, Charlie."

Lowering himself to a seated position, Henry held the rope between his legs and wiped his sweaty hands onto his jeans, then he looped it around his fists and pulled. He gritted his teeth, feeling the weight pulling him down. His face grew hot as he wrenched on the rope with what little strength he had. Then, Charlie began to rise. His bulging, strained face floated upward, like a toy in a grab machine. The others watched Henry, oblivious.

Charlie's body rotated in the air, his limbs hanging. A gasp forced itself from Henry's mouth. His arms shook. Spittle flew from his cracked lips.

"*Gah*! Come on! Come *on*!"

The rope went lax. Henry, toppling bassackwards, heard a wet, ripping sound. Something struck the wall behind, then rolled to a stop. Panting, Henry forced himself up. He looked over the edge.

The headless carcass of Charlie Harris rolled on the dead like a crowd-surfer from hell. His body jittered and bobbed as it was passed about, eventually splatting to the grubby floor. Henry spun, already knowing what he'd find.

The head of Charlie Harris lay a few feet away.

Charlie's glazed eyes burned holes in him, his mouth snapping like a fish out of water. Trails of inners streamed from his shredded neck, leaking over the dusty floorboards. Henry screamed and almost lost his balance. Below, the dead cried in a choir for brains. Henry toppled forward and sidestepped around Charlie's head, seeing the splatter of gore on the wall where the head had smacked.

Henry took a deep breath and shook out his arms. "It's all right. The plan's still working. I got him up here. Part of him, at least. Come here, Charlie. Fat Henry finally got you."

Henry lifted Charlie's head by the temples, careful not to touch the ruined burrow in the top of the skull. The skin, cold and soft, felt like old fish. Drops of crimson tapped the floorboards. Henry grimaced. He could feel Charlie's jaw still working, trying to bite at him.

"I've lost it, Charles," Henry said. "It's the end of the world, and I need to eat. Guess we all do."

He flipped the head, viewing the serrated opening in the neck, and got presented a mess of gore leaking icy blood over his hands. His grip went slippery, but Henry held tight.

Then he began to weep.

"Just couldn't stop eating, could I?"

Holding the head with one hand, he wiped his eyes into the sleeve of his shirt. "Never good enough to fit in with assholes like you. Not handsome enough. Never fit enough to play football...Not that I ever wanted to. It's not my fault, you know. I never asked to be this way." Henry wiped away a new stream of hot tears. He chuckled. "Well, none of that matters now, Charlie. At the end of the day, we both lost our heads."

Henry slowly raised the grotesque gauntlet to his mouth. His tongue slid slowly along the soft, cold line of a severed jugular. Like licking a slug. The taste of copper filled his mouth.

Then a gunshot rang out.

Henry dropped Charlie's head and screamed. The head thumped to the floorboards, and Henry listened. An engine revved.

Dread suddenly flooded Henry's body, making him nauseous. At the drop of a hat, the adrenaline coursing through his veins disappeared.

"What the hell did I just do?"

He kicked out at Charlie's head like a football, sending it sailing back down into the barn. He heard the dead scurry about to inspect as he made his way to the broken hole in the wall, wiping his tongue on the way.

Outside, a battered and filthy jeep bobbed and rocked over the rough terrain in the morning light, a trail of dust hitching a lift. Two men stood in the open flatbed, holding the cab. One had a shotgun. A shuffling figure fell towards the jeep as it sped through the empty field, and the shotgun raised.

A splatter exploded from the figure as the shot boomed out, the two men whooping from the back of the jeep. Headlights cut a path in the dirt ahead, casting the soil in relief. Then the jeep began to turn to the right, towards the main road. Henry's stomach fell.

"Hey! Over here!"

He waved his arms frantically. He called again, his throat stinging.

The jeeps break lights went up and it fell still, dust drifting by. The two men in the back looked towards the barn as one pointed.

They see me!

The jeep crunched dirt as it U-turned and veered towards the barn. Below the loft, Henry heard the dead shuffle about, seeming to sense the newcomers.

Hurry up! Please, hurry.

The engine cut as it skidded to a stop just below the hole in the wall. The two men peered up at him. Henry wiped his face on his wet sleeve, hoping there were no signs of what he'd done.

"Well, I'll be a son-of-a-bitch. Henry Miller?"

The two men laughed. Great. George Thompson and Douglas Peters. Two of Charlie's crew. Henry couldn't see the driver, but it had to be Jerry Carter, completing the four.

Douglas called up. "We came out here to see if Mary-Ann was around. Whole family are lurchers. Such a shame, right? How'd you get through the night, fat ass?"

Their faces blurred for a moment as a dizzy spell washed through Henry. He shook his head to clear it.

"Don't shout so loud," he said. "There's about twenty of them in the barn. They don't seem to realise the door's open, but if they do, they'll be on you."

"Shiiiiit." Douglas planted his hands on his hips. "Then we better get the hell out of here, eh?"

The driver revved the engine.

"Hey! You can't leave me here!"

George and Douglas honked a laugh.

"S'pose not," Douglas said. "Looks like you're going to have to jump, lard-ass. And soon, too, if they're in the barn like you say."

Henry's stomach gurgled. He blinked fast and stayed focused on the guys below.

"It's too far."

His voice sounded alien to his own ears. His shook his head again, trying to concentrate.

"Well then there ain't nothing we can do, Henry. Sorry about that."

"Hold on!"

With a whimper, Henry pushed himself through the hole in the wall. The broken wood jabbed at his belly. He placed his hands onto sides of the opening and braced himself.

"Clear the area!" George called out, hands cupped to his mouth. "Big load, coming through!"

Douglas leaped from the flatbed, scurrying a few feet away. George looked up, shielding his eyes. "Bombs away, big boy!"

Henry took a deep breath. And jumped.

The pit of his stomach elevated as the ground disappeared. The jeep soared towards him as the air ripped past his ears. Then came a metallic *thunk* as he landed in the flatbed, rocking the suspension.

Panting, Henry opened his eyes and looked around. The two men were doubled over laughing, their eyes wet with tears.

"Oh man," Douglas said. "Like a goddamn whale!"

A long horn beep cut them short. Henry looked towards the barn, his eyes widening.

"Shit!" George shouted. "Go, go, go!"

From around the barn, the dead shuffled, bathed in headlights. The vehicle rocked as Douglas leaped back inside and banged the hood.

"Step on it, Jerry!"

They took off, veering in the direction the road. Henry jumped as the shotgun burst to life. The smell of gunpowder filled the air.

"Dropped one!" George cried, his voice muffled from the ringing in Henry's ears. "Think it was Mrs. Jefferson!"

The jeep rocked and bumped, and Henry lay down, the cold metal digging into his back. He didn't care. He needed to close his eyes for a moment. After a while, he asked, "What's happened?"

He kept his eyes closed, feeling hot and clammy.

"Not listening to the radio?" George said. "Something to do with a virus in the water. Shit, the warning's been broadcast since last night. How'd you not know?"

"Our water comes from the well. Don't have a radio. And Momma only ever watched VHS tapes because we don't get any stations."

"Well that's what happened. Don't know specifics, fatty. Seems the virus killed a whole bunch of unlucky S.O.Bs that drank the water. Then yesterday, they all come back to life. Eat people's brains!"

"Don't talk about food."

Henry's eyes shot open. *What had he said?*

George squinted. "What's that, now?"

"Nothing."

George and Douglas exchanged a look, George arching an eyebrow. "We're going to Millington. They've set up some sort of safe zone for anyone who makes it. Some sort of government protection area. Say they might even be flying all survivors out of the US. All of Tennessee's been put under quarantine." George banged on the dirty plate of glass that separated the cab from the bed with the stock of the gun. "Here's good. Stop it here, Jerry!"

The jeep screeched to a halt. The engine cut.

"Take off your shirt, Henry."

"What?"

"You heard me. Take your shirt off."

Henry's stomach dropped. "Please, don't make me—"

"We need to see if you've got the marks. See if you've been bitten. Can't be bringing you along if you're carrying, can we? And I'm not talkin' lice and the butt-tonne of extra weight! Come on now, Henry. Take your shirt off."

Henry stood and began to slowly remove his shirt. He couldn't think straight. Something felt wrong. The cold air prickled his skin as the two men began to laugh.

"*Shhh*," George said. "Shut up, Doug. This is serious, now. We need to-," The sentence cut with a snort of laughter. "We need to see if Henry here has any marks."

Henry wasn't embarrassed about having his shirt off. Didn't mind at all. His mind went elsewhere. His mouth salivated, and he swallowed.

"Turn," George said. "Give us a twirl, Chunky."

Henry did, his bones aching. He imagined the taste of something salty, something creamy. Something *firm* like ripe yogurt. He laughed. So did George and Douglas.

Suddenly warm and comfortable, Henry closed his eyes and swayed. Then something hit his face. Henry's eyes flew open.

"That's the third time," George said. "You ain't with it."

Third time? Had he been *smacked* three times? How had he not *felt* that? Henry noticed he'd been drooling. He chuckled. It was kind of funny.

George shook his head. "You're delirious, fat boy. I asked you a question."

Henry didn't speak. George's voice came in and out like bad radio reception.

"I'm only going to ask you one more time, fat ass," George said. "*Are you hungry*?"

Henry smiled. "Of course I am."

KING OF THE GYPSIES

"**SO, YOU'RE REALLY** going to do it?"

Michael drained his second pint of beer and wiped his mouth. Even though it was only ten in the morning, the stale scent of smoke and vomit still hung in the pub from the night before. Thin Lizzy played quietly on the jukebox as a lone bartender went about setting up for the day's business.

"Of course I'm going to do it," Michael said. His voice was low and steady. "What other choice do I have?"

Henry nodded. "I know. You have to do it."

Henry had always been a good friend, an understanding friend, and the only one who'd support Michael in a decision as ridiculous as this. The idea was foolish, but Michael saw no other choice. With a baby on the way, he needed the money.

"How long ago was it?" Henry asked. "The last one, I mean. When it happened."

Michael's brow creased, his callused fingers drumming the wooden tabletop. "Ten years, give or take. '85, I think."

"Jaysus."

Looking out the window of the pub, Michael watched the light drizzle fall in the sunlight. A summer shower spat down on Dublin city centre. Good weather for a fight.

"I remember it like it was yesterday," Henry said, shaking his head. "Still remember the O'Connells trying to blame the mud for him slipping the first time he went down, even though he was clearly pissed. Sure, I could even smell the whiskey from where I was. All hell broke loose, man. Jaysus. Still have a scar on my ribcage from where Patrick O'Connell smashed me with a bottle."

Michael remembered that night. Of course he remembered. "Horrible," he said flatly.

Far up the Wicklow Mountains, a two-hour drive from Dublin, through back roads and steep inclines covered in nothing but forests and woodland, lay The Ring. At least, that's what it was known to the bare-knuckle boxing community. The Ring was a clearing near the top of the Sally Gap, a place where gravel crunched beneath your feet and the sound of harsh wind tore by your ears. Up there, there was no interference. And on that night, ten years ago, Michael wished there had been. If there was, things might be different. The young Brady O'Connell might still be alive.

The Gardai had gotten a tip-off, and raided The Ring back in 1992. The news covered it extensively. The entire country had spoken of nothing else for weeks but the traveling gypsy families who staked money on fist fights for a living. That was, until something better came along. Some bigger news always did. What didn't get publicised, though, and only because they were never discovered by the media, were the VHS tapes that made big money down on Moore Street. His tapes sold door to door. Michael *the Mountain* Rourke was something of a celebrity.

"When are they meant to be here?" Henry asked.

"Any minute now. Going to try for one more pint before they do."

Henry laughed. "You always have to go one more, don't you? I'll get it. Stay here."

Michael breathed a sigh of relief as Henry went to the bar. He hoped that would happen. He hadn't had money since he retired from bare-knuckle boxing eleven years ago. That night, the O'Connells, the self-proclaimed *Kings of Gypsies,* had sabotaged Michael's fight against Brady O'Connell when they saw their fighter losing. They'd turned off their car engines, plunging The Ring into total darkness and chaos.

Michael knew that Brady had been drunk off his ass that night. Everyone did. Still, a lot of money had been placed on that fight, and the O'Connells couldn't afford to lose. In the dark, accusations were screamed, punches were thrown, and a now legendary brawl exploded between the O'Connells and the Rourkes.

Brady had been stabbed in the back of the neck with a broken bottle and trampled underfoot. And even though a decade had passed, the finger still got pointed in Michael's direction. But Michael hadn't done it. On his life, he'd never killed a man.

Michael had retired from the scene after that. But even though the O'Connells were enemies of the Rourke's, he'd never wished any of them dead. The fights were just easy money to him, that's all. And Michael *the Mountain* Rourke was a safe bet when it came time to pull the money out. The odds were on his side every time.

The money had been great, and the traveller families, sometimes even the settled families, would look forward to the fights like a professional boxing season once those VHS tapes got around. Michael had even seen a woman wearing a homemade *Up The Mountain!* t-shirt once on Grafton Street. That'd been surreal.

"Here. Cheers."

Henry sat with a grunt and raised his pint. Michael did the same, draining it halfway with a couple of mouthfuls. The booze went down far easier than he expected it to, or wanted it to, in the morning.

"Shit," Henry said, looking out the window. "Blue van just pulled up. Looks like...Yeah, it's Willie The Lookout. Think he has Tommy Fenton with him. Time wasn't too nice to either of them, eh?"

Willie *The Lookout*, real name William Byrne, had been a main creator of The Ring. The land it was on belonged to his family, and he'd leased it out for a handsome sum anytime it needed using by the boxers. Tommy Fenton, his right-hand man, served as a non-biased referee for all matches, and had become legendary in his own right. Rumour had it he'd once stopped Johnny *The Fox* from ripping off Ken Leary's ear back in '81.

Fishing a crumpled carton of cigarettes from his jeans, Michael lit one, watching the smoke curl to the ceiling. The jukebox had switched to Rory Gallagher now. Taking a deep breath, Michael waited for Willie and Tommy to enter.

"They see us," Henry said, not taking his eyes from the window. "Coming in now."

The bell chimed over the door of the pub, and in walked Willie *The Lookout* and Tommy Fenton, both sporting dark green raincoats that glistened from the drizzle. When Michael had first met Willie back in 1990, Willie had been a large man. Now he was an absolute gargantuan shit-house. It looked as if he was trying to smuggle a bag of footballs beneath his coat. He caught Michael's eye and nodded, then made his way over. Tommy Fenton trailed behind like a loyal puppy, his beady eyes scanning the pub.

"Michael," Willie said. He smiled, flashing nicotine-stained teeth. "It's honest-to-god good to see ye again. You know how long I've been waiting for you to come to your senses and get back into bangin' a few heads? Fuckin' ages, man. Wasn't I only saying it to you, Tommy, last week, and then who calls me? Michael the feckin' *Mountain* Rourke."

Michael took a deep drag of his cigarette and held it in his lungs. "So, the O'Connells are happy enough with the rules, Willie?"

"Daylight fight, no chance of them knocking out the sun, now is there? Wouldn't have come if they didn't agree. The O'Connells can't wait for a match. Should have heard them when I called, boy. Even the big man, Georgie. He wants it worst of all. Says you're a dead man walkin'."

"Georgie O'Connell's going to come?"

"To see one of his pups get a rematch against you? He'd walk from Donegal if he had to."

Georgie *Wolfman* O'Connell was the self-titled *King of the Gypsies*. He'd never lost a fight in his life, or so the story goes.

Brady O'Connell had been the man's youngest, and by far the best fighter. The three others, Derry, Patrick and Sean, were boxers, too, and each was as mean as a battered bulldog.

"Georgie must be in his sixties now," Michael said.

Michael had never actually seen The King himself, and the idea of seeing him triggered an old thrill deep down in the part of himself he fought to leave behind. But try as he might, a pull to this lifestyle existed that he never would admit. *Like attracts like*, he supposed. He never could admit that to Angie.

One time, last year, when he heard that Ken Leary had been granted a rematch against Johnny *The Fox*, he'd tried telling Angie about it, because the idea of seeing that fight had made his heart race. Fortunately, he had some self-control. The words had stuck in his throat like a brick, and that's where they'd stayed. Angie couldn't know about that part of his past. She would look at him and see a monster.

Angie was a South Dublin girl, a college graduate, and a hard worker. The Michael that she got to know laid bricks on the weekdays and enjoyed playing the guitar on the weekends. He was quiet, reserved, and liked to read crime novels to her while she curled up on the sofa next to him in their small City centre apartment.

To her, Michael Rourke wasn't a fighter.

He'd told her that he came from a family of travellers, but at the age of eighteen he'd gotten a series of part-time jobs and scraped his way through school. The latter part was true. He had, in fact, paid his own way through school. The rest had been a lie. It wasn't any part-time job that had earned him his money, and it wasn't any small amount, either. Michael had been fighting since childhood, right up to that final fight with Brady O'Connell in 1985. That had been ten years ago.

The money he'd earned, he'd mostly pissed away. He drank with Henry and tried to wash the taste of guilt out of his mouth. But of course, that hadn't worked. Renting a room in the city centre, he'd landed a job on a construction site. He'd been straight ever since.

But now, Angie was pregnant, and they needed the money. Bad.

For just the two of them, they earned enough to get by, but that wouldn't last with a baby on the way. Michael wasn't prepared to ask for help from his family. He didn't want them involved in this. He was going to give his child what he could, by himself. He was going to make sure that kid never had to see the inside of a damn mobile home. Not if he could help it.

The fighting had been the only thing he'd ever kept from Angie.

"Georgie is definitely coming," Willie said. "Dying to see you go down, lad. Sure, he's touching seventy now, but I'm telling ya, he wants to see your blood spilled, Michael boy. And he's setting up ringside."

Michael swallowed. His mouth had gone very dry. "How many are we expecting?"

"I'd say nearly fifty," Tommy chimed in. His voice was wheezy and high, and in any other context, it would have been comical. His long, stubbly face jittered as he spoke. "Not sending word out to anyone. This one's personal, Micky. You know that."

"I do." Michael stubbed out his cigarette on the table and stood. He nodded for Henry to do the same. "Well, let's go then."

Outside, the rain beat down, sounding like white noise. It had picked up heavily in the last few minutes, splashing off of windowsills and rolling down the gutters. The overcast sky hung bloated overhead, and the red cobbled road of Grafton Street was slick with water. It reminded Michael of blood. Lighting another cigarette, he made his way over to his Triumph motorcycle, the others following behind. His heart kicked at his chest and he felt lightheaded. *This was really going to happen*, He thought.

Willie's blue van was parked next to his bike, and Tommy climbed into the passenger seat while mumbling something about the weather. Willie unlocked the driver-side door, turning to Michael before getting in. "So you're going to follow behind us, Micky, yeah?"

"Yup."

"Don't worry, I'll have me lights on full the whole time."

Tommy spluttered a laugh from inside the cab. Michael didn't reply.

"Touching eleven now, so it is. We'll be there by a half hour or so, so plenty of daylight left for ye. Let's hope you've been getting some training in. Must be hard with the baby on the way and all."

Michael's blood turned to ice. "How'd you know about the baby? What do you mean a half-hour? We're going to The Ring, right? That's at least over an hour from here."

"Really, Micky? You don't think we've been keeping tabs on ye? Course we have. Angie's a good lookin' young one, so she is. So let's hope you make it back to her with some money for that little baby now. But listen, Micky." Willie's fat lips curled into a smile. "You're one of us and you know it. Always will be. This isn't something you just walk away from. And there's been a change of plans. Georgie wants it up Montpelier Hill."

"Montpelier?" Michael shook his head. "You mean at the Hellfire Club?"

"It's their stompin' ground, Micky. Their home, their rules." With that, Willie slammed the van door shut and started the engine.

Michael turned to Henry. The rain continued to beat them. "They've been watching me?"

Henry shook his head. "Can't believe it. Doesn't surprise me though, if I'm honest. Bad bunch of assholes you ran with Michael. Bad bunch."

Michael climbed onto his Triumph. The seat felt soaked but he didn't care. He only wanted to get this over with and go home to Angie with his pocket bulging. He still didn't know how to explain the cash to her, and Henry's idea of saying that he'd won the lottery looked more and more appealing by the minute.

Michael put on his helmet, the flower sticker that Angie had slapped onto its black surface making him feel silly now. "Hellfire Club. Can you believe it?"

"They live around there, man. I can't say I'm not worried about you. Could be a setup. But you don't need to be told that...So just be careful, yeah?"

"Yeah."

Henry patted Michael's shoulder. "Sure you don't want me to come?"

Michael shook his head. "Just make sure you're by your phone between five and six. I'll get to a payphone and call you if I need you to come and get me."

"Vincent's Hospital, yeah?"

"Jesus, Henry." Michael lowered his visor. "Only if I lose, you morbid prick." He started the engine, the bike vibrating soothingly beneath him. "Which I won't. I'll be back in one piece. And if worse comes to worst, I'll say I got in a bar fight after one too many. Got it?"

Henry nodded in understanding as Michael eased his way out of the parking space. He gave his friend a wave goodbye and Henry returned a salute. Then Michael took off.

The Triumph's tires splashed through dark puddles collected on the city streets. The bike trembled beneath him, as if it knew it headed for danger. Ahead, Willie's filthy blue van bounced along, waiting for him to catch up. Michael flashed his beams, indicating that he was behind them and Willie took up speed.

They drove out of the city, the urban landscape slowly giving way to greenery. Trees, wet with dew, blurred past. Within the hour, they were deep in the Dublin mountains, a notorious spot for gang members to dump bodies, and god only knew the number of rotting cadavers that still lay undiscovered within the hidden thickets. Gradually, the road became a single lane, lined with potholes. To either side, the steep, vast body of trees descended while the road continued to climb, leaving a threatening drop should one lose grip on the steering wheel.

Michael's ears popped. The temperature crept steadily lower, leaving his denim jacket cold against his skin. He shivered. The noise of the Triumph's engine filled his ears.

Ahead, Willie's blue van swayed like the hips of a geriatric, his brake lights hardly ever lighting in the darkening day. Dusk was coming fast.

The bends became increasingly tricky to manoeuvre, and Michael thought, *Can't be much further...*

Finally, Willie's brake lights went up, painting the dark road red. Michael lowered his kickstand and cut off the ignition. Smoke from the blue van's exhaust drifted by in the cold air like a ghost. Removing his helmet, Michael lit another cigarette. Ahead, Willie plopped out of his van and lumbered back to him.

"Leaving the van here, so I am."

"Why?"

"In case the Gardai come. Blocks the road off. Only way up is here past Killakee house, we'll see their lights from a mile away. Either way, they'll have to stop here and walk up. Give us time to get the fuck out. It's only a banger of a yolk anyway, not registered, have three others so it's no skin off my back if they take it."

Michael nodded, not mentioning that his bike was his pride and joy, and if it was taken, Willie would be in hospital.

"Come on then."

Willie led the way, joined by the ever-scampering Tommy. They'd been walking for less than five minutes when the fat man's breathing became annoyingly loud—he wheezed out phlegmy breaths that occasionally called for a sloppy spit. Tommy shuffled along beside the man, hunched over like his evil sidekick. And in a way, Michael thought, that's exactly what Tommy *The Lookout* was to him.

"Did you know that this place is called the Hellfire Wood, Micky?" Willie wheezed. "Did ye?"

"Nope."

"But you do know the stories of the Hellfire Club?"

"I know it's meant to be haunted. That's all."

"Sure there's more to it than that. The clubhouse used to be a hunting lodge, built by William Connolly himself. Georgie's ancestor. Big, mad, rich fucker. Do you know what they used to hunt?"

"Deer?"

Willie shook his head. "Back in the seventeen hundreds, the Connolly lads knew where to find some special animals. Did you ever hear what the Hellfire Club is haunted by?"

Michael wasn't interested. Still, he answered because he *did* know what the place was said to be haunted by. Most people in Dublin knew some version of the Hellfire Club legend or other. "A big black cat."

Willie laughed. "Big black cat, sure. Chinese whispers ruined that one. Wasn't a cat at all, at all. No. It was a fuckin' wolf."

"A wolf? In the seventeen hundreds? In Ireland?"

Willie smirked and answered, "Not that farfetched, Micky. Sure, Ireland used to be known as Wolf Country to the foreigners, didn't you know that?"

They hit a crossroads and took a right, heading higher up the hill. To the left, the Dublin Mountains rolled out in all directions, peppered here and there by lonely homes.

"Sure, but that was a long time ago. They went extinct," Michael said.

"Not extinct. They went into *hiding*. There's a reason Hellfire Wood has such a mental name. If you listen carefully..." Willie stopped and held up a finger. "You'll hear that some of them are still here."

A rustling came from deep within the forest, quickly followed by another on the other side of the road. Then silence returned.

Michael sighed and wiped at his forehead. “Can you cut the ghost stories, Willie? I have business to get to.”

Willie’s face fell. “They’re not stories. These are words of wisdom if you’re smart enough to hear them.”

An uncomfortable silence settled. Then Tommy Fenton spoke up. “Ever hear about the giant hamsters around here?”

“Rodents, Tommy. No one said they were giant hamsters.”

“They did, actually, ye plank. Big mad hamsters, runnin’ around eatin’ people. Sure, Paula Butler said she saw one eat a tree one time. Didn’t have a camera with her, though. But I’d trust her about anything, so I would.”

“Just ‘cause you want to give her one. Now shut your gob.”

They continued to walk, the crusty road crunching beneath their feet. Michael saw a tree with deep scrapes etched across its bark and said nothing. He didn’t want to draw attention to it. He’d had enough of Willie’s spook stories. But unfortunately, Willie saw it too.

“See what I mean, lad? Werewolf claw marks.”

Michael couldn’t help but chuckle. “Werewolf claw marks? Where are you going with that? First wolves, then giant guinea pigs—”

“Hamsters,” Tommy corrected.

“*Hamsters*, right, and now fucking *werewolves*?”

“You’d do well not to laugh too much about that, Micky. I’m tellin’ ya. It’s too late either way. Look where we are.”

They rounded the last corner, revealing the clearing at the top of Montpelier Hill. The wind blew heavily up there, and thick clouds hung plump in the sky. Michael counted at least fifty people wandering about, talking and smoking and drinking. Ahead stood the Hellfire Club itself, its stone structure both horrible and amazing at the same time. It was two stories tall, the front dotted with long holes that used to be windows. In front of the building, over the edge of the hill, Dublin city spread out in all directions like a twinkling sea.

"Michael!"

"Here's the man himself," Willie said, patting Michael on the back. "Bet you didn't expect him to be here, eh?"

"Dad?"

Michael's father panted. "You didn't think the rest of the Rourkes wouldn't know you were coming here, did you? Are you completely thick? Jesus, Michael, this is the fight of the century. Everyone's here."

Everyone except Brady, Michael thought. "I'm sorry, Da. I didn't think you'd want to know about it."

"Doesn't matter." Michael's father gave a half-smile. "Now look up beside the far wall of the Club there. See your man?"

Michael looked at the man standing just outside the main door of the Hell Fire Club. He looked to be in his late sixties, dressed in an over-sized leather jacket and drinking a bottle of whiskey. His whiskered face moved as he talked to the men surrounding him. Michael didn't have to be told who he was—Georgie Connolly needed no introduction.

"Who do you think he has me against, Da?"

Michael's father shook his head. "You should have just stayed where you were, you know that? You were done with all this shite. Do you have any idea how hard it was for me to keep the Connolly lads off your back all this time? Then what do you do? You go and call them and walk right up to their doorstep. Why'd ye do it, Michael?"

Michael scoffed. "You know damn well why I did it, Da. Angie's six months along now. We need the money. And judging by how many people showed up, I'm guessing that's a five-figure fight we're dealing with here. Right?"

His father didn't answer. Michael knew from experience that at least ten of the men here tonight were brokers, taking bets for some privileged assholes back in their homes. They'd be sitting in their cosy living rooms with friends all around, getting drunk and waiting for regular updates. Two brokers stuck out from the crowd already, their second-hand suits giving them away. They shouted into their large phones to be heard over the wind and the people.

"Just remember that you did this to yourself then. That's all."

"Thanks for the support."

Michael shouldered past his father and pushed further into the clearing. Heads turned instantly. Some cheers went up, but not many. To support a Connolly opponent on their own ground was a very stupid thing to do, so even though many were there for Michael *the Mountain* Rourke, they wouldn't show it. Folks slapped his back with good nature as he passed by, but most only glared. They wanted his blood spilled.

Michael made a beeline for Georgie Connolly. He kept his posture under control, breathing slow and deep through his nose. *The sooner it's over with*, he thought, *the better.* Besides, what was the old saying about wandering into a new environment? Seek out the biggest guy and go straight for him. In this case, that man was clearly Georgie Connolly.

Georgie's voice cut in mid-laugh as he turned and watched Michael walk towards him. He whispered something to the man next to him and the crowd that were surrounding him dispersed. Georgie lowered his half-finished bottle of whiskey to the ground and stood back up, adjusting his leather jacket as he did. He hocked a wad of phlegm at the Hell Fire Club wall and waited, his face unreadable. One by one, the onlooking crowd fell silent. Michael stood face to face with the King of the Gypsies.

"Georgie Connolly?"

"Yer damn right Georgie Connolly."

The wind blew, whistling through the trees. From behind, somebody coughed.

"Back in '85, I fought Brady Connolly. But I did not kill him. I think it's important for you to know that."

Georgie arched an eyebrow. "I think it's important for you to know that it doesn't matter if you did or didn't. He's still dead. Now, what's the reason for you to get back in the game?"

"I'm here for the money, Connolly. That's all. I have a child on the way, and I only want the money. Nothing more."

"Well there's sure to be a lot of green on the table for this one. But you won't be getting any of it."

Georgie waited for a response, but all he got was a nervous chuckle from someone in the crowd. Michael didn't take the bait. Instead, he asked, "Who is it you're having me fight?"

Georgie smiled and made his way past Michael, addressing the crowd. They backed away, matching him step for step. "Who is it I'd have Michael *the Mountain* Rourke fight?"

No one replied.

"Would it be my youngest, Sean?"

A resounding *no* from the crowd, followed by a few laughs.

"How about me middle lad then? Patrick Connolly?"

Another *no* from the crowd, this time louder.

"Well then, would it be me eldest? Derry Connolly? Derry the *Widow Maker*?"

A cheer erupted from the assemblage, fists punching towards the sky, feet stomping. Their words garbled together in a sea of white noise. Michael continued to breathe low and steady, keeping his nerves in check. If he let the fear take him over now, he knew he wouldn't stand a chance in the fight.

Georgie Connolly yelled for quiet and the crowd shut up instantly.

"No. No, this one is special, lads. Michael the feckin' *Mountain* is out of retirement, after all. Isn't this a special occasion?"

A mumbling from the crowd, too afraid to voice their agreement.

"Well, it is. It's very special. I don't give two shites about it, meself, but I do know that a lot of you think he's a good fighter. One of the best, in fact. So you know what? Two people are coming out of retirement today, it seems. Lads..." Georgie smacked at his chest with a balled fist. "*The King* is fighting the fuckin' *Mountain*."

With that, the gathering went crazy. The noise sounded like an old train ripping along a dodgy line on a stormy night. Men slapped at each other, jumping from foot to foot, and in their eyes lurked a look of wild excitement. The men on their phones broke away, updating their clients on the change of events. Michael knew that many of those clients were sure to be putting their money on The King now.

The King of the Gypsies had never lost a fight in his life.

Michael's body shook as he pulled a breath deep down into his lungs to try and steady himself. The crowd was too busy with the news of *The King* to pay him any attention. *Good*, Michael thought. He didn't want anyone to see *the Mountain* shaking like a tree.

Georgie clapped his calloused hands and the audience fell silent once more. "All right, listen up! I want the circle going, lads, just like old times. Make sure it's as big and tight as an ol' nun's cunt. There's no gettin' out until one of us is down and not getting back up, Mikey. You know the rules. In front of the Hell Fire Club, come on!"

The crowd shuffled towards the front of the old building, moving like a single organism. The wind blew their overcoats and hair every which way, but their faces were filled with wild anticipation. Georgie didn't spare Michael a single glance as he followed them. The last to leave was Michael's father.

"You should have stayed well away from this life, Michael,"

he said. "But it just called you back, didn't it? Back home...It's where you belong. It's in your blood. We're family, not just me and you, lad, but all of us. This is a pack. And you don't just leave a pack, do you?"

"I guess not," Michael said, making his way towards the ring of people. "But it's just this one time. One more round, that's all."

Michael's father bared his teeth like an angry dog. "It's always *just one more* with you, you *gobshite.*"

Ignoring the man, Michael approached the circle. The fifty or sixty men with their arms locked around each other's shoulders created an inescapable cage of bodies. Two of the men broke away to allow Michael entrance, and once he got in, they closed the gap. All eyes were on him. Despite the high winds, the smell of sweat hung heavy in the air. Michael stood in the ring.

One man shouted for Georgie to "*Go on and knock the shite out of him.*" The cheer that followed sent a shiver up Michael's spine. On the other side of the ring stood Georgie Connolly, a smirk on his face.

Georgie dropped his leather jacket to the dying grass and kicked it away into the crowd. One of the audience members caught it and placed it behind the ring, out of sight. Georgie flexed his large arms, the tattoo of a crown showing on his hairy right forearm. His plain black t-shirt clung tightly to his large stomach. That stomach, Michael thought, wasn't loose and flabby like most old men's. It might seem that way at first glance, but Michael knew that that stomach was hard as a rock from years of built-up muscle. The old man's hands were like hardened concrete as he slapped them together, large and tough. Through rumours, Michael had heard that Georgie would soak his fists in petrol for an hour each day to harden the skin, make it like leather. From the looks of them, that seemed highly plausible.

Michael sighed and removed his denim jacket. The howling wind made the hair on his arms prickle, but he knew from experience that leaving the jacket on was a rookie mistake. Once adrenaline kicked in, his body temperature wouldn't matter, and besides, with all the moving he'd be doing, he'd be hotter than an oven either way. A jacket could also be yanked and used against you. Michael wasn't taking any chances.

"All right, lads," Georgie shouted. "Shall we give young Michael his birthday present early?"

The crowd went crazy, stomping their feet and roaring, their faces wild with excitement. Michael began circling the ring, breathing through his nose and balling his fists, looking to their faces for an answer as to what was about to happen, but the men only leered and shouted as he passed, some salivating like rabid animals. They leaned their heads forward, screaming in his face.

Georgie barked a laugh from the far side of the ring. "Look to the door of the Hell Fire Club, young Michael. Look!"

Michael did, and his legs nearly buckled.

From the darkness of the main door, out stepped a nervous looking young woman. At the sight of her, the crowd began to dog-whistled and howl. She was beautiful. Blonde, fair-skinned, and all too familiar. Those brown eyes had melted Michael for the past number of years. Angie stood and rubbed at her belly, comforting the growing child within.

"Wha—" Michael's voice deserted him. His throat felt like sandpaper. "What's happening?"

"We've made a deal with the lovely lady, Michael," Georgie said. The place roared with laughter that sounded too loud. "You know that we've been keeping tabs on you. Sure I thought Willie would have told you by accident and blown it!"

The audience giggled, including Willie.

"See, we told little Angie about your stunt you were planning. Told her all about you and your past, and you know what? Turns out she wasn't too impressed. Turns out, actually, she *hates* being lied to. Who would have thought that, eh? Even said to us she told you a *million times* she hates being lied to! Now, as it also turns out, all she wanted from you was the little bah-bah in her belly!"

The words hit Michael like a bullet, each one smacking a little deeper. He squeezed at the bridge of his nose, trying to concentrate. It seemed the air had gotten too thin and he suddenly found it hard to breathe.

Just beyond this circle of testosterone-fuelled madmen stood the love of his life. But if what was happening was true, she was a liar and a traitor. All she wanted was a baby. An involuntary sound escaped Michael's mouth and he began to shake. Had the child been the only reason for him and nothing more? Did she ever really love him? How could she look him in the eye each night and let those words fall from her lips if they weren't true? Michael's whirling thoughts were cut short by the sound of Georgie's voice.

"We've agreed to give little Angie all of the winnings from the fight, regardless of the outcome. How nice is that, eh? Money's not an issue to us, lad. She can have that. Don't worry, the baby will be well taken care of. Just as long as we can have you. You don't just *leave* this lifestyle, Michael Rourke!" Georgie bellowed a laugh that sparked a chuckle from all the other men around. "Especially not when you've spilled blood of our own! Your da knows the rules, and he's held us off for long enough, us pesky O'Connells! But then, then Micky, you actually had the cheek to *call us out*? You had the *nerve* to walk right back to us?"

"Stupid cunt!" Someone yelled. To Michael, it sounded like Willie.

"She gets the money, lad. And we get you. Deal's a deal, and fair's fair."

Michael finally found his voice. Adrenaline was coursing through his veins now, and all he wanted, all he *needed*, was to plant a good solid fist into *The King*'s face. "What do you mean you *get me*? No one *gets me*."

"Oh, but we do...We do. Welcome back to the pack, brother."

Two things happened simultaneously.

The first was that Georgie Connolly dropped to his knees. He wailed in agony, his thick neck standing out in fat veins, looking like slugs wriggling just beneath the surface of his red skin. Spit flew from his lips, his body seeming to *vibrate* in pain. There was a sharp snapping noise as things beneath his skin began to protrude all over. *Bone*, Michael thought. *That's the sound of bone breaking. What the hell?*

Some of the men from the circle tried backing away, looking terrified and confused, but others held them back. The ones who tried to run, Michael noticed, were his supporters. The ones who had given him a sly, brief smile when he'd made eye contact. The ones doing the holding were the Connollys. They giggled like hyenas as they kept the men in place. Patrick looked to his father. The old man, he noticed, hadn't tried to run. When Michael caught his attention, he shook his head, the message clear—*I told you to leave it be, Michael. You shouldn't have come back.*

The second thing that happened was that Michael pissed himself.

He was terrified. The supporters of Michael began shouting for help, but they were silenced by fists. A riot broke out. Screams mingled with wet thuds. People fell about, the brawl in full swing. Michael stalked about the ring, looking for an exit. An escape. But it was useless. The similarity to '85 when he'd fought Brady Connolly made him sick to his stomach.

But there was one difference between that night and this—No one was dead. Yet.

Michael searched for Angie but couldn't see her. He guessed she'd slunk back inside the Hell Fire Club when things had started to go down. Maybe, if what Georgie said was true, she'd gotten scared and had second thoughts. Perhaps she was hiding away until the entire nightmare ended. If that was the case, then he could go to her later. Talk. If he lived through this, that was. The chance of that happening looked less likely by the second. But if he *did*, he could hear, in her own words, the reason for this. Maybe salvage something of the relationship, and if not, then at least give the entire catastrophe some closure. Ignoring Georgie as he wriggled on the ground between the mob's feet, Michael spotted a break in the circle and made for the Hell Fire Club door.

Something grabbed at his ankle.

The ground whooshed towards his face but Michael managed to get his hands up at the last moment. He thudded down, the pain zapping through his arms. With a grunt, he turned—and screamed.

The *King of the Gypsies* was no longer human. What crawled towards him on all fours was an abomination.

The creature's scrawny body looked freakishly out of proportion to its mutated head. Two large eyes pulsated, full of primal aggression. Thinning grey hair stuck out in clumps all over its blackened skin. Michael spotted something crawling around there, what looked like giant ticks. That creature looked sickly, spotted here and there with fat warts and blisters. A large tail whipped back and forth, slapping at the earth. Then the Wolfman stood, forcing half the crowd to scream.

Scrambling on his back, Michael pushed himself away, scampering through the dead grass and staring at the demon before him. All around, the Connolly crew linked arms again, gaining control of the situation and recreating The Ring. Even some of Michael's supporters had given in. The men linked with the others. Including Michael's father. The ones who didn't give in were already dead. Michael saw some of them from the corner of his eye, stab wounds visible on most of their bodies. The Connolly supporters had gutted the opposition.

The circle of men looked at the Wolfman with awe and admiration, completely enraptured. One of them was crying.

The King of the Gypsies howled, the earsplitting noise like a canine wailing through a Marshall amplifier. Michael's hair stood on end and his legs went weak. When the howl finally died down, he noticed he'd been screaming the whole time.

"Hail Georgie!" One man hollered. Another replied with, "*Hail the King of the Gypsies*!"

Standing at full height, the beast easily reached six and a half feet. His balding skin stretched tight across his visible ribcage and his legs shook from the upper body weight. To Michael, the Wolfman looked like a rotting, wild beast from a nightmare. He muttered a silent prayer under his breath.

Then something happened. A familiar feeling began to build inside Michael. In the past, his body had gone into autopilot whenever he couldn't take any more physical or mental pain, he retreated somewhere in the back of his mind while someone else seemed to steer the wheel. As far as he could remember, it had only happened three times before. One of those times being the infamous fight with Brady Connolly. His fists had flown, his legs had moved, but he hadn't been conscious of it. Now, it was happening again.

Michael shouted, "Hey!"

The place fell still. All eyes were on him, including the beast's.

"It's typical, isn't it, Georgie? You get some curse, or gift, if that's what you want to think of it, and it makes you thin, huge, and scary as shit, but it couldn't make your cock bigger, could it?"

The beast grunted, hot air shooting from its wet nose.

"You want to go? Come on, you rancid sack of shit."

The crowd stepped back together as the monster formerly known as Georgie Connolly staggered forward, its huge claws balling into fists.

The creature swung and Michael ducked. The stench of wet dog wafted by. Michael kicked out, smashing the beast on the kneecap. If it hurt, the Wolfman didn't let it show. Instead, it threw its head forward, bearing those long, yellowed teeth in front of Michael's face. Michael didn't allow himself time to think. He head-butted it.

Michael's forehead collided with the creature's wet nose. A sickening *crack* came as the bone broke. He stumbled backwards, cradling his aching head. The Wolfman howled in agony, its shovel-like hands reaching up to its face. Dark crimson leaked from between its fingers, soaking its fur. With a roar that made Michael want to vomit, it charged.

The Wolfman crashed into Michael, sending them both to the dirt. Despite the malnourished look of the creature, its weight bore down as heavy as a car. Michael's lungs screamed for air. He could *taste* the bitterness of the beast's breath, all brown and wrong. His eyes blurred from the pressure in his chest and his vision started to go dark.

Hot blood trickled from the monster's nose and spattered Michael's face. He shook his head from side to side, trying to avoid it, but it was everywhere. The Wolfman brought its head closer, the stink of foul meat unbearable. Its lips shrivelled away from its hideous teeth, putting them on display. It was taking its time, Michael knew, savouring the struggle of its prey.

I'm going to pass out, He thought. *I can't take it.*

With a grunt, Michael quickly raised his hands, clamping them around the creature's snout. He felt the jawbones work beneath his palms, trying to open, but he pressed harder. Those jaws shuddered like a mechanical toy, trying to pry themselves wide. The stress increased, shaking. Bloody bubbles appeared and popped from the beast's nostrils.

Michael's skin crawled as cold, rough nails clawed up his right side. He needed to roll away, but to do that, he'd have to release his grip on the snout. He knew he had to think quickly. Or not think at all. Both had served him equally well in the past.

Freeing his right hand, Michael promptly pounded the beast in its already broken nose and pushed all of his weight to one side. The Wolfman yelped and threw its head back, still holding Michael tight between its thighs, the pressure like a vice grip. Michael rocked from side to side, trying to free himself, but it was no use.

Then the Wolfman slammed its face down. Michael screamed, bringing his hands up to grab at the monster's neck. He managed to get two fistfuls of fur and pulled with everything he had, keeping the creature's face inches from his own. Warm liquid dribbled from the beasts injured nose and continued to coat his face. All around them, the crowd cheered on.

Michael's arms stuck out in veins from the force as the Wolfman's teeth came closer, its nose now pressed to his. It curled its lips back and hot saliva dribbled onto Michael's face. Its mouth opened freakishly wide, giving him a clear view of the hellhole within. He wanted to scream like a lunatic. Instead, he forced out, "Get the fuck off me!"

The Wolfman's head jolted forward, its jaws snapping shut. At first Michael felt nothing, then slowly, his cheek began to burn. The resistance in his hands let up, the pressure gone. The Wolfman stood, shambling back to its full height as Michael sucked in fresh air and looked to the clumps of torn, greasy fur in his hands.

Did that bastard just bite me?

Fear flooded Michael's body. He wiped his palms shakily on the dirt to remove the oily hair and stood, putting his sweaty forearm to his cheek. He winced at the pain. With a whimper, he staggered about, not knowing where he was moving exactly, only knowing that he needed to *go*.

Hands pushed from behind, forcing him back to the centre of The Ring. Michael fell in the opposite direction, but the same thing happened again. Laughter came from everywhere. Eventually, Michael stood in the middle, confused, shaking, and feeling feverish. Ahead, The Wolfman watched on with those sickly yellow eyes.

"He bit me," Michael said, speaking more to himself than anyone else. A headache began to bloom behind his eyeballs. "He actually bit me..." He looked up. "That's all you wanted to do, Connolly? Bite me?"

Then he doubled over as his stomach sloshed and cramped. He moaned before vomiting to the dirt. In his vision, blind spots danced and swayed. Wiping at his mouth, he forced himself to straighten back up. The crowd seemed to find all of this as amusing as a new circus act.

"What are you all looking at? *Huh*? Are you all in on this?"

Before anyone could answer, the Wolfman began to shudder. Michael backed away, and this time, the crowd didn't push him back. They were scared too. Together, they slowly paced away, not removing their eyes from the spectacle before them. It was an atrocity, but one that Michael couldn't help but watch. The King of the Gypsies was becoming human again.

The creature's snout began to retreat into its head with

a crunching, crackling sound. Its body slowly shrank, its weight compacting back to Georgie Connolly's previous state. Its stomach bulged outward, the girth returning as its hair shrivelled and went grey. That black and pitted skin began to lighten, becoming more human by the second. The entire process lasted at least one full minute, and in that time, no one spoke. No one needed to. Michael had forgotten about the throbbing sting in his cheek. What they were witnessing was the stuff of fairy tales and fantasy. And yet, somehow, here it was, right in front of their eyes. No one, Michael noticed, had even remembered to run.

Not even when Michael began to scream.

Hot needles began jabbing at every inch of his body. The world seemed to spin, his head reeling from the pain. He fell to his knees and raked his fingers through the muck, dry-heaving and retching. It felt as if someone had taken a hatchet to his brain. All around him, people shouted in a blind panic.

"What were you thinking, Georgie?" That voice, Michael recognised, belonged to his father. "*You can't do it out in the open*!"

"It can't be happening already!" This time, it was Georgie speaking. His voice sounded as if he'd been on a week-long drinking binge. "The shortest it ever took was with my Derry, and that took hours."

"It's a *full moon*, you bastard. And you're forgetting why Michael was called *the Mountain*. Oh, let it be on your head, Georgie. You've poked a sleeping bear."

Georgie scoffed. "How feckin' poetic is that? Bollocks, that's what it is. Lads, grab him and take him down to the tombs. He's in the pack now. That was the deal. He's *ours*."

The words drifted around loosely, as if in a washing machine, but some of them managed to stick in Michael's brain like flies to Velcro. He managed a gasp before another fit of agony shook his body. "What the hell are *the tombs*?" he asked.

His father replied. "The *tombs*, Micky. This whole mountain is hollowed out with them. This vermin bastard and the rest of the Connollys have lived there for decades. But we had a *deal*, they were to stay in there on nights like this."

"*Nights like this?*"

The searing pricks of pain once again shot through Michael and he shuddered. A rusted razor blade sliced across his brain. "Make some fucking sense, please!"

"Full moon nights, son! They're lycanthropes! Werewolves!"

"Enough!" Georgie roared. "Lads, get him below, *now*. The fever's burning through him quicker than I've ever seen. He'll be turned soon."

He's scared, Michael thought. *The* King of the Gypsies *is afraid of me! He knows I'll rip them limb from limb if they can't get me down there in time.*

Michael began to laugh. "Try it, lads. This fucking disease is racing through me like a horse on coke. Let's see you get close."

Something began turning inside Michael's stomach, forcing him to clench his teeth. He tried to hide the pain from his face but his lip twitched intermittently.

Bone moving, he thought. *Dear god, that's my bones reforming...It's happening.*

A bead of sweat dripped from his nose.

"*You* fuckin' do it, Georgie!" That was Willie the Lookout talking. "I'm not touchin' Michael *the Mountain*. Not a chance in hell."

Georgie stomped his foot. "Get the lads out of the tombs, then!"

"They can't control themselves! You feckin' know that! *You* turn and take him down!"

"If you think I'm putting myself through that again, you can think again, Willie! Not a fuckin' hope. Grab him by the arms and legs. Let's go, now!"

Michael whipped his head around, trying to focus on the men but they doubled and blurred. The edges of his vision grew black. Consciousness began to slip away as slopping and crunching noises filled his ears. These noises, he knew, were coming from inside of him.

Screams.

Darkness.

Rage.

These were the things that Michael was aware of. He could *smell* those bastards, rank and sour with fear. They were different from him. They ran away and yelled and smacked at him when he got close. His body felt like a solid cement brick, large and powerful. He lashed out at these pathetic creatures, hating them.

They smelled of shit and looked like weak little ants. He knew he could destroy them. In fact, that's *all* he knew. And that was all he wanted, too – total elimination.

He swiped, watching as body parts flew away, the coppery smell of blood flooding his mouth with saliva. He had to stop them screaming. That noise aggravated him to no end, like an unreachable itch.

Howling, Michael ripped through the troublesome creatures. He wanted them gone. He needed this to end.

And then it did.

Cold, wet grass pressed against his cheek, and Michael rolled onto his back. A blanket of grey clouds covered the sky. *Morning*?

Sitting up, he shivered at the freezing cold air. He was naked. His head throbbed and his stomach ached, as if he'd been on the world's worst bender. He closed his eyes and they twitched beneath their lids.

I'm at the Hell Fire Club, he thought. *There's no way that nightmare could've happened. They drugged me.*

He wanted to stay there, in the cold, his eyes shut. But he knew he had to look.

Michael opened his eyes and scanned the clearing of the Hell Fire Club. Body parts lay scattered like the discarded toys of a bored child. Brown patches and chunks of god-knows-what littered every inch of the grounds. Even the walls of the Hell Fire Club itself were splattered in gore.

"No..."

He'd torn each and every one of them limb from limb. Even the King of the Gypsies.

Michael tried to stand but his legs refused and dropped him back on his bare ass. He sighed and tried again. This time, slowly, he got to his feet.

Shambling about the clearing, his stomach roiled at the shredded pieces of flesh. "Lucid dreaming," he said aloud. "It's all a very lucid dream."

Then he began to laugh, jittery butterflies tickling his stomach.

"Angie?" He shouted.

No response...He'd never have hurt Angie. Never. She must have run. She was out there somewhere, with his child inside of her, scared and alone. Somehow, he decided, he would find her.

Voices. Male voices.

Michael moved towards them, past the decrepit Hell Fire Club and onto the bumpy earth out behind it. His breath ghosted away like fog. All around, the forest sat in silence, as if every living creature were afraid. Perhaps they could smell the disease coursing through his veins. Maybe they could smell the danger.

Someone called out in a worn voice, "Micky?"

A man-made footpath lead downwards through the dewy grass, and Michael followed it, his bare heels icy and wet. He knew where it led. Ahead, the entryway of the tombs that lay carved within Montpelier Hill came into view. The entrance was blocked by long iron bars, and behind them lurked only darkness. Those tombs were sealed off from the public, Michael knew, because they were in danger of caving in at any point. But now he saw they were sealed for a whole other reason.

This is no dream.

A face appeared in the space behind the bars, dirty and haggard. Michael recognised the man instantly. He looked so much like his brother, after all.

Derry Connolly smiled. "You did it, Micky? You killed them all, eh? Plan didn't go as it was meant to, then...My da might have been tough, but he wasn't much in the brain department. He should have taken you down here and did it in the darkness. We told him to. But he wanted to make a show of you. Backfired on him, didn't it?"

"Where are Sean and Patrick?"

"Sleeping. I'm sure you've felt it, yourself. When that disease goes through you, it knackers you out. They'll be asleep until noon. I would be too, if I didn't hear you calling out." Derry chuckled, slacking against the bars. "Cold out, eh, Micky?"

Michael swallowed, his throat bone-dry. "So you all live down here? In the tombs? The whole Connolly clan?"

"Better than a caravan, that's for sure. Me da was meant to have you down here and locked up before the night was over. But I'm guessing there's nobody left?"

"No."

"So...Why not let us out? Help you clean up that mess you've made. People will be up here soon. Hikers, all sorts...Maybe even the Gardai? Come on...My da had the keys on him. They must be up there somewhere. Wouldn't take you ten minutes. Let us help you."

"I don't need any help." Michael turned and started up the pathway. "If the Gardai do come, they'll find three naked men locked down in the tombs, rambling about a werewolf. Doesn't sound like they'll be looking for another suspect."

"Michael? Ah, come on now."

"See you on the other side, Derry. I've got business to attend to."

Derry shouted after him, sounding like a crazed animal, and Michael smiled. At the clearing, he removed a black t-shirt and jeans from one of Georgie's men. The t-shirt felt greasy with either sweat or dew, but fine otherwise. The clothes fit just fine. After dressing, he searched for the keys of his bike and found them beside his shredded pants. With that, he started down the mountain.

Angie was out there somewhere. She had to be. He'd never hurt her. That meant his kid was out there, somewhere. And all he wanted was an explanation, and to one day see that child's face. He deserved that much. Hell itself couldn't stop him.

Michael kicked his Triumph into gear and set off towards Dublin city. Behind him, the woods came alive.

THE FAERY TREE

"IT'S A MIRACLE," Patrick's mother cried. "A God's honest *miracle*. Do it again, please..."

With a grunt, Patrick hoisted himself from the wheelchair, legs quivering. He placed one bare foot onto the floor, slowly followed by the other. He continued to hold onto the arms of the chair for support, his face scrunched in pain. When his feet found purchase, he released his grip from the chair and raised his hands up above his head. He breathed in short, tight bursts.

"See?" he said. "I'm standing. I'm actually *standing*! My legs are working, Mom."

"A miracle," She repeated, shaking her head. "I just can't believe it. How do you feel, Pat?"

"That's just it, isn't it? I *can* feel! Something, anything! I swear, my legs just tingled all morning. I was calling out for you, but you weren't home. I felt *cold* on them, I could actually feel temperature. I mean it. I prodded them for hours with my fingers, I couldn't believe it. I never thought I'd feel again..."

With that, Patrick squeezed the bridge of his nose and cried. The tears came hot and fast, heating his cheeks. His mother scuttled forward and held him tight. They stayed that way for a long time, until she finally brought him back to arm's length. She pulled his hands away from his face and looked him in the eye.

"No more wheelchair, Pat. No more medical bills, no more physiotherapy. It's done."

Pat sniffled. "I just don't understand how it's possible."

"God works in mysterious ways. That's all there is to it. You're a very special boy."

The door burst open, and Patrick's father stumbled into the room, red-faced and panting. At the sight of Patrick, his eyes fluttered.

"No...It's not real..."

"It is real, Dad." Patrick raised his arms. "*Ta-da.*"

"Oh, sweet mother of...I think I'm going to faint. Pass me your wheelchair, would you? You don't need it anymore, but I think I will!"

They all laughed. Patrick's father ran to him and squeezed him with enough force to cause his vision to blur. He buried his face into Patrick's neck, his beard ticklish and his hair smelling of tobacco smoke. He nuzzled his head back and forth. "You're back, Pat..."

Patrick laughed. "I never went anywhere, Dad."

"No, of course not. You know what I mean."

"Yeah."

"You'll be able to play basketball again. You'll be able to ride a bike. You can do anything you feckin' want!"

"I guess so."

Patrick's father released him from the hug and looked to his wife, still rubbing Pat's shoulder with one strong hand. Patrick got the impression that his Dad never wanted to let him go.

"Helen," his father said. "Can we talk?"

Helen's eyes darted around the room, then landed back on Patrick's father. "What, now?"

"Yes."

She sighed. "Okay, Dennis. Let's go to our room, though. All right?"

Dennis nodded then turned back to Patrick. "You're a wonder-child. I always knew you were." Then he and Helen left the room.

In the fireplace, a warm orange-bellied fire blazed. Patrick walked, *actually walked*, over to it, and warmed his legs. The cotton material of his grey sweatpants slowly grew hot, pressing against the smooth skin of his thighs. He sighed, savouring the feeling. If this were three years ago, he'd most likely have worn a pair of shredded jeans and a Black Sabbath t-shirt, but ever since the car crash, he hadn't seen the point in looking how he wanted anymore. He hadn't felt like himself, so why bother look it? For those three awful years, Patrick stuck to grey sweatpants and a comfortable Aran sweater. It was easier that way.

Closing his eyes, Patrick's thoughts drifted to the accident.

He'd been sixteen.

The weather forecast had called for snow on the radio of William's brand new Honda Accord that night. The two boys had listened to the report before switching the channel to 100.5, the only classic rock station in Ireland. AC/DC blared from the speakers, and they sang along at full volume. They were driving through the Wicklow Mountains after a short trip to Dublin to try out the new car, a present for William's eighteenth birthday from his father.

Patrick had been secretly jealous of William for his present. The boy's parents were rich, unlike his own family. Patrick's father worked six days a week but the family barely managed to scrape by. Patrick had hunted for a job for nearly five months to try and help out, but he'd found little work since the recession hit. He'd gotten some odd jobs at a local garage, but his father had told him to keep the money and spend it on himself. After all, he'd earned it.

"Think the snow'll catch us?" Patrick had said, peering through the window at the thick clouds in the night sky.

"We'll be back in Gleannloch in the next half-hour, so I doubt it."

What William hadn't taken into account, however, was the ice.

It glistened on the patch of illuminated road ahead, shining in the headlights like diamonds on grit. AC/DC had given way to Pearl Jam, and they sang along with that too. They rounded a sharp corner, and that's all it took.

Patrick remembered an invisible hand, like that of an angry God, flipping the car in slow motion. He'd heard stories of when you believed you were going to die, your life flashed before your eyes. But nothing of the sort happened. Instead, the entire process had gone very slowly, as if time warped. The car landed on William's side, glass shattering and raining down on them. Their screams mangled together with a wailing guitar solo on the radio and the crunch of busted metal. The car screeched as it slid on its side, sending them towards a ditch.

Patrick could remember hearing a crack, which he later found out to be William's head as it slapped the road through his non-existent window. Then all had turned black.

In hindsight, William considered himself lucky that he'd been knocked unconscious from the disaster. That way, he'd never felt a thing. Not even when his face had scraped along the cold earth and peeled like an onion.

The next day, a trail of red had painted the road for more than ten feet.

"...There? Patrick?"

"Huh?"

Patrick's mother eyed him from the living room doorway. She pulled her blouse tight across her chest. "I asked are you there?"

"Yeah, sorry."

"The heat from the fire..." She nodded towards it. "How does it feel?"

"Wonderful."

She smiled then, her eyes puffed from crying. "Your father just stepped out. He's just so overwhelmed, you know? Probably gone to tell the lads at Lynch's the good news. Scrounge a couple of free pints out of them. You know, if you went up there some night, you'd be drinking free for at least a month."

Patrick laughed. "True. Should we call a doctor, Helen?" Patrick had always called his mother by name. If he didn't, she was inclined to smack him for a *Mom*, or *Ma*, or *Mother*. Not seriously, of course, but the message carried clear. "You know," he said. "To make sure everything is all right?"

"Everything is fine, honey. You're standing, aren't you? You're walking. It's a miracle."

"You know I don't believe in any of that. I'd like to know, *scientifically*, what's happened to me. Get a doctor's opinion."

Helen smiled. "We'll call the GP on Monday, I promise. It's the weekend, they won't be open. Then we'll see what's happened, okay?"

"Okay."

"I just can't believe it."

Patrick shook his head. "Me neither. Can I...Can I go for a walk?"

Helen stayed silent for a moment. "Sure...Just promise me that you'll bring your phone with you, okay? I know nothing will happen, but just in case. Please. And call if you start to feel funny in any way. All right?"

"Of course." Patrick chuckled. "Not much faith in action there, Helen, if you think it's going to be taken away from me just after being given to me."

"Ah sure, God's a wanker sometimes. Now go on. I'm going to call your Aunt and tell her the good news...And Pat, I love you. You know that right?"

Patrick's chest tightened. He couldn't remember the last time his mother had said those words to him. If ever. "I love you, too."

With that, Patrick left the house.

The first step outside felt overwhelming. The soles of his trainers pressed onto the hard concrete driveway, creating a welcome pressure in his calf muscles. He'd expected some pain, some wobbling from lack of use, but his legs felt strong. How was that possible? There had to be some scientific explanation behind all of it, he thought. There just had to. Without walking for three years, surely his muscles would need to be trained back up to a point where he could walk without a problem?

But that didn't seem to be the case. He walked the length of the driveway just fine.

Bill Montague watered his garden next door, and when Patrick called out a hello, Bill smiled and nodded before returning to his chore. Then he dropped the watering can and stared, wide-eyed.

"You have to be joking me."

Patrick laughed. "No joke, Bill. Helen calls it a miracle."

"She says it's a miracle? Is she inside?"

"Yeah."

"I'll drop into her." Bill gave a smile that never reached his eyes. "I'll go in for a chat. This is...something else."

"Sure...I'm going for a walk. An actual goddamn walk."

And he did. He passed by the houses of the small council

estate, each one a direct carbon copy of the last. He looked at the windows as he drifted by, wondering if the residents had any idea that Patrick Mulligan was walking outside, just like he used to three years ago.

He hung a right at the end of the estate, passing through the football field that lay beyond the row of homes. There, he removed his shoes and socks and worked his toes into the soft, wet grass. He sighed. Overhead, the sun shone down out with a glorious warmth and some birds sung from a nearby patch of trees. Taking his shoes in his hands, he pressed on, through the football field and onto to the Green Road that lay ahead.

The Green Road was a forest trail, carved by walkers and vehicles that passed through the dense woodlands. It stretched for three miles with nothing but forest to either side, eventually ending at the Visitation centre of Gleannloch where tourist buses would park in the summer. In those months, Gleannloch would be swarming with visitors from all over the world, each of them hiking or sightseeing. The local businesses thrived and survived on them. But now, in April, the area sat in silence, exactly as Patrick liked it. Shimmying back into his shoes and socks, he entered the forest by the Green Road and listened to the birds.

"Hey! Pat!" a voice called to him. "Wait up!"

Patrick turned and watched as an old man jogged towards him. He wore a tie-dye shirt and sweatpants that made his fashion sense seem frozen in the sixties. His face was somewhat familiar, but Patrick had a hard time recalling where he'd seen him before. He waited for the old man to catch up.

"Pat," the man said, leaning over to catch his breath. "It's true, you're walking. I just can't believe it."

Patrick smiled. "Yes, I am...Sorry, do I know you?"

"I'm sorry, I should have introduced myself. Justin Godly. I run the retreat centre up by the church in town."

"That's it, the retreat place. I knew I recognised your face."

The pamphlets, Patrick thought. The ones posted through the letterbox each month with your beaming face on them. That's where I know you from. The holistic healing centre.

Patrick could see the green and yellow paper of the pamphlet all too well. Become a Reiki Master for €500 on a two-week course, it claimed. Laugh yourself better with Madam Hughes' positive energy Fridays. Reflexology training from €50 a week. Crystal balls and tarot cards and energy rocks for sale and in stock.

Ludicrous, Patrick thought. His father had put it perfectly, saying, "Simply replace the word God with the word Universe and you've got yourself an industry. Religion for the non-religious."

The Green Road called out to Patrick. "Mr. Godly," he said. "I don't mean to offend you, but I *really need* to go for a walk."

"Of course, of course." He nodded frantically. "But, Pat...I think your mother did something terrible."

Patrick cocked his head to one side. "What...What are you talking about?"

"Your father, he came to Lynch's to spread the good word. The place was overjoyed, of course. But I'm just glad I caught you in time."

"Caught me in time? Mr. Godly, you're worrying me here. What's going on?"

"Your mother came to me," he said. "Seeking advice on how to make you better. This was some time ago and—"

Patrick interrupted, "First off, I didn't need to be *made better*. I was still me, even in that chair. And secondly, are you talking about *holistic* healing?"

"That's what I thought she wanted, too, of course. But no, what your mother wanted was my personal insight into other areas." Justin Godly paused. "Black magic."

Patrick snorted a laugh. "Okay. Sure. Black magic."

"Pat, for God's sake!" The change in the man's voice sent a shiver down Patrick's spine. He stepped back. "There's a reason so many people travel to Gleannloch each year," Justin said. "Not just because of its beauty, no. This place is *magical*, you know that, you grew up here, you've heard the stories from school about the monster in the lake and all the rest. Mystical stuff. The *healing* that happens here."

"The monster in the lake, right." Patrick nodded. "I forgot about that one. A Saint befriended it and wowed the locals, right? And that Faery Tree that's at the end of the Green Road where people hang their wishes for the faeries to grant, too."

"That's exactly what I'm here to talk to you about."

Patrick arched an eyebrow. "The Faery Tree?"

"Exactly."

"Oh for Christ's sake. Mr. Godly…"

Without warning, Justin firmly grabbed Patrick's arm. "Your mother made a wish to the faeries. Against my warnings, I might add. But I never thought she would go through with it. I told her again and again, the hidden forces of Gleannloch are not to be taken lightly. They are ancient and powerful. They're not good, not bad. They simply *are*, and for that, they must be respected."

Patrick sighed. "So, what? You're saying that my mother placed a wish onto the Faery Tree, and that wish was for me to walk, and now I can?"

"Exactly."

Patrick stayed silent a moment, studying the man's face. "Look, Justin, you might be able to con stupid American tourists with your pseudo-scientific crap, but I won't be tricked."

"This is not about my beliefs, Patrick. This is about black magic. Something I do not practice, nor do I advise."

"But you study it?"

"As an interest. Like some atheists might study the Bible, just to broaden the mind and have both sides of the argument on file, so to speak. How long have you been out of the house, Pat?"

"Like, five minutes?"

Justin's face fell. "It could already be too late."

"I've had enough of this."

"Go home, Pat. If the faeries have had a hand in granting your mother's wish, they'll be after their payment."

"Hold on," Patrick said, holding up a hand. "What do you think their payment is?"

"I don't *think* I know what their payment is, I *do* know. Celtic mythology dictates that in return for a granted wish, the faeries demand a sacrifice. A *human* sacrifice. That, or a job gets done on their behalf. The jobs are usually something unspeakable, and most people don't ever agree to the terms. So, to my logic, a sacrifice would have been your mother's choosing."

Patrick's mother's voice ran through his mind, speaking those three words he'd never heard her say before.

"This is bullshit," he said. "Pure and utter bullshit. And who, exactly, would my mother be willing to sacrifice for my ability to walk again?"

"I think any mother would give their own life to give the best to their child. Don't you agree?"

A silence hung between them for what seemed like hours. Patrick knew the conversation to be ludicrous. But something deep down stirred, all the same. What harm could it do, to go home and check? He could say he forgot his keys when he saw his mother, because, of course, she'd be there. Then he could go find this Godly man again, and smack him on the head for ruining his first walk in three years. That sounded like a reasonable plan.

"You're going to go check on her, aren't you?" Justin asked.

"Of course." Patrick shook his head. "She's my mother. If anything has happened to her, I swear to God, I'll find you, and you'll be sorry."

"No, I won't." With that, Justin Godly started up the Green Road. "You'll find me by the Faery Tree. I'll wait there for an hour. If something's happened to your mother, I'm sure you'll be there. If it hasn't, forget I ever mentioned it and let sleeping dogs lie."

Patrick turned and left. With his back to Justin, his skin crawled. Something about the man unnerved him. To Patrick, he had *that look* in his eyes, one usually reserved for fundamentalist Christians. It seemed to infect new-agers, too, he'd noticed. A look that made you wonder if they had a hatchet behind their back.

Justin called after him. "I will wait for one hour, Pat."

Patrick ran. The muscles in his legs cried out in ecstasy with each stride but his mind was filled with anxiety. Halfway across the football field, he picked up speed, like a car grinding up through its gears, not seeming to go fast enough. He wanted to move like lightning, to use every ounce of strength within his newly working legs to full effect. His heart punched at his chest and sweat beaded down his face as he shot through the field and out into the estate. The place stood still and empty as Patrick zipped through. He climbed the driveway, fumbled with his keys, and finally opened the front door.

The lingering scent of tobacco from his father's cigarettes welcomed him home, but the house sat in silence. Patrick called out for his mother.

No response.

Quickly, he went from room to room. In the spare bedroom, his father's art canvas and paint sat alone by the open window. A half-finished watercolour of the Round Tower in Gleannloch was in the works. Patrick spared it a glance before noticing a notebook and pen nearby. Without overthinking, he snatched them from the table and stuffed them into his back pocket. If worse came to worse, he had a plan.

Knocking on his parents' bedroom door, he didn't wait for a response before entering. The bed was mussed and empty, as was the walk-in closet. The curtains were drawn and the room was clothed in darkness. A clock ticked too loudly on the wall.

Patrick's stomach knotted as he spied his mother's sewing machine with a piece of beige material still inside of it. She never left a project unfinished.

It's all right, he told himself. She just stepped out to go to the shop. That's all. Probably needed milk or bread. Maybe she dropped by a neighbour's place?

An idea hit Patrick like a slap. Bill Montague! He'd said he was dropping by for a chat. His mother must have gone next door for a cup of tea and a talk, that's all!

"Up yours, Mr. Godly," Patrick said to the empty house. "Stick your black magic up your hole."

Patrick made for the Montague house next door. Bill lived there alone, ever since he and his wife divorced nearly five years ago. He liked to keep to himself, and Patrick thought of him as kind and quiet. He had an impressive science-fiction paperback collection, and had loaned many to Patrick over the years.

Patrick knocked on the door.

"Come on in."

The house smelled unmistakably of cannabis smoke. Old Bill must have been onto his afternoon toke already. Patrick closed the door behind him and made his way through the hallway. The walls were painted a faded green, the floor covered with faux wood floorboards. In the living room, Bill sat half-sunken into a beanbag, the sound of an old John Lee Hooker album drifting from a nearby stereo. Smoke danced in the sunlight of the open window.

"Bill, you okay?"

The man shook his head. His eyes looked red and puffy. "Your mother, Pat..."

The world seemed to spin on Patrick just then, and not because of the smoke in the room.

"What about my mother?" He asked.

"She went through with it. She actually did it."

"Please, please don't tell me you're talking about that stupid Faery Tree?"

Bill's eyes widened. "You know?"

"I don't know anything!" Patrick's lips tightened to a slit. "I'm fucking confused as hell right now! I can *walk*, for God's sake! What the hell's going on? That guy who runs the holistic place up by the church stopped me on the Green Road. Told me about it. But, I mean, it's *bullshit*, of course, yeah? Come on."

Apprehension crept through Patrick like a burglar. He wanted Bill to start laughing and tell him it was all a joke. His mother was just using the bathroom. She'd be out in a moment. Instead, he began to cry. "Gleannloch is a magic place, Pat. That's—"

Patrick interrupted. "I've heard all this before. Too many times."

"Then it would do you good to listen. You know that's why so many unique people come here. You must have noticed. Artistic types, religious types, the musically gifted. Because they know the powers this place holds. They can feel it."

"What are you getting at?"

"Ask any of the older folk about The Faery Tree and they'll all tell you the same thing. Stay away from it. Bad things have happened here, and all because of that damn tree, and the creatures that own it."

"The faeries?"

"They live in the mountains, Pat. *In* the mountains. Have you ever been to it before?"

"Of course I've walked by it, but it's always been roped off. Being removed because it's a hazard is what I heard."

Bill laughed. "A hazard? That's poetic. It's roped off during tourist season so that no one will put a wish on its branches. Not only that, it's watched by some of the more *extreme* locals day and night. But that didn't stop your mother getting to it and making a wish."

"If this is all for real, Bill, I don't think I'll be able to handle it. This is crazy talk."

"So is you being able to walk." Bill leaned forward. "Listen. She did it. She made a bargain with the faeries. Your mother wouldn't have a bad bone in her body to do those monsters' bidding, so my guess is she made a sacrifice. Have you heard that before?"

Patrick nodded and repeated what Justin Godly had told him.

"Right. I went over to your place just as you left, but she was already gone. The faeries are sneaky, crafty little things. They wait until no one is around to do their work. That's when they took her."

Pat shook his head frantically. "Took her where? Why didn't my father stay with her? He must have known."

"Oh, I'd say he knew something once he heard the news that you were walking. And I doubt he went to Lynch's to spread the good news. My guess is he shot off like the wind to the Faery Tree to try and catch those little creeps before they made off with your mother, before they take her to the Otherworld."

"I've got to get up there, I've got to try and save her."

"The deal has been made." Bill began to get up. "You're walking and they've got Helen. What's done is done."

"Then I'll make them another deal."

Bill's eyes widened. "Pat, no!"

But Patrick had left before Bill could object. Leaving the front door open, he sprinted back towards the Green Road. Bill's calls echoed after him.

Thoughts fell around inside his head like loose items in a moving truck. Faeries living inside the mountains of Gleannloch? Taking his mother to some other dimension where mystical beings and deities resided? That was the stuff of folklore, and folklore was nothing but campfire comfort. Cautionary tales. Not real.

The forest blurred past as Pat pumped his legs. Some agitated rooks took flight from a nearby tree, but other than that, the road stood in silence. Patrick watched the birds fly ahead, thinking to himself about a childhood story of how rooks, ravens and crows were messengers from the afterlife.

"Going to the Otherworld, are you?" He shouted after them. "*Tell them to be fucking expecting me, then*!"

Rounding the final corner of the dirt path, the Faery Tree rolled into view. Yellow plastic tape stretched around four trees surrounding it, squaring the Faery Tree off from access.

His lungs burned from exhaustion and his legs screamed in pain but he kept moving. Two figures stood just outside the tape, seemingly deep in conversation. Patrick could tell it to be his father and Justin Godly. They looked to him as he ran.

A wooden sign reading NO ACCESS was planted at the side of the road and Patrick slapped it as he passed.

"Pat," His father said. "Stay back, we need to think about this."

Patrick eyed the two of them, sneering. "There's nothing to fucking think about."

Swooping below the yellow tape, he stumbled towards the Faery Tree. Dark moss mottled the trunk. Here and there, thick bark splintered away like dead skin, revealing dry, grey wood beneath. The tree's branches were scrawny and long, like the legs of some giant, dead spider. Each one had coloured ribbons attached, and tied to those ribbons were folded pieces of paper.

Wishes, Patrick thought. Frightened people's wishes. People with nowhere else to turn.

Patrick yanked one from a nearby branch, making the limb bob and sway. From behind, Justin Godly cried out as if Patrick had ripped wax paper from the man's own skin. Patrick glared at him before unfolding the paper and beginning to read.

Please, take these tumours from my Willem and take me instead. He has so much to live for, and all I want is to see him happy. Yours, ever faithfully, Killian Barns.

Patrick's father screamed. "What the hell is that thing?"

Lowering the paper, Patrick's legs nearly buckled. A creature unlike anything he'd ever seen stood before him. It looked to be about three feet tall, its head bulbous and bald. Its skin looked to be the same texture as porridge, dark grey and splotchy. A potbelly mercifully hung enough to cover its genitalia. Its three-fingered hands ended in long black nails and were disproportionate to its arms. Its head cocked from side to side like a curious dog, two beady black eyes studying him.

"Pat, don't move," His father warned. "Stay still."

Patrick didn't. He turned. And his breath froze in his throat.

Behind him were three more, while another two crawled from the well beside the tree. They moved slow and clumsily, but a dangerous intelligence burned in their eyes. Patrick slowly backed towards the yellow tape, but the first creature shuffled after him as if it wasn't done with its examination. When the tape pressed into his back, Patrick ducked and kept moving, backing up towards his father and Justin Godly.

"They're here," Justin said. "They're real..."

The faeries shuffled about the tree, inquisitively looking at their surroundings like newborns. They seemed fascinated by everything. One of them plucked a wish from an overhead branch and studied it, the motion slow and purposeful.

"Do you think they understand the words?" Patrick's father asked. His voice sounded like gravel.

"Maybe they just get the intention," Justin offered. "The *feeling* of what's been asked. I have no idea."

"I need to sit down," Patrick said. "I think I'm going to be sick."

Patrick's father reached for him but Patrick shook his head. He wanted to be alone. Besides, he had a plan.

Patrick slowly made his way to one of the trees that secured the tape. There, he leaned against it and removed the paper and pen from his back pocket. Deep down, he'd known he would do this from the start. He just didn't want to admit it. Not to his father or Justin Godly, and not to himself.

His hands shook. Patrick took a deep breath and wiped the fresh sweat from his forehead. Then he began to scribble on the paper.

Insurance, he told himself. So neither of them can change this. This is my choice.

Patrick made his way back to the tree, his legs seeming to move by themselves. If he paused for thought, he knew he wouldn't be able to follow through.

"Pat," His father shouted. "What are you doing? Those things could be dangerous."

Patrick didn't reply.

"Pat!"

The creatures stumbled towards him, their tiny feet lurching through the fallen leaves on the forest floor. They circled him with their heads curiously lolling from side to side. Giving them a proper look, Patrick noticed something new. A growth poked from each of their backs, like two weak bones protruding from the skin. Patrick guessed they must have been wings at some point.

"Move aside, you little creeps."

Patrick waded through them towards the tree, his father and Justin Godly watching silently. The creatures parted, letting him pass. Their little claws flexed, and although their hands were small, the black nails clicked sharply, sounding as if they could shred through skin as easily as a knife through cream. One of them made a mewling noise, deep in its throat, and Patrick got the impression it was trying very hard not to take a swipe.

Maybe they don't know what to do with me...

Reaching for the nearest branch, Patrick pulled it towards him. It was cold and slimy, like a decomposing limb. Two more faeries began making that mewling sound, but still made no attempt to attack.

Patrick removed one of the wishes tied to the branch, one secured with faded yellow shoestring. He unfolded the paper and dropped it to the earth, causing one of the creatures to shuffle forward and sniff it. When Patrick looked down, the creature darted away with a high yelp.

"Pat, stop!" His father ordered. "Get out of there."

Ignoring him, Patrick popped the shoestring through the top corner of his own wish. He tied the string tightly around the branch, yanking it to make sure it felt firm. Satisfied, he held the branch for a moment and looked around. The creatures were closer to him now, one close enough to touch. They were getting too comfortable. He needed to get out of there, and fast. His father and Justin Godly watched anxiously.

Patrick let the branch go, causing it to flop back up and sway. The faeries scattered away from the noise, bunching together at the edge of their well. Patrick saw the opportunity and took it. He darted for the yellow tape and ducked beneath it, back to his father and Justin.

"What have you done, Pat?" His father asked. "We should have talked about this. You can't go taking matters into your own hands!"

"Someone should have told Helen." Patrick looked his father in the eye. "I was fine in my wheelchair, you know. I *accepted* it. That was not her choice to make, and if you had any sense you should have tried to talk her out of it. Both of you. You should have told *me*."

Clearing his throat, Justin asked, "What did you wish for, Patrick? What did you write?"

Patrick smiled. "Simple. Bring my mother back."

With that, he collapsed, sensation suddenly swiped from his legs.

At the same time, something lurched from under the tree. Something stinking of soil and rot. Something with an all too familiar face.

SWAN SONG OF ROBERT ENSLIN

REVIEW TAKEN FROM 'Like It Loud' magazine, January 1996:

"The most recent offering from Pennsylvania-based Slow Grind *is their twelve track, independently released studio album,* State Of Mind. *A triumph of modern rock laced with blues, this monster record is guaranteed to turn heads on the live circuit. Built upon a thunderous, tight rhythm section, composed by DeLong bothers Andy and Sam, this album does not let up from start to finish. And while stand out tracks such as 'Pushed Too Far' see vocalist, Gary Richardson, soar up the octaves with his whiskey-ridden voice, the real treat on this juggernaut is hearing guitarist Robert Enslin rip out a solo. Although staying primarily in the predictably stale minor pentatonic, Enslin manages to put a jaw-dropping twist on such an old thing that you need to hear to believe. You can catch* Slow Grind *live at Jacob's Bar & Lounge this Saturday the..."*

Robert lowered the magazine from his face and looked to Gary.

He laughed. "God damn it. If only these good reviews reflected our financial state, huh?"

Gary nodded. "Same shit, different day, man."

They had been driving for a little over an hour now, speeding down the highway on their way to the last show of the week. The radio in the old van (a present from Gary's dad when they put out their debut release) had gone bust a week before, and only the sound of an occasional car whizzing by punched the silence.

"Got to stop doing these freebies, dude," Gary said, eyes not leaving the road. "At least if we can manage to flog a few copies of *State Of Mind,* we'll just about cover our gas. If we're lucky."

They pulled into Jacob's just as it started to rain. The van's heavy tires splashed through a black puddle as they parked. Heavy drops tapped at the roof and the engine ticked as it cooled.

Sam and Andy pulled their jackets over their heads to run inside to the bar and ask about a back entrance so they could unload the equipment. Gary and Rob stayed in the van, watching the raindrops race down on the outside of the windshield. They sat for a while in that comfortable silence that only old friends are capable of.

"Another line of shows finished..." Gary said, opening his door. "Well dude, let's rock and roll."

A little over an hour later, they stood on stage. Plugging into his Marshall stack for the third time that week, Robert smirked as all the burdens of everyday life melted away like snow under blistering heat. He swelled the volume knob on his guitar as air from the speakers pushed at his back. Andy stood to his left, and Robert eyed him a wink. *This* is where he belonged. With his friends, on stage. He was *born* to do this, had known it from the very first time he'd picked up his dad's old parlour acoustic in the attic when he'd been twelve years old.

He, Gary and the DeLong brothers all belonged here. Music coursed through their collective blood, and they knew they were powerless to do anything about it. You either had *it* or you didn't, and boy did they have *it.*

The blinding stage lights lifted, and Robert basked in their neon glow, eyes shut. The unseen crowd cheered, and as the noise grew and washed over him, a chuckle rose to his lips. *Home.*

From behind, Sam clacked the drumsticks, counting into 'Pushed Too Far', the lead single off the new release. For the next hour, the four friends were in a world of their own. A world they had created together. A place where they could momentarily transcend the troubles of everyday life, if only for a short while.

After the show, Gary said he'd pull the van into the alleyway around back, while Andy, Sam and Rob packed up their gear.

Robert's cables had tangled themselves into a Chinese knot and he pulled them apart as the odd crowd member approached the stage.

"Fucking *sweeeet* playing, man!" A drunk man pointed to Rob, spittle flying from his mouth. "*Dananananana*!"

He began playing air guitar while swinging his head.

Great, Rob thought, *not awkward at all.* He politely smiled and nodded to the man, all the while making his way around him towards the back door, his bag slung on his back. His smile dropped as soon as he passed. Catching up to Sam and Andy at the fire exit door, he chuckled.

Sam winked. "Could do without *that* every show, huh? Oh well, that's the price you pay for being a rock star."

The brothers clapped him on the back as they stepped out into the hissing rain. A cold rush of air made Robert sigh as it blew his sweat-slicked skin. He closed his eyes and tilted his head, greeting every drop with a satisfied groan. Ahead, Gary climbed out of the van, banging the door closed.

"All right, let's get it loaded, ladies." He tossed the keys from one hand to the other. "Nice turnout tonight. Shame we only got five albums sold. At least that covers our fuel."

"Yeah," Sam said from the side of his mouth, lighting a cigarette. "Not a bad show at all." He blew smoke from his nostrils, making him look like an angry cartoon bull. Robert laughed. His smile faded when somebody spoke from down the alleyway.

"No, not a bad show at all, little dude."

The four of them turned. A skinny man with long hair stood in the mouth of the alley. He approached, his shadow elongated and falling behind him. He had a happy *hippy* stride, head bopping and swaying. His boot heels clicked pleasantly on the blacktop, and in one hand, Robert spotted a battered, leather guitar case. Coming into the light, the man's toothy smile appeared from his long grey beard. *He's stoned*, Robert thought. The 'crow's feet' around his eyes gave him away.

When he reached the boys, he clasped a hand on Robert's shoulder and puffed a tight laugh through his nose.

"Mean guitar playing, man." He sounded to Robert like Tommy Chong, the actor. Looked very similar, too, with his John Lennon style glasses.

The man's smile widened across his weather-beaten face. "You and I got a lot to talk about."

Robert's brow creased. "Hey, no disrespect, but if it's got anything to do with the band, you can talk to all four of us."

Gary regarded the man, arms folded across his chest. "Yeah."

"Oh don't worry, Paul Rodgers." They all laughed at that, used to the comparison by this stage. "Ain't gonna steal your boy. Nothin' like that. Just want an old chinwag with yours truly here, that's all. Care for a drink, man?" He gave Robert's shoulder a little squeeze.

"Okay, sure." Robert realised he'd pulled what the band called a 'Robby face'. One that always led to trouble. "Why the hell not."

"All right then." The old man put his free hand on the fire exit and pushed it open, squeezing himself past the DeLong brothers and into the venue.

"When you're ready, I'll be at the bar."

The door slid shut.

Looking to the band with his 'Robby face' still on, Robert waited for an answer.

"Go on, dude." Adam laughed. "I'm not your parent. At least it will be an interesting story in our biography if you get murdered."

With that, they shook hands and parted ways, the DeLong brothers getting a lift from Gary while Robert went back inside to talk with the old man.

The mostly empty venue stunk of stale beer and sweat. Some hangers-on staggered about while the bartenders cleaned. Spotting the old man, Robert took a seat next to him at the bar, the stool squeaking.

"So what's your name?" Robert extended his hand for a shake and the old man took it firmly, his palm dry and calloused.

"I've been called many names in my day, little Robby. But you can call me Frank. Frank Carpenter. At your service, son."

They both smiled, as if old acquaintances. Robert got the impression that Frank must've been a fan of the band to know his name. He felt good knowing their only demographic wasn't the drunken college type.

"So, Frank," Robert said, pointing to the case leaning against Frank's stool. "What's in the case? I take it you play?"

He'd been eyeballing the old, brown leather case since entering the bar. Frank cast his gaze to the case and then back to Robert.

"We'll get to that soon, little brother. But first of all, what's your poison?"

"Tequila, on the rocks."

Frank raised his bushy eyebrows. "Tequila time, eh? The Devil's water. I like your style."

He turned to the bartender, waving his index and middle finger, indicating two drinks.

"You really do play a mean guitar, dude, and I know a good player when I hear one. You don't just *masturbate the neck*, if you catch my drift. Guitar is all about the *feel*. Don't you ever forget that." He cocked a thumb towards the jukebox. "Richards, man...Keith Richards can play with feel. That guy really riffs."

Robbie nodded. He'd been a Stones fan for as long as he could remember.

"I met him once," Frank continued. "Back in '65, on their first US tour. Nice guy."

"No way?" Robbie shifted his position. "You're kidding, right? I'd give my left nut just to jam with Richards."

"Yeah, a lot of people would give away a lot of things to go further in this business, am I right?" Frank regarded Robert for an answer.

"Fuckin' A man. Fuckin' A."

Two shots of tequila were placed in front of them and Robbie downed his as quickly as it arrived, slamming the glass back down to the bar. It burned a good burn as it traveled to his stomach, making his eyes water a little. Frank raised his index finger to the barman again, indicating a second shot. Then he patted the guitar case.

"I got a 1957 Gibson Les Paul gold top in this here case." The old man looked Robbie straight in the eye, clearly waiting for a reaction. "Believe that?"

"Are you serious? I've always dreamed of owning a vintage Les Paul, but we didn't make as much money off the first record as I'd hoped, so I guess I'll just keep on dreaming on. You're a lucky man, Frank."

"Nah." Frank waved his hand dismissively. "Ain't nothin' lucky about it, kid. Had some money back then, wanted one, bought one. And I played it—not professionally, mind you, just for fun. Always been a huge music fan, not a music player. Never had the commitment. No *luck* involved."

Frank lifted his shot glass and sipped. He licked his lips before slowly swallowing the entire shot, placing the glass gently back on the table. "In the music biz, it's all who you know, not what you know. But luck can help, I believe. That's why I'm here."

"What are you talking about?"

"It's yours if you want it, kid."

Robert couldn't find his voice. The lights over the bar blinked, indicating last orders.

"What?...I couldn't take it, Mr. Carpenter, sir."

Frank laughed. "Mr. Carpenter, sir? Robbie, I'm a dude, a Frank, but never a mister, and certainly never a *sir*. Let's get that straight, man."

Robert lowered his head, embarrassed. "Sorry, Frank. I mean, it just wouldn't feel right, taking a guitar. And it's not just any guitar, either. I mean, a proper vintage gold top. From a stranger, at that. Why not just sell it if you don't want it anymore?"

Frank sighed. "Because the only type of person who could afford this baby would be a collector. Do you know what a collector would do to it?"

"What?"

"He'd put it in a glass case and stare at it, and it would never get played, man. You and I both know that. I'm not going to live forever, and my hands are seizing up because of this condition I've got. They call it *old-fuck* syndrome. I'm sure you'll find out all about it someday. But if giving you the guitar means it will still sing—well then, I think you owe it to the old girl."

"You're serious, aren't you?" Robert's breath had begun to come in short, shallow bursts.

"You're damn right I am, little dude."

Frank's face blurred as tears dampened Robert's face. He sniffled and wiped his eyes with the sleeve of his shirt, his hand shaking. "Shit...I'm sorry. I..." He tried to speak but his voice came as barely a whisper. Catching the tequila from the corner of his eye, he snatched it and downed it. Clearing his throat, he tried again. "Thank you...God, that sounds so ungrateful for what I really mean. *Thank you a million times over.* I honestly don't know what to say. I feel like I've just won the lottery. Is there any way I can repay you, if you're serious about this?"

"Ah dude, don't *cry*!" Frank honked a laugh and, bizarrely, twinkled his fingers above his head. "You could give me your soul, little dude!"

Robert snorted louder than he expected at that. The couple at the end of the bar shot him an annoyed look, making him laugh harder.

"If that's what you want, you got it, Frankie, my man. I'll give you my damned soul for this here guitar."

"Let's get that in writing then, huh?"

Still chuckling, Frankie stood, fishing a pen from his jeans pocket while swiping the tequila receipt from the bar. He handed both to Robert. “Well, go on then.”

“If this will make you happy.”

Robert read aloud as he wrote: *“I give one, unused, and still sealed-in-the-box, partly damaged soul, to Frank Carpenter in return for his 1957 Gibson Les Paul gold top—Robert Enslin.* There. How does that sound?”

“Like music.”

He dotted the final period with a firm thud of the pen and handed the paper back to Frank. “Here’s your receipt, Mister Never-a-sir.”

Frank took it, folded it, and stuffed it in his pocket. Then he bent and closed his fist around the leather handle of the case. The old leather creaked as he lifted it and placed it on the counter with a grunt. The couple at the end of the bar looked to them, this time with curiosity.

Frank spread his arms above the case. “Go ahead,” he said. “Open it.”

For a moment, the idea that perhaps Gary or one of the DeLongs put Frank up to this, hit Robert. *There’ll be nothing inside*, he thought. The bar would explode with laughter and he’d hightail it out of there, embarrassed beyond belief.

“Robbie? You gonna open it?”

Wiping his hands on his jeans, Robert stood and slowly snapped open the case’s four golden locks. He placed his hands on the lid and looked to Frank, who smiled back politely. Then he opened it.

The purple plush interior greeted him warmly, and slipping away the purple silk cloth that covered the instrument, he gasped.

Inside, a golden, well-worn Les Paul lay sleeping. At parts, the lacquered finish had been completely stripped away, revealing dark mahogany. Robert's eyes stung. He realised he hadn't been blinking.

"She's a beauty, huh? Got character, too, that's for sure."

Robert reached in and lifted the guitar by the neck. The weight felt wonderful, as natural as an extra limb. He turned it over and inspected the back as well. Golden-brown mahogany made up the back and neck, the finish completely stripped away. Dulled silver hardware adorned the headstock from years of use. *Character,* Robert thought.

"If you're serious, Frank, I hope I never get that receipt back."

"Don't worry, little dude, this is for keeps."

Review taken from 'Bulldozer' magazine, October 1999:

"Released posthumously, one month after vocalist Gary Richardson's untimely death (27), Slow Grind*'s third studio effort* 'All Or Nothing' *finds the band at the top of the charts for the third consecutive week. The album went gold when...*

Robert lowered the magazine and looked to the photo of Gary in his right hand. He still couldn't believe it. He knew the royalties from the band's back catalogue would keep him afloat for life, but that didn't make matters any easier. Mentally, he was drowning.

The band had never known of Gary's heroin vice, had never suspected a thing. The only drug they'd ever taken together, and before they formed Slow Grind, was acid. Now, on Gary's anniversary, as if in ritual, Robert took a trip. This year was no exception. "Here's to you, Gar."

Robert slurred as he raised his glass of raw whiskey. He took it dry, just as Gary had. “Cheers.”

He slipped a blotter of acid onto his tongue, washing it down with the burn of liquor. The liquid sloshed up the bottle too quick, spilling some down his front. He coughed. “Sonofabitch...”

Reaching with his left hand, he slapped blindly for the old ‘57 Les Paul gold top. Not *his* gold top, he thought. *The* gold top. It’d never been his, even after all those years.

Pulling the guitar to his lap, Robert banged out a sloppy melody. He stopped every so often to take a drink. As he played, he thought of days gone by, days when things were fine, when money wasn’t great, but the band was like family. Good days. He sat, feet folded beneath him, for another hour. Then he slept, curled on the floor in the foetal position, with the guitar as his teddy bear.

A noise came from the living room. His record player?

The slow hiss and crackle of vinyl made him bolt upright. The bedroom smelt musty. Outside the window, night seeped in. The only light came from the hallway, a sliver of gold across the bedroom floor.

Robert took a deep breath and shook his head. Someone, or something, had begun walking up the hallway, the shadow bobbing in the light. Slow Grind’s first album, *State of Mind*, began playing from the living-room.

Frank stopped outside the bedroom door, his shadow elongated on the far wall. He let out a light chuckle.

“Duuuuude...”

Robert crossed his legs beneath him and waited for the show to continue. *I’m like a child watching a puppet show!*

He clasped his hands together, snorted a laugh, and began rocking back and forth. *What’ll happen next?*

On the bedroom wall, Frank's shadow brought its hands above its head, imitating a ghost, just as the old man had done at the bar. The fingers wriggled. "*Bugga-bugga-bugga*!"

It sent them both into a fresh fit of laughter. And after a moments thought, Robbie lay on his back to relax, the guitar lying across his stomach. He knew what would come next. Slowly, he began to strum.

"So you've come for it?"

"You said it was mine, little dude. Deal's a deal, ain't it?" Frank stepped into the room. He towered over Robert, peering down, his long, grey hair swinging.

"You haven't aged a day," Robert said. "Just as I expected."

Frank smiled. "Shut up and listen, Robby. You hear that song?"

Robert strained his ears, expecting Slow Grind's *State of Mind*. His brow creased. Something else played now. A wash of tritones, layered over feedback. Dissonant and slow.

"What is it?"

"It's your swan song, Robbie, man. Your very own." Frank tilted his head to the side. "You like it?"

"Yeah..." Robert said. "I really do."

He meant it, too. A deal *was* a deal, after all. A gold record and three consecutively well-received albums were a lot to accomplish in twenty-seven years. If this happened to be the price, well then, he wouldn't change a thing.

"Not feel bad about Gar?" Frank asked, as if reading his mind. "Sacrifices have to be made to get where you want to go. You know that. In this world, it's all or nothing. You boys gave it all."

With that, Frank's smile grew impossibly wide, his features distorting in the dim light. The music swelled in volume, but Robbie ignored it. He closed his eyes and got lost in a new world. A world of his own music.

NO ONE GETS OUT ALIVE

"I DARE YOU to jump."

"No way, *you* jump."

They peered into the rushing water below. Whitewater bubbled and rushed around the few sharp protruding rocks. Alan placed his glasses onto the rough yellowed grass by his feet and looked to his older brother.

"If the jump didn't kill you, Mom would."

"Mom talks the talk but she's far too drunk to actually do anything. Come on, don't be a wuss."

Alan approached the edge. His stomach fluttered as his legs carried him forward. He would do it, but he felt as if he were watching someone else through their eyes instead of his own, like an out-of-body experience. Some part of his mind had decided this without his consent.

The bristly grass crushed beneath his bare feet. The ground felt warm and dry. This summer had been a real scorcher, and here in Harlensburg, West Virginia, it was hot as hot could be.

Alan felt wonderful. There were no Lewis brothers here to beat the shit out of him, no four-eye name-calling, no school, no worries. There was Eddie of course, but just like most siblings, they tolerated each other just fine when needed. Anyway, it was Alan's birthday, so Eddie had to be nice.

Eddie laughed. "Al, I was kidding. Come on, dude. It's like fifteen feet. You'll break your damn neck."

Alan closed the gap with one final step towards the edge. Hypnotic dark water rushed below. The butterflies inside him grew restless and his toes tingled, but there was nowhere else to go. He was thirteen this year, and for a fresh new start, that meant changing what he could. Exfoliating the bad and creating the good. He'd never been courageous, but if he could *act* how a courageous person would, that would be a great start.

"Quit being such a baby," he heard himself call back to Eddie. "Can't be scared of everything."

With that, his feet left the cliff. He felt the world disappear beneath him, and from somewhere far away, he heard Eddie yell. His stomach lurched and as his balls shrank back inside of him as he fell, as if they were trying to escape the coming impact.

Air rushed past him as he tore towards the glassy black surface. The plummet only lasted a few seconds but it felt eternal. It was amazing. Alan smiled as he smashed down into the drink. The roar of the river was replaced by the rush of bubbles. The coldness of the water disappeared in an instant, and he kicked back towards the shimmering reflection of sunlight overhead.

Alan's head broke the surface as he swallowed the hot summer air. He laughed and hooted, listening to the sounds echo throughout the wood. Some rooks took flight from their trees, cawing in their displeasure. He continued giggling the whole doggy paddle back to the bottom of the cliff.

Eddie was rushing down the embankment, skilfully avoiding the prickly bits. They knew this wood better than any anyone.

"You fucking lunatic!" Eddie said, but he was laughing. Good. That meant no trouble. "How was it?"

Alan pulled himself out of the water, the cool air already drying his skin. "Why don't you find out for yourself?"

"Uh-uh. No way. You were about an inch away from one of those rocks in the river; no chance in hell I'm trying that. Besides, you don't have a towel."

"Look at this weather; I'll be dry in no time." Water dripped from his arms and ran from his legs, making a dark pool around him which the thirsty dirt drank around his feet.

Eddie was being surprisingly nice today, and that alone was better than any birthday present he could ask for. Well, he couldn't be a bad brother all the time. A friendship needed balance.

Alan grabbed the transistor radio and turned it on, switching to the AM dial. The show was Big Mike's Countdown, a pirate radio channel that played decent rock music, which was something that both brothers couldn't get enough of. Eddie always listened to it, but this summer was the first time Alan had been exposed.

Last month the Stones' new single "Satisfaction" had just been released, and since the lyrics were too *suggestive*, the mainstream stations wouldn't play it. But Big Mike played it all the time—that, along with a truckload of other rock staples like The Beatles, James Brown, and best of all, Muddy Waters.

As they ascended the steep, dry hill to leave, Big Mike's disc jockey voice called from the top: "All right, you crazy kids. Mikey's got a spoonful more to feed you, so open wide and prepare yourself for another helping of fresh hot Rock 'n' Roll, doctor's orders! It could be a spoonful of coffee, it could be a spoonful of tea, but one little spoon of Etta James is good enough for me."

The brass section filled the summer air just as they reached their spot on top of the cliff. Etta's soulful voice always gave Alan gooseflesh, and that, mixed with the cold damp of his skin, made a powerful combination. He sat and put on his glasses, listing to the song as Eddie fished out a crumpled carton of smokes from his jeans pocket.

"Want one?" he asked.

"Sure."

Alan had only started smoking two months ago himself, and although he didn't like the nauseous feeling that came with it, he did love the smell. He caught the cigarette and motioned for the lighter. Eddie sat across from him against the large oak, nesting his back into it. They sat, smoked, and listened to the rest of the song.

"Only one more year and I'll be driving." Eddie swirled his cigarette in his fingers, watching the smoke drift away. "Just one more year, man. Getting out of here the minute I do. Or maybe sooner."

"Yeah, and you're taking me with you."

"You? You're never leaving this town, Al. Sorry to break it to ya." He popped the cigarette back into his mouth and drew the comb from his side pocket, running it through his greasy black hair. "You'll work at the dam, just like Dad. Probably knock up some chick just as you're getting ready to go to college too. Then it's all downhill. Hit the bottle pretty hard after that I bet." He laughed.

Alan flipped him off. "Why do you always have to be such a dick?"

"Oh, come on, lighten up. I'm just kidding with you. You'll leave sooner than you think."

"Well," Big Mike's voice interrupted from the radio. "The summer of nineteen sixty-five has just begun. Let's leave behind those winter blues and slip inside our dancin' shoes.

Time's running out kids, and those pesky parents of Harlensburg are so unfair, so blow 'em sky high and y'all get outta there!"

Alan choked on his cigarette. It burned the back of his throat as he hacked and coughed. "What—" His voice was cut off in another coughing fit. "What did he just say?"

The smile fell from Eddie's face. "It's about time you learned all about what Big Mike said, Al." He flicked his cigarette over the edge of the cliff. "Harlensburg is a dark place, and you're lucky it's your birthday, because I'm going to give you the best damn present you could ever hope to get: your life."

"What are you talking about?"

Eddie pushed himself from the oak. "I won't tell you. I'll show you."

He made his way towards the thicket of trees behind him. They were mostly birches. Their spindly grey trunks leaned towards each other as their skeletal branches intertwined.

"Through here."

Alan followed his brother silently. Their feet crunched the dead leaves and yellowed grass. The river ran loudly out of sight. The sharp pine needles poked at Alan's soles as he tiptoed over them.

Alan kept his gaze on the ground beneath him, stepping carefully. The sunlight and shadows patterned the carpet of debris.

"You're not a kid now," Eddie said. "We have got to make this quick. Keep up."

Ahead, the thicket cleared, and across the overgrown field in front stood their home. Their *home*. That old familiar wooden structure their dad had inherited from *his* father. It was a comforting place with the newly fitted shingled roof. It wasn't much, but it was more than most had.

And now Alan saw—Mom and Dad were on their knees in the garden, coming in and out of view as the tall grass swayed. Mom's golden brown hair blew back over her shoulders as the wind picked up. Dad's brown puffy coat, the old one Alan had known all his life, was zipped up to his neck.

Sure, they might have drank a little too much, and Dad might have spoken with his fists on a few occasions, but they were his parents, and deep down he loved them.

"What are they doing?"

"Praying."

"Praying? Oh, come on. We're not religious."

Eddie barked laughter and slapped his knee. "Religious? Damn right we're not, at least as far as God is concerned."

He looked to Alan, shaking his head. That familiar *you're such an idiot* expression filled his face. "They're a damn cult, Al. Mom and Dad are part of a cult. The whole damn town is." He looked to his brother for a response but got none. "Remember Sammy Hogan? His big scholarship last year? What a laugh that was. He didn't go anywhere. He's six feet under back in the wood and the whole damn town knows it too. Him, along with about a hundred others."

"What are you saying?"

Eddie imitated Big Mike, "No more than one per couple, those are the rules according to the scripture."

"What scripture, Eddie?" Alan almost shouted.

"The book, it's been here for years. Loads of small-town folk practice magick and old traditions. They'll play it down if you ask them of course, but they believe it."

"Eddie, this isn't funny."

"It gets worse. Remember the Flatwoods Monster over in Braxton County the year you were born? Big Mike told us over the radio that it's all true. That thing exists. They say the second born is to be sacrificed in *his* name, before adulthood, so the family can live on. Only one for every couple. The second child is killed, but you're going to be the first to escape it."

Alan's stomach cartwheeled. Eddie wasn't the most imaginative person, and this was one hell of a story. He tried to poke a hole in his brother's logic. "What? And you believe this? Why wouldn't anyone ever put a stop to something like that?"

Eddie laughed. "You ever see a cop around here? No one gives a shit about our small town, man. We're on our own."

"You're playing a joke, Eddie. If you're serious, why wouldn't our parents just kill me when I was born?"

"Because the rules say you must die when you reach lucky number thirteen. Usually kids are killed at birth, so the parents don't get attached. Hell, I don't know. All I know is that I'm getting you out of here. Big Mike told us everything."

"About Big Mike...why wouldn't other people hear his broadcast from anywhere else?"

"It's a local pirate station, and no one knows who he is. We've had meetings to discuss this, all of the kids. Did you know there are only sixty-seven kids in the whole town?"

"I never thought about it."

"You've never noticed that every child in this town is an only child?"

"So what are you saying we do?"

"We're already doing it. We're getting out of here. Johnny's got the car running. Your stuff's already packed."

Alan's head was fuzzy. It was as if when he came back up from the water earlier, he had emerged into some horrific parallel existence. One where parents offered their children in sacrifice to some monster in the woods.

Was he ever going home again? Was he never going to step through that familiar whitewashed door to the smell of a fire burning in the living room? His comics! Was he never going to read another in his bed by torchlight?

This was one big elaborate prank. Had to be.

Eddie turned and headed back towards the thicket. Alan gave one final look back at their parents on their knees in the garden before following his brother. Could they really be in on this? Big Mike's voice grew as they approached the cliff through the wood, fighting for sonic real estate against the river's roar.

"...the night, kiddies. You've all been training for this real hard, and it's going to go great, I just know it. They say Rock 'n' Roll is the Devil's music and then they read their sick book and practice their sick, utterly unmentionable acts. Hypocrites! Each and every one of 'em! But we're not playing their game anymore, no way. Tables have turned, folks, and we're making the change. Our first escapee is Alan Peterson led by his brother Edward and we're all going to pitch in just like we talked about."

Alan's feeling of disorientation and lightheadedness increased hearing Big Mike speak his name. The DJ's voice grew distant as Alan's thoughts whirled. His parents were going to kill him? His stomach felt as if its bottom had been removed, just like when he had jumped from the cliff. *I'm going to vomit...*

From Elm Road, though really more a dirt track than a road, came the growing noise of a large engine.

"Good, Johnny's almost here." Eddie's voice snapped Alan back to reality. "Get the radio, squirt, then wave a happy bye-bye to Creepsville, because it's the last time any of us will ever see this place."

Alan picked up the transistor radio just as The Beach Boys started "I Get Around." He was running on autopilot. The happy harmonies came from both the radio in his hand

and the radio from the car that came into view through the spindly trees.

It wasn't Johnny's usual beat-up ride. What came down the dirt track was a new, pearly white Ford Shelby Mustang.

Johnny in a Mustang? Alan thought. What sort of crazy dream is this?

Golden dust swirled in the mighty car's wake as it pulled to a stop. Two dark stripes ran the length of its blinding white body. Johnny honked the horn.

"Time to rock, man!" Eddie called, rushing to the car.

Johnny smiled at them. "Hey!"

Johnny Morris had been Eddie's best friend for as long as Alan could remember. "I thought if we were finally leaving, we should leave in style." Johnny threw his hands up as if he were weighing something invisible. "Nabbed it from my dad's showroom. What a pony, huh?"

He had on sunglasses and a black muscle shirt, and Alan figured that Eddie was thinking the same thing he was—Johnny Morris looked like the coolest kid to ever walk the face of the Earth.

"Johnny, you old dog!" Eddie shouted, clapping his hands and moving like he needed to pee. He popped the door, hopped into the passenger seat, and bounced on the leather.

Alan moved slowly towards the car, the radio clutched tightly to his chest. He still felt as if he needed to vomit.

The great white's idling engine purred. Johnny climbed out and popped the seat down so that Alan could crawl into the back.

"Johnny, is it true?" His voice sounded weak.

"True as true can be, kid. Sorry to tell you, but happy to tell you happy fucking birthday, 'cause we're getting you the hell out of here." He slapped the white metal of the door impatiently. "Come on, Daddy-O, we got to get moving."

Alan let himself slowly into the backseat. The new car smell made his stomach even worse. Johnny slammed his door shut and shot off so fast that Alan's head hit the leather headrest. He was once again knocked back to reality.

A tingle of excitement crept through Alan. He despised that he *liked* the rush, but he couldn't deny it. He wasn't a kid anymore. He thought that maybe his parents had told Eddie to take him to the river as they set up a surprise party, but that had been far too hopeful.

The picket fences swished passed as they sped down Pine Street. Once a picturesque quiet slice of suburbia, those pickets all seemed like jagged teeth now. This town was bat-shit crazy.

"There's Mrs. Stewart," Eddie hissed, looking out the window. "All right, slow down."

Johnny did. Mrs. Stewart stood with a hose, watering her front lawn, a slim woman with a pretty polka-dot dress. Her home behind her was a replica of every other home on the perfectly manicured street.

From the radio came Big Mike's voice again: "All right, kids, we've reached it. It's Big Mike's Countdown! Is everybody ready? Ten! Nine! Eight! Seven! Six! Five!"

Mrs. Stewart lowered her garden house to wave to them, her face a wonderfully warming, country smile, but Alan now knew behind that smile lay dark and twisted secrets... In anticipation, his balls crept back inside him as Big Mike's countdown continued. Eddie smiled back to the woman, and slowly raised his middle finger.

"Two! One!"

Johnny hit the gas, and suddenly Mrs. Stewart's home exploded. *Boom!*

A rush of hot air shot past the car, bringing the scent of gasoline and charred wood. Alan shot his head out of Eddie's window to look back down the street, wind around his face. Fireballs of all shapes and sizes rained down to the perfectly maintained garden below.

Where the Stewart's home once proudly stood was now a black and flaming gap, like a cavity in an otherwise perfect mouth. Alan's adrenaline rushed through his bloodstream, making his heartbeat drum in his ears.

Mrs. Stewart's body lay on Mr. Roger's lawn across the street, a black slump surrounded by burning debris.

Both Eddie and Johnny were whooping at the top of their voices. "Did you see that? Laura did it, she actually planted the bomb! What a gal! You think the rest of them had the balls to do it?"

A second explosion answered his question. Alan ducked back inside from the window in shock. It sounded like the Rogers' place. He was surprised to hear himself cheering with the other two.

Once again, a rush of hot air blew past the speeding white Mustang, carrying smoke and screams. Those screams were deserved. Another extraction from the rotted gums of Pine Street.

They hit the intersection at the top of the road and waited. Behind them, more homes exploded. The engine purred, the homes roared, and The Beach Boys sang. Alan could feel and hear the impact of flaming objects hit the street behind the car. The charred and burning smell became overwhelming. How many homes had gone sky high by now? Six? Seven?

From the end of Hazel Street to their left, where the public entrance to the woods lay, came the unmistakable roar of engines. Alan positioned himself in the backseat of the Mustang to get a better view. He watched the rushing black, toxic smoke of Pine Street as cars came into view from the Hazel Street wood entrance.

A pack of oddball hatchbacks and old, beat-up classics came from hiding, crawling slowly towards them. Cars of all shapes, sizes and colours. Alan counted at least forty. The sun gleamed off their metal surfaces, and between the earth-shattering explosions on Pine, The Beach Boys grew in volume from the combined radios on Hazel.

“The cavalry has arrived, gentlemen,” Eddie said, now quiet and serious. He swung back to face Alan. “Happy birthday, shit-for-brains. Your present is your life. Let’s ride.”

The roar of the engines kicked into life to their left as Johnny led the way straight ahead, towards Bull’s Point, the kids’ make-out spot—the highest point in all of Harlensburg, West Virginia.

It dawned on Alan that one of those explosions must have been his own home. He was shocked to discover a smile creeping across his face.

Mike’s voice blared from the radio once again: “It worked, you crazy kids! Now go, go and don’t look back. What’s to come next is the real Big Mac. Get to Bull’s Point as quick as you can. A treat for the eyes is my present to the newly free man!”

Alan’s heart punched his ribcage as his glasses fogged. He laughed hysterically as Eddie banged the roof with one hand and Johnny honked the horn repeatedly. They drove that way for a long time, a constant barrage of noise as they barrelled further up the dirt road.

When they reached Bull’s Point, Johnny cut the engine as the other vehicles approached. He left the radio on, and The Kinks began to play. To either side, Alan listened as the first of the other kids parked and cut their engines, too. The three boys climbed out and stood at the edge of the cliff overlooking the whole of Harlensburg. From up here, it seemed tiny, surrounded by woodlands, nestled away from absolutely everything.

Flames throbbed on Pine Street. From behind, car doors popped and slammed and chatter grew as the other kids joined them on the edge of Bull's Point. As they watched, another home went up in flames with a satisfying boom—the biggest one yet. Every tree within a mile radius leaned backwards as the house rained down in bite-sized pieces.

From either side, the crowd cheered. They clapped, hugged, and danced on the spot.

Alan looked to his brother and said, "Dare you to jump."

Eddie grinned. "Not when I know what's still down there." He pointed to the far side of town. To the woods. "Look."

From the thicket came a noise like a freight train, cutting through the explosions and the cheers. A frightening hoot of anger made Alan's hair stand on end and his eyes bulge. The roaring triumph from the gathered crowd died down. Nothing in existence could make a sound that terrifying...

"What is that?" Alan asked, his eyes wide. Eddie nodded towards the woods again.

As they watched, the creature emerged. Bending trees in its wake, it stood at least ten feet tall. Alan's nerves sung and his heart tried to escape his chest. A united gasp came from the crowd, but that sound seemed very far away.

The creature's body was slim in proportion to itself, its arms slender and long like birch tree branches. Alan's head slowly shook from side to side in disbelief. Its skin was an ashen grey, and its spider-like fingers flexed, visible even from where they stood. The figure's head was round and bulbous, with two sickly dark holes for eyes, reminding Alan eerily of a skull.

The creature lurched slowly through the pines, trembling and quivering. Alan's stomach twisted as it slapped one grotesquely long-toed foot in front of the other.

"We need to get out of here," he said.

Eddie smiled. "Calm down, man. It's *Saltushom*. Known to some of the folks around here as the Flatwoods Monster. The one I told you about."

As they watched, the creature leaned its gaunt frame over the bleeding, sprawled body of a parent and scooped it from the road. Its lower jaw seemed to dislocate as it stuffed the person shakily inside. A sharp sound, like a snapping branch, drifted to their collective ears. The crowd let out a combined *eeew* and one kid screamed.

"I don't think we need to watch this," Eddie said. He turned to Alan. "Where do you want to go?"

Alan thought about it. "Everywhere."

"Good." Eddie smiled. "Let's go everywhere."

The fires roared from below and the engines purred all around, as The Kinks played on the radio.

AN ANGEL AND A REAPER

"**GRACE, GET IN** the car. Right now."

Grace ignored the sound of her husband's voice and kept moving. The marshy earth sucked her feet with each step. The rain came down hard and heavy, rushing around her in deafening white noise. When she reached halfway to the Sitka spruce forest, she paused.

"Go home, Fred," she said. "There's something here I need to see. I need to prove it to myself."

Fred sounded tired. "Grace? You're soaked to the bone. Come on, get in the car and let's go home. We'll go and see Father Doyle, okay? Talk this over."

That got her attention. Grace turned and faced her husband. He stood by their car on the isolate back road, wearing a dark green jacket, hunched against the bad weather. His hood obscured his face.

"Don't you dare try and force your religion onto me ever again, Fred," she said. "This is my choice, my life, and I'm doing this for me. Understand?"

Fred sighed. "I saw your computer history this morning, Grace. What's it all about? Will-o'-the-wisp, and such? You've got to be kidding. I mean, this is childish, you know that, right? Aliens, Bigfoot, monsters...Father Doyle has answers if you need them...Real answers. Now, come on."

"Go home, Fred."

Grace turned and continued through the marsh. She doubted very much that Father Doyle had answers. He couldn't pray away the tremors in her hands, or the rigidness in her body. Couldn't stop the aches, the depression, or the constant fear of degradation. Most definitely, he couldn't stop the bronchitis that'd developed.

Grace wiped her wet face and looked at her husband. "Fred, I need evidence. I need the cold, hard truth. And you can laugh all you want, about the lights, the video, if you think it looked staged...But that video was shot right here in the Wicklow Mountains, and it's as close as I'll ever get to the truth." She sighed. "I'm sixty-eight years old, Fred. I need this for me, before I go."

Fred scoffed. "Before you go? Go where?"

"Oh don't be such an old fool! I don't want to live with PD, Fred, why can't you understand that? I want to go on my own terms, doing what I want to do, even if that's something as silly as seeing Will-o'-the-wisp. I'm done with Father Doyle's praying, all right? The government thinks euthanasia is wrong, and I'm taking matters into my own hands. If going out here is dangerous, and I die, that's on me. But this is my damned life. Not yours. Now go home."

"This is all because of that man, isn't it?" Fred said. "Darren Cross?"

Grace's stomach fell. She'd had enough. "How many times are you going to ask me about Darren Cross, Fred? He runs the cryptozoology website, that's all. He knows I live in Ireland so he sent me that video last night. This is still fresh. The people who uploaded it haven't answered any email, so, yes, a hoax is looking likely, but it's got me feeling *alive*. I'm not asking you to understand that, just to go home. Darren Cross is my friend."

"Friend. Sure."

Grace shook her head. "You had to be an asshole, right up to the end, didn't you?"

"What did you call me?"

There it is, Grace thought. *The tone that developed when you lost your brother. Same time Father Doyle became your best friend.*

"Say it again," Fred said, his eyes narrowed. "Go on."

"Asshole." Grace licked at her lips. "Asshole, asshole, *asshole.*"

"That's it." Fred started across the road and into the marsh, the earth slopping beneath his boots. "You'd do well to learn your place, Grace. A woman shouldn't be calling a man those kinds of things."

"Oh, for fuck's sake. Don't you take another step towards me, Fred. Listen to yourself. That ancient tortoise, Doyle, has filled your head so full of shit that it's starting to come out your mouth. When did you get like this?"

But Grace already knew. It had been the night Fred's brother, Kevin, had been taken out by a drunk driver while walking home two years ago. After that, Fred had never been the same. Father Doyle stepped in, happy to help in his time of need, and having another male around seemed to comfort Fred. Grace's husband had never been one for emotional conversation. If he didn't want to talk to her, then maybe some time with Doyle wasn't such a bad idea. She'd been wrong, of course. Now her husband acted like one of those evangelical preachers on public radio. And when the Parkinson's developed, *praise Jesus*, Fred and Doyle had all the answers.

Fred grabbed her arm, but Grace yanked it back. "Don't. Don't you dare. Do you know how much pain I'm in?"

Rain tapped on Fred's plastic hood. "Then what is it you want, Grace, eh? To sit out here until the damn lights come? All because some Yankee charmer sent you a video? Is that it?"

Grace shook her head. "You know what, Fred? Yes, that's it. That's what you want to hear, right? Darren and I have been having an affair through the magical interweb, fucking on Skype and going on virtual dates. For God's sake, Fred, grow up. Darren sent me a video, one that looks like nothing I've ever seen before, and for the first time in my life, something impossible is looking plausible. So save your damn prayers."

"Blasphemy. These freak lights, Grace? You know how stupid you sound?"

"I feel the same way about you, Fred. At least I have the possibility of proof. Don't like it? Then tell it to someone who cares."

Grace began walking away, and coughed. She looked at her shaking palm, at the blood washing away in the rain. Her throat stung.

"We might not be in love, Grace. But I vowed on our wedding day to take care of you. In sickness and in health. I might not like it, but that's just the way it is."

"If you want to take care of me, Fred, then let me do this. I'm not going back to Father Doyle to pray the sickness away. It's a terminal illness. I've accepted that, why can't you?"

For once, Fred had nothing to say. The rain continued smashing around them, turning the marshy land into a soup. A low mist curled at knee level, giving the place a cheap B movie vibe. Under any other circumstance, it would have been pretty to Grace. Now it looked creepy.

"This mist was the one thing in the video I thought gave it away as a hoax. It looked too *staged*. But, here it is." Her forehead creased. "And there's the large moss-covered rock that stuck out in the background. This is where it was shot. Right here."

"Then where are your Will-o'-the-wisp, Grace?"

Fred's voice sounded very far away, masked by the blood thrumming in Grace's ears. A dizzy spell hit and she would have fallen if not for the vacuum of the mud. "They're right there, Fred," she said, not believing her own words. "In the Sitka. Look."

Ahead, three dim lights bobbed through the trees. They swayed like glow-sticks, casting long, moving shadows on the wet foliage.

"Looks like your reporter people beat you to it," Fred said, but Grace could tell he didn't believe it. "Look, it's kids pulling a prank."

The rain filtered Grace's vision. She squinted to see more clearly. No use. "I think this is it, Fred. I think we're seeing Will-o'-the-wisp."

The three lights floated closer, brighter, making the slick bark of the trees look as if they were caked in some sort of transparent, glistening goop. They glided soundlessly, about a football field's length away now. Something inside Grace flipped.

"Fred?" Her mouth had gone dry. "Fred, are you seeing this?"

The lights were attached to figures.

A trivial piece of information floated to the surface of Grace's mind. Something she'd seen in a documentary about deep-sea fish. Anger fish, to be specific. A light protruded from the fish's head as a means to lure prey, coaxing them with dangling light. But behind the light, lay teeth...

As the lights advanced, Grace began to shake. The skin on the back of her neck crawled and the hair on her arms stood like tiny strands of cold steel.

"I don't know what I'm seeing..." Fred's voice came as barely a whisper.

The creatures were humanoid, but certainly not human. They were too *long*. Besides, no human could scuttle on all fours that that fast. They were...*Wrong*.

"Grace, we need to get back into the car, now!"

Grace agreed, turned, and ran. The sloppy terrain gulped her boots, making every step a chore. Fred looked to be having the same problem. Grunting, she pushed forward, rain streamed down her face and dripping from her nose. She chanced a look back and a scream work its way up her throat. The creatures scuttled forward like spiders, their scrawny limbs arching through the marsh. They didn't make a sound.

"More of them!" Fred shouted. "Look!"

He pointing to the right, where further up the slender road, two more glided from the forest, lights bouncing. Their odd movement reminded Grace of oversized, four-legged insects.

Fred reached the car first, Grace still bogged down in the muck. She watched as he forced the driver-side door open and jumped inside. The ignition turned as she reached the road, finally pulling her leg free with a wet, slopping noise. "Fred! Wait!"

The engine spluttered, refusing to start, as Grace shambled across the road. She reached the passenger door and jerked it open, throwing herself inside.

"You asshole!" She punched him in the shoulder. "You were going to leave me out here?"

"What? No. I was just trying to get the car started!"

"You fucking *asshole*!"

The engine wheezed. Ahead, two abominations slithered forward. Grace looked out the driver-side window, her skin crawling at the sight of the other three as their dull headlights illuminated the marshland and cut through the mist.

"They're nearly here, Fred..."

Fred growled as he twisted the key, willing the car to start. Grace heard him pray beneath his breath. Then the car came to life.

"Ha! I told you! Thank you, Lord, *thank you, Lord...*"

"Or thank Bobby Peters down at the garage for having a look at this damn thing last week," Grace said. "Get us out of here."

Fred forced the gear stick into reverse and the car began to roll with a whine. Then the engine cut. Slamming his fist into the steering wheel, he turned to Grace. "This is your fault, woman! This is where your damn blasphemy gets us! This is what you get for cursing the God Almighty! You and your godforsaken suicidal thoughts!"

"No, Fred. This is what you get for not taking Bobby Peters' advice and letting him fix the car. This is what you get for being a cheap, stubborn bastard, and not listening to anyone but Father Doyle. This is what *you* get."

The creatures were around them now. Branch-like legs clicking off the tarmac, their swinging lights throwing shadows. This close, Grace could make out their facial features. Their faces did look eerily similar to an anglerfish, lower lip eating the upper. The rain splashed down the window in a waterfall, warping the monsters as they scurried around the car like lions circling an unfortunate wildebeest.

The car rocked and creaked.

Tip...Tip...Tip...

A light invaded the back window as if a curious police officer wanted to see inside. Craning her neck, Grace looked behind, where one of the creatures stood on its hind legs, underbelly exposed against the glass.

"It's got a mouth on its stomach!" Fred shouted. "Demons, Grace!"

"My God..."

The creature's stomach had split down the centre. Small, ragged teeth ran down the sides. Grace had a sudden image of being gobbled in, those lips working eagerly. *Like going inside a body bag,* she thought. *That's why their torsos are so long...*Once stowed away, she could imagine acid hissing, like some sort of hellish car wash, melting her flesh down to the bone.

Fred shook his head with a disgusted high yelp. "Let me get through this, Lord. Please, get me through this."

"What are you doing?"

Before she could stop him, Fred had reached for the hand brake, slamming it down with a scream. The car didn't budge. He pushed back into his chair, trying to force the wheels in motion. "Come on, you piece of shit! Roll!"

"Stop it, Fred!"

"If we can get it rolling just a few feet, we'll be on the hill." He threw her a look as if she were a slow child. "*We'll roll down to the village, Grace*!"

"I understand physics, you patronising fuck! I just don't think it's a good idea! Sit still!"

"No!"

Outside, the Will-o'-the-wisp continued prowling the vehicle, their lights gliding like dorsal fins through the window. They moved in front, as if sensing Fred's plan and not wanting to be behind when the car began to roll. Her stomach knotted and jumped, and her hands were beginning to shake. She could feel another coughing fit wanting to escape but resisted. *What if I* do *cough, hock up some blood, and they sense it?* She worried.

"Stop it, Fred...Stop it, Fred...*Just stop!*"

"*What*?"

"Look!"

Two of the creatures had moved to Fred's side of the car. They scurried back and forth as if trying to figure the vehicle out.

"Don't talk," Grace said. Icy cold fingers worked up her spine. "Stay still. I think they're planning something."

Suddenly, the two creatures began to spasm. Their spindly limbs quivered and their heads twitched from side to side, sending dull light swinging. Then their bodies began to pulsate and grow.

They were sizing him up, Grace thought. *They're preparing their bodies to fit him in...*

The creature's stomachs elongated and fattened, a sickening slopping sound audible, even from the car. Then, as Grace shrieked, their underbellies fell open, loose lips flapping, splashing the tarmac with running liquid.

Fred's voice was barely audible. "Like snakes...They're probably able to swallow anything. *Anything...*"

With that, he opened his door.

Grace screamed as he leapt from the vehicle, the rain forcing its way inside the car and smacking her face. Without thinking, she grabbed the swinging door and slammed it shut, locking it. She patted her own lock. Already down. An involuntary noise escaped her lips.

From the rearview mirror, she watched as Fred jogged down the country road. He moved faster than she'd ever seen, but even if an overweight serial killer chased him, he'd be caught. He was an old man, after all.

Grace's skin crawled as one of the creatures shot past the car, the road ahead lit by its headlight. Its legs arched like a spider, the shadows amplifying nightmarish shapes. A thick slug-trail of transparent liquid slopped from its midriff. Fred had made it only a few meters before it caught him.

The fact that the rain tapping the car roof blocked out all other noise made it somehow worse to Grace.

The Will-o'-the-Wisp circled Fred, its light turning each wrinkle on his face to a deep crease. For a brief moment, Grace saw the terror in her husband's eyes, how he balled his hands to his chest, shaking, and she began to cry. "Fred!"

He turned, looking towards the car through the sheeting rain, his lower lip quivering. Then the creature attacked. It shot up suddenly, towering above him, the hideous lips of its underbelly trembling like an over-eager lover. Then the monster came down, engulfing Fred whole.

"No!"

The Will-o'-the-wisp walked in circles, slowly pacing the wet road. Its stomach bulged and kicked as Fred thrashed about inside, desperate to escape. *Digesting*, Grace thought, a wave of nausea washing over her. Her marriage to Fred might've ended when her husband had met Father Doyle, but she'd never wished him *dead*.

Then, slowly, thick red liquid began to slop from the monster's underbelly, slapping the road in a shower.

"Fred, you goddamn fool…I'm so sorry."

The insistent rain lashed down on the car and the marshy landscape. Grace closed her eyes and listened. She had always liked that sound.

"If this were religion," she said to herself. "You would be angels. Fallen from heaven. Physical proof." She opened her eyes, seeing the car surrounded. "Darren Cross's angels."

In the rearview mirror, the swollen creature had slipped back into the marsh, a dim light swinging through the fog. Back on the road, the crimson mess it left behind washed into the trench.

"And my reapers…" Grace continued, smiling nervously. "How about that? I was right, all along."

With a sigh, she tried steadying herself, but her hands shook. *I'm doing this for me,* she thought. *No matter how gruesome, no matter how painful. It's my choice. And I want it. Yes.*

Grace opened the car door, the hiss of the rain filling the air. The creatures stood back, cautious. They stayed a few feet away, a solid block, fencing her in.

"It's okay," she said. "I'm not going to run. Not anymore."

Grace stepped from the car.

MATT HAYWARD is a Bram Stoker Award-nominated author and musician from Wicklow, Ireland. His books include *Brain Dead Blues*, *What Do Monsters Fear?*, *Practitioners* (with Patrick Lacey), *The Faithful*, and *A Penny For Your Thoughts* (with Robert Ford). He compiled the award-winning anthology *Welcome To The Show*, and is currently writing a novel with Bryan Smith. Matt wrote the comic book *This Is How It Ends* (now a music video) for the band Walking Papers, and received a nomination for Irish Short Story of the Year from Penguin Books in 2017. He is represented by Lane Heymont of the Tobias Literary Agency and can be found on Twitter @ MattHaywardIRE or at his website www.sundancecrow.com

ALSO AVAILABLE FROM
POLTERGEIST PRESS

BRIAN KEENE
DARK HOLLOW
(RUSSIAN EDITION)

AARON DRIES
A PLACE FOR SINNERS
(ENGLISH EDITION)

ROBERT FORD & MATT HAYWARD
A PENNY FOR YOUR THOUGHTS
(ENGLISH EDITION)

Lightning Source UK Ltd.
Milton Keynes UK
UKHW040849240719
346696UK00002BA/7/P

9 781999 341930